THE FALL

THE FALL

Ryan Quinn

a novel

Published by AmazonEncore
P.O. Box 400818
Las Vegas, NV 89140

ISBN-13: 9781612182100
ISBN-10: 1612182100

For the courageous.
It gets better.

Haile: new girl, a cappella

When I awoke the train was aboveground, far from Penn Station, moving west through an amber hay field. It's startling to drift off among the canyons of Seventh Avenue and Broadway and wake up in the middle of nowhere. Not even the middle of nowhere. This was just an anonymous stretch of lazy green hills, cool rivers, and rural valleys: the things that fill the places between the real places. No marquees shouted celebrities' names or boasted of upcoming concerts. No billboards were propped against the sky. The landscape was beautiful in the most obvious ways, but it started and ended outside anything I'd ever experienced.

My name is Haile. I'm a twenty-one-year-old girl, and I may or may not be making the biggest mistake of my life.

To settle my nerves, I tried to imagine that these hills and fields and towns—one of which would be my new home—represented a counterpoint to the urban, coastal cities I'd come up in, a quiet necessity like the silences between notes of a melody. My reflection in the window was sleepy and ragged. I pulled my long black hair into a ponytail and rubbed the sleep from my eyes.

On the next seat, my cell phone blinked. My mother. I wasn't ready to hear her message. I'd been relieved that she hadn't insisted on escorting me to the train station. This was part of the game she thought we were playing. By not coming to see me off, she'd hoped to trivialize my decision to go to Florence University and finally get through to me that, as she'd maintained all along, I was simply going through a "stage." Sure, I'd gone through stages. There was the stage when I wished I had a sister or brother, any other human body that could absorb my mother's attention so that it wasn't all concentrated on me. There were stages where I wished she hadn't divorced my father and moved us across the country to start our own life. And there were stages when I wished she had a boyfriend, even though it would be weird and I probably wouldn't get along with him. *Those* were stages. And even as I moved through them, I never really lost track of the fact that it really *was* just the two of us and that I would always be the sole target of her ruthless devotion.

This, though, was not a stage. Almost as soon as I'd been approached by Ms. Rivera about the music program at Florence University—which is not in Italy, as I'd first assumed, but in rural Pennsylvania—I'd known that it was where I needed to be. I had decided what I wanted to do with my life. My mother didn't understand it then or now—and maybe she never would, considering the way things had blown up on tour with the Atlantic Quartet— but *I* knew it, and that had been enough to get me through the university's application process and onto the train.

Until only a few hours ago, Florence had remained to me a somewhat hypothetical notion, like having a crush on someone I was unlikely ever to meet. Drawing from pictures on the campus Web site where I'd submitted my application last spring, I'd constructed in my mind a life so rich with detail that at times it felt as if I'd already transformed into my new college self. The interesting new girl with the confident smile studying in the library?

That was me. The diverse, laughing students relaxing with open textbooks on a campus lawn? People like that were going to be my friends. And they would be friends who didn't think of me first as a violinist.

Then, this morning, faced with the tiled floor and grayish fluorescent light of Penn Station, dragging everything I could carry in a suitcase and my handbag, the adventure felt a little too real. The confidence that had coaxed me to this point ran out like thread slipping off a spool. When the announcement came for my train, my limbs turned to jelly. Passengers around me stood, rushing to be the first to board. But I couldn't move.

Once, I read an article in an old *National Geographic* about an adventurer's quest to reach the summit of the world's ten highest mountains. I remember a photograph of the climber scaling a towering cliff, gripping the ice with metal picks as the wind whipped dry snow into his blistered face. I remember thinking then that I could never do something like climb mountains because no matter how wonderful the idea of standing on the world's highest summit might be, I could never get through those moments when you crossed the line between climbing and merely hanging on for dear life. Hearing the boarding call for my train, I thought of myself in that *National Geographic* picture, only I'd gotten halfway up the cliff and was suddenly paralyzed with terror, without the means to go forward or back.

This is it. I can't go through with it.

The truth is, had Mother been with me I'm not sure what might have happened next. She can smell my fear. I could picture the look in her eyes, sensing that she'd won, that all she had to do was hug me and tell me that the easiest thing in the world would be to change my mind and not get on the train. But she hadn't been there, and somehow I'd gotten on board.

Now what? I felt a stinging behind my eyes. *No*—I wouldn't second-guess myself. Not yet.

I dug my iPod out of my handbag, eager for the soothing sounds of the Traci Rice Trio. When people ask me what kind of musician I want to be, I tell them to go see Traci Rice. Her music is vintage soul driven by R&B beats that support her fearless, bare vocals. When she opened Jazz at Lincoln Center last year, I left the theater feeling that the story of that night would be the one I'd mention to interviewers when, years later, they would ask me about the moment I knew I wanted to be a performer. I longed, then and now, to earn the power that Traci Rice holds over an audience.

In a place called Coatesville, the clicking and lolling of the train car slowed and then stopped. Two passengers in my car got off; a new passenger got on. Moments later the train jerked forward without warning and began its labored acceleration. My stop was next. The passenger opposite me, a graying woman knitting a small child's hat, eyed me from across the aisle. She looked perfectly sweet but also a little nosy, the sort of chatty travel companion you end up beside on an overbooked plane when you just want to sit in peace. I wasn't prepared to discuss my story, where I'd come from and where I was going, and it made me anxious to be reminded that I would eventually have to answer questions like these. I still hadn't decided what about myself I wanted to take with me into my new life.

I turned away when the woman looked again. If I'd been on a plane, I could claim a fear of flying to explain my anxiety and silence. But there's no official fear of riding on trains, not that I'm aware of. It probably exists—that's what you learn in New York City, everything exists—but that wasn't a conversation I was interested in having, either.

We entered a valley slung between green hills sloping toward the blue-white sky. The tracks fell in sync with a river nestled like a fat, stone-colored snake along the bottom of the valley. Then suddenly we were above the water, suspended in a claustrophobic cage of steel. As we surged for the far bank, the swift current flowed diagonally below while blurred steel trusses flew by at irregular intervals, inches from the window. The moment was dizzying, a discordant symphony of motion violent enough to rupture the thin bubble of courage that I'd managed to stretch around my adventure. My wits were at last restored once the train rolled off the bridge and was swallowed softly by a thick forest; we were coasting now to the silent staccato of bright sun breaks in the trees.

In the retreat from all this commotion, something clicked in my head: the missing line to a song I'd been struggling to finish. Funny how the mind works, how it can perform instantaneous chains of associations to arrive at a seemingly irrelevant thought.

Can you trace it back?

The way the line came to me made it seem more like a gift than my own creation, which, I admit, is not unusual. I get these little thought-gifts every so often, though unfortunately they come without any instructions on which to throw out or how to assemble the ones I'm inclined to keep. I wrote the words down in the notebook I take with me everywhere and read them back to myself. *Can you trace it back?* The basic idea was right but the line, which would take us into the refrain from the second verse, contained too few syllables.

Can you trace it back to you?

Closer, but still a little awkward. Still missing two beats. Then it came and I felt like it was right even before I could test it with the melody.

Can you, can you trace it back to you?

The simplicity seemed profound. The syllables and vowels and sounds captured the larger thrust of the song, but the line also stood on its own, groping at something universal. Who couldn't ask this question of themselves and not be haunted by the answer?

I'd collected my handbag and suitcase by the time the doors opened to the platform with a soft hiss. My first taste of the country air was clean and wild and terrifying. This was River Bend.

As Ms. Rivera had instructed, I took the Florence bus system to the campus's main entrance and lowered my suitcase to the curb, clicking onto the sidewalk after it in my red heels. Coming through town to campus, I was struck by how River Bend was so dominated by the university, with its large-scale, institutional architecture and symmetrical sprawl. The door folded shut and I was left with a blast of hot air and the passing smell of diesel fumes. There were several days before the start of classes and I'd apparently arrived ahead of my classmates. A restless peace hovered over the massive campus. I could hear the muted sounds of a riding lawnmower and the harmless-seeming clatter of colliding helmets on a field a few blocks away. A silver Jeep crested the bridge from town and then turned off to a side street.

Few pedestrians wandered the sidewalks crisscrossing the deep green lawns. I would have to find Ms. Rivera's office in the music department on my own.

With a flutter of exhilaration and independence, and using all my strength to lug the suitcase in the right direction, I crossed through the front gates of Florence University.

Scene: Interior & Exterior. Car. Daylight.

A silver Jeep crosses the bridge to campus. Behind the wheel is IAN (good-looking, athletic, slightly taller than average) gazing warily up through the windshield as if he's not sure he wants to be here.

Approaching campus, two roads diverge beyond the bridge tethering River Bend to the university that supports it. You can see the town's namesake, that abrupt kink in the river, curving out of view downstream. The channel narrows slightly at the bend, hurrying the currents and frustrating the crew teams that have been rowing the otherwise straight and gentle waters for the last fifty years. At the spot where the road splits, the well-maintained right fork sweeps up to the main gate, a stone and iron behemoth that loomed in my windshield as I faced my return to campus. The left fork—the road less traveled—makes a dash for the woods, disintegrating into a potholed strip of gravel as it enters the trees and narrows toward its terminus at the fire-gutted remains of a small church.

My name is Ian, and I have a secret. Something I have to confess. But I'll get to that. It's only a matter of time. So much is only a matter of time.

In the meantime, I'd driven all day. Driven and driven and now I was back here, back where things remained the way you left them. Students converged on campuses around the nation— a great autumn migration webbing out across the country like the route maps in airline magazines. Millions of students— the vast majority of us never meaningfully encountering one another, like planes that never collide in flight—living out more or less the same College Experience. I'd chosen Florence in a last-second momentum shift, bailing on my parents' plans for me to play Division II football in the Pacific Northwest, close to home. Florence quickly emerged as the top candidate. It's my parents' alma mater, and they remain active in alumni initiatives, so they could hardly object with much enthusiasm. The deal was sealed when I was offered a modest scholarship to play on the Florence tennis team, which, though nationally competitive, is not so deep as to have no use for me.

But three years at Florence and I'd learned, if nothing else, how hilariously arbitrary was my decision to come here. What's here in this whitish-toned melting pot of formative youth that I couldn't have found closer to home or farther away? The gate up ahead says only *Est. 1950* in small, engraved letters on a moss-covered stone. It ought to proclaim: *Welcome to Florence University—not quite Ivy League, not quite New England, not quite what you thought you were getting.*

But that's life. That's your education. A series of opportunities and missed opportunities. Exams and grades and blue books and blue balls and majors and minors and liberal arts and liberal minds. The scam of it is, no matter how much you paid or how far you traveled, everybody's receipt says pretty much the same damn thing. BA, MBA, JD, PhD, MA, BS.

BS. That's all it is, right?

Even though senior year was about to begin, I was still thinking seriously of transferring. Not simply changing my major, but transferring schools. The drive down Main Street, with its one coffee shop, gift shop, used bookstore, gas station, diner, and sports bar, confirmed for me that I needed a bigger city. Main is the unnerving kind of street that townspeople put a great deal of effort into keeping quaint, as though that were some kind of virtue. I vowed to look immediately into the application deadlines for colleges that were located in actual cities. Something even farther away from home.

As I turned onto the quiet streets lined with off-campus housing, my chest thumped wildly as if its most vital organ had slipped out of place, like a fish on land. I never should have agreed to live here. For the past two years, I'd lived with a tennis teammate who'd graduated last spring. Before I had a chance to see who else on the team was looking for a roommate, I'd run into Casey one spring afternoon in the weight room and he mentioned that they'd have a vacancy in the fall. It had made sense at the time. Casey and I had been best friends and football teammates in high school, and though I was done with football, at least a part of my decision to come to Florence had hinged on knowing that he'd be here, too. But then he'd gotten swallowed up in the football machine, and I, newly devoted to tennis, saw him only in passing. Now, living in the same house, we could reconnect.

The house was on a cul-de-sac at one end of Oak Street. I'd passed the property many times before without retaining any specific memory of it. As I climbed the front lawn, I saw that the two-story bungalow was larger than I'd imagined. I heard laughter and clinking bottles from the backyard. The smell of charcoal drifted on the breeze.

Casey met me on the front porch, grinning in his familiar way. The dilemma over whether a hug or a handshake was
expected flooded me with panic. I'm telling you, it was awkward.
But Casey switched his beer to his left hand without hesitation,
thrusting his right to meet mine. It seemed at the same time inevitable and unlikely that we'd be able to pick up where we'd left off
in high school. I spoke first.

"Hey."

"Hey."

"Nice place."

"Your bedroom is upstairs. Did you come on the train?"

"No. My car was at my aunt's in Boston."

"Then you've been driving all day. You must be completely
sober. Come on back, we're barbequing."

Woods bordered the backyard on three sides. The dark façade
of the baseball stadium rose above the trees, looming massive in
the dusky light. The underside of the stadium's upper deck sloped
out like an overhanging cliff. Though the ballpark was dark, you
could imagine how it would transform the yard during a game,
the banks of lights casting their artificial moonlight over the
neighborhood and the sounds of a healthy crowd ebbing and
flowing like waves crashing against rocks.

Case introduced me around. A broad-framed guy named
Jerrell rose from a lawn chair by the grill. At the ends of thick
forearms, his hands seemed small and delicate. Tabular trapezoids
raised the fabric of his tee shirt on either side of his neck. His grip
was solid and steady and lacked any display of extra strength. No
need to prove anything here. He called me man, as in how you
doin' man, and then he lowered himself back into the lawn chair,
supporting both hands on the armrest in a way that activated

ridges of triceps descending from his short sleeves. Case explained that Jerrell played tight end and was one of our housemates.

Next Case introduced me to Todd Fleming. The guys call him T-Smalls. He was shorter and white and didn't live in the house. Two girls who had come with Todd were leaving for a party and I wasn't introduced to them before they went. Todd dug a beer out of the cooler for me and you could tell from his first two attempts at the bottle cap that he was gone.

Case disappeared inside and Jerrell and Todd laughed about something that had happened at practice. I stood alone by the grill, picking at the label on my beer. When I turned to sit on the porch steps, where I hoped at least to appear less uncomfortable, I bumped into a girl in tiny pink shorts and an oversized sweatshirt coming out of the house. She looked me over and then sat down on the top step, hugging her knees to her chest.

"It's *you*. You used to play football with Casey? And your dad is like some famous coach or something."

"Right."

"I'm Krista."

Of course she was. You might have guessed Mandy or Brittany or Tara, but Krista definitely was one of the first names that sprung to mind. She was pretty, as in pretty average. You couldn't have picked her out of a lineup of the sorority-ish girls I imagine she goes around with.

"I'm Ian," I said, struggling in my mind to give Case the benefit of the doubt.

"So how long have you and Casey been friends?"

"Junior high, I guess. That's when we started playing football together."

"And then you quit." She smiled—pure bitch.

"Yeah, I stopped playing ball after high school."

"Why'd you switch to tennis?" Her tone left no doubt as to where my new sport fell in the hierarchy of acceptably cool activities.

"It's just the way it worked out," I said a little too defensively.

"I was just asking." Bitchbitchbitch. "Casey likes you a lot," she added after a silence. "He talks all the time about how you guys used to be such good friends in high school. He's glad you're moving in."

If she was trying to make peace or flatter me or make me uncomfortable, it was all working. I'd finished the beer I was holding and was prepared to use the need for another as an excuse to duck away. But suddenly I felt obligated to hold up my end of the conversation.

"What do you do here?" I asked her. "I mean, why'd you come to Florence?"

"My parents thought it was a better school than OSU. They both teach there, lifetime Buckeyes. I didn't get into any of the Ivy League schools like I wanted. But Florence's reputation is almost as good so I worked really hard on my application and I got in."

"That's really great." This is really lame. "What are you studying?"

"Psychology. I started premed. That's how I met Casey. But premed is *really* hard so I changed my mind. I want to be a psychologist."

Krista was plainly boring and completely harmless except for her attachment to Case. She talked as if they'd be together forever. I was indiscreet about checking my watch but she got off another question before I had a chance to stand up. I'm telling you, this girl will terrorize patients if she ever becomes a psychologist.

"What about you? You got a girlfriend back home or something?"

We were interrupted by singing. It was a male's voice. The song was reggae-ish, clear and effortlessly in key. A giant man in a Hawaiian shirt filled the doorway behind the screen, and the first thing I thought was that his singing voice seemed much too high for a man of his size. He was wearing sunglasses despite the hour and most of his deeply tanned arms and legs were marked with tattoos. Case followed him through the door.

"This is Afa."

"Hey, man. Welcome," Afa said. "Case told us everything about you."

Afa picked up the plate of beef patties he'd set down on the railing to shake my hand and hummed to himself as he wandered to the grill. After we ate burgers, it was dark enough to see stars. Case plunged a hand into the cooler's watery bed of ice.

"Anyone wanna 'nother beer?"

"Oh yeah, baby."

I felt a remote sense that I was drunk—*did I just say Oh yeah baby?*—but my self-consciousness paled in comparison to my emerging enjoyment of the evening.

"Let's break into the stadium and steal the bases," said Todd, the stocky safety everyone called T-Smalls, from across the lawn.

Everyone looked at Todd.

"Dude," Case said. "Don't be gay."

"I'm serious. Let's *do* it. Who's in?"

Todd had either had the most to drink or was the least capable of handling it. He was pissing at the edge of the woods, his body turned only slightly away from us. His head was back and tilted up at the rim of the baseball stadium. The moonlit upper decks were chalky white through the tops of the dark trees rising abruptly at the edge of our backyard.

"Come *on*. We can climb over the back gate."

"You want to do it that way, you gotta go through the woods," Afa said. "You're on your own, man."

"What are you afraid of?" Todd said. He finished pissing and zipped up, but he stood with his back to us, staring into the woods.

"I'm just sayin'," Afa said. "Those woods are haunted. You wouldn't be the first person to walk in there and not come back out."

"Whatever. That happened once. One time, like ten years ago. And, for the record, he *did* come back out."

"Yeah, in a bag. Point is, his ghost is still in there."

"The fuck are you talking about? He didn't die in the woods."

"How do you know? They beat him pretty near to killing him."

I listened to this exchange quietly, gauging everyone's reactions. The story had stuck with me ever since I'd heard it, days after first arriving on the Florence campus for freshman year.

"They didn't kill him. He killed himself," Todd said. "Besides, that happened over in the old church that burned down."

"Don't matter," Afa said.

"Casey? Jerrell?" Todd said. "Someone please tell Afa he's a fucking fruitcake."

"Why you always get so crazy when you're drunk?" Jerrell said.

Todd raised both arms triumphantly and a new intensity electrified his impaired gaze. He flashed us wild eyes.

"It's not 'cause I'm drunk. It's 'cause I'm invincible. And if I ain't invincible I don't want to be anything. Now, who's with me? We're going through the woods and over the back gate, we're stealing the bases, and then we come back here. Okay? I got dibs on home plate. I'm gonna hang it in my room."

"You want to sit and have another beer and think it over?" Case said.

"Hey, I got a better idea," Todd said. "We should do this for the Homecoming ritual."

Everyone turned to Todd like he'd said something wrong.

"Dude, shut up," Case said.

"What's the Homecoming ritual?" Krista said.

"It's just—"

"Shut up," said Afa.

"Seriously," Jerrell said. "What will it take for you to shut up?"

Krista looked at Case. "What is it?"

"It's nothing." Case glared at Todd, like *Now look what you've done*. "It's just something the team does. And we can't talk about it. Sorry. It started with the very first Homecoming game and it's continued as a secret that only the players know about."

Krista turned to me. I shrugged, like *Don't look at me. I don't know what they're talking about*. She jabbed Case in the side with a finger. "Bullshit," she said. "You're telling me stupid football players have been able to keep a secret for a hundred years?"

"Sixty years," Case said.

"I still think we should steal the bases tonight," Todd said.

"Shut up," everyone said.

Todd shrugged. "Okay, you're right. I'm gonna sit and have one more beer first."

He settled into the hammock on the porch. Nearby, Krista had cuddled up with Case, imposing her head into the crevice between his chest and shoulder so that he'd wrap his arm around her. Something occurred to her and she lifted her face to look at him.

"This place has only been around for sixty years? I thought it'd been around as long as Yale or Harvard."

"That's what they want you to think."

"I thought it was founded right after World War Two," Jerrell said.

"Yeah, a few years after. June 20, 1950."

Everyone looked at Case.

"Man, are you shittin' me?" Jerrell said. "How the hell you remember something like that?"

Afa let out a loud, high-pitched laugh and wrapped an arm around Case's shoulders. "I love this guy. Never doubt anything this guy says if it's got anything to do with numbers."

"Seriously," Jerrell said. "He's shitting us. How you know that?"

"I read it somewhere. I don't remember where. Numbers just stick in my head if I can attach them to something important."

"What's so important about June 25, 1950? Or whenever it was," Krista said.

Case was quiet for a moment and then nodded as if confirming it for himself. "June 20. When DiMaggio got his two-thousandth hit. Against the Indians."

Jerrell shook his head. "Unbelievable."

Krista kissed Case on the mouth. "You're so weird. I'm going to bed."

Case stood and looked down at Todd snoring on the hammock.

"I guess Mr. Invincible is staying the night. Let's get him inside on the couch."

In my new room, I lay awake for an hour before sleep came, restless with a fear that change—change that had been building for years—would begin, finally, inevitably, like summer turns into fall.

Casey Boyd joined the group "Suck my stats: The numbers don't lie"

Casey Boyd changed his profile picture

Casey Boyd is bruised in the ego after sucking at practice

Finally, it was late August. The grass on the practice field smelled like the dry end of summer. Thirsty-looking yellowish-green blades split the cracking earth at the center of our huddle. Everything on this field was thirsty. We buckled over between plays with hands on scraped knees and spat dust through the grid of our face masks.

Not one of us wished to be anyplace else.

We had four days until Syracuse came to town for the season opener. This should have been just like any other Tuesday afternoon practice, but each time we broke out of a huddle and set ourselves on the line, we played as if it was the only day that mattered. One glance at the sideline and the row of dark sunglasses perched on the faces of the coaching staff was enough to remind us all that we were being watched.

My name is Casey. I'm a senior receiver on the Florence University football team, and I've paid my dues. It's my year to kick ass and prove that I can play in the NFL. So far, however, things aren't going as I'd expected.

Kyle Brown, our quarterback, was the only player already locked into a starting position. Kyle retrieved the play call from Coach Evans, the offensive coordinator, and then leaned into our huddle and told us to line up Razor X. All eleven guys clapped in unison as the huddle disbanded. My first maneuver off the line was a quick stutter-step to throw my defender off balance. By the time I'd accelerated forward and slanted inward at fifteen yards, the ball was airborne, converging on my route through midfield.

Although plays are meticulously choreographed, scrutinized on film, and rehearsed to the point of heat stroke, there is still a moment of shock when the coordinated movements of eleven guys manage to unfold according to plan. Of course, plays are designed to succeed, but since they so rarely *do* succeed exactly as planned, there is an inadvertent flicker of awe, a quick pump of adrenaline, that sends a two-part signal to the brain: *Holy shit, it's working!* And then, *Don't fuck it up.*

The ball made brushing contact with no less than seven of my fingers before it continued on, reentering the open space beyond my grasp and then skidding off the ground, taking a series of awkward, unpredictable football bounces before eventually rolling to a stop ten yards away.

"Boyd!" Coach Draper barked. I'd been wide open and I dropped the ball. It was not the play that failed, it was me. Inexplicably, this had been my third bobble of the day, and by far the most flagrant. Coach Draper strolled over and picked up his playbook, which he'd thrown on the field after being treated to the disgrace I'd made of its contents. I hated letting down Coach Draper. He'd taken a chance on me three years ago when I'd failed to land a scholarship with UW, and I'd spent every day since trying to prove that his risk would pay off. This was going to be my year. This was going to be *our* year.

I remained on the ground, hoping in vain that I could avoid drawing attention to myself. The worst thing in practice is to be singled out.

"Boyd, that was the laziest goddamn cut I've ever seen. There isn't a cornerback in all of college football who couldn't have beat you. Get over here!"

I got to my feet and ran over. Draper was silent for a moment when I joined him at the sideline. He was collecting his thoughts, preparing his words. I'd insulted him personally. He didn't even need to say anything. The real punishment was this feeling, the sickening knot of failure, regret, injustice, and self-loathing that continued to intensify in my chest. I'd never drop another ball in my life. I just wouldn't.

"Casey," Draper began, unrushed, like he had all day to humiliate me. "Son, it's on the bad days, the days when you're struggling, that you have to demand the most of yourself. Tough days are when champions are made, not when it's coming easy." He paused again, as if his words were something to savor. "That's the good news. The bad news is that these NCAA pricks allow me only so many hours on the practice field with you. So when you're here, I've got to have your mind focused only on football."

"Yeah, I know. Sorry. It's just, uh, not my day."

"Nobody said it *was* your day. But everyone on this field knows what you're capable of when you've got your shit together. A bad day is a bad day, but you can't let on. If you've got cracks in your game today, Boyd, cover 'em up. Understand?"

"Yes, Coach."

Coach blew his whistle. "Line it up again, gentlemen. Nate Orton, where are you?"

Orton is probably the only other receiver as quick as I am. The guys call him "Nato," like the treaty organization, because he's mild-mannered enough to get along with nearly everyone.

"Nato, you're gonna run Boyd's route for him. And Boyd, you're gonna guard Nato. You understand? You're gonna get a front-row seat of what a cut on my football field's supposed to look like."

This was the worst possible scenario. I knew exactly what it meant. After three weeks of camp, I still hadn't convinced the coaches I was the number-one receiver. They still had their eyes on Nato.

We lined up facing each other across the line of scrimmage. It was hot. Unbelievably fucking hot. Suddenly that's all I could think about. It was ninety-five fucking degrees and we'd been out on the field going back and forth for three fucking hours. Nato could hardly look at me. It wasn't his style to drag someone's dignity all over the field because of a dropped ball. Maybe he was secretly enjoying this. I couldn't tell; he never said a word. Any of the other guys would have said something by now. "Sorry, man," or, "Don't worry about it." Or, even better, he could've gotten in my face a little and called me a pussy or told me I run like a fag. It would be easier if Nato was a dick, if he were some prick underclassman who thought he could trash-talk his way into a starting spot that wasn't his.

But Nate Orton, Mr. NATO, hands at his sides, a smudge of blood and dirt on his shin, just stood there waiting for the line to get set. What scared me, I realized because I had too long to think about it, was that Nato was above all a competitor. He'd earned something today and he knew it wasn't to be taken for granted. Meanwhile, I'd let the idea enter my mind that I could lose. The last thought that went through my head before the ball was snapped was that maybe Nato wanted it more than I did.

The snap caught me off guard and I had to sprint just to stay even with him. We were shoulder to shoulder when—bam! There came the cut. The move was impressive: instantaneous, fluid, effective—and he wasn't finished. He'd been holding back and his new acceleration was devastating, immediately opening daylight between us. I'd been burned and all I could do was flail my arms helplessly as he grabbed the ball cleanly out of the air.

Coach didn't say anything this time. He didn't need to. *Cover the cracks*, I told myself, joining my teammates for the weary trudge from the field into the weight room. *Be a leader.*

I tried again not to think about the approaching four-year anniversary of Mom's death.

Haile, *andante*

Campus came alive the day before classes began. Students crossed purposefully in and out of the bookstore and hauled boxes and duffel bags into the residence halls; many had parents in tow. Everyone appeared to be smiling—real smiles, happy and comfortable, not the kind that masked anxiety—or at least that's how I perceived them. They were returning to a familiar way of life with friends they looked forward to seeing. To me—technically a senior, though I'd never set foot here—everything was new and intimidating. Every decision, even the most minor, like whom to talk to or smile at or where to sit in the cafeteria, felt loaded with potential humiliation.

Ms. Rivera had given me a ride down to campus, where she had last-minute work to do at Shostakovich Hall, the boxy concrete building that housed the music department. The day was sunny and warm, and as I wandered around alone, I tried to appear as if I was going somewhere with a purpose instead of looking like the new girl who is clearly lost. In fact, I was never lost, because I'd already practiced walking to the buildings where each of my classes would be held. Encouragingly, now that the entire student body was back on campus—I knew from the school catalog that there were twelve thousand undergrads and four thousand grad students at Florence—it felt easier not only to blend in but to believe that I wasn't the only person who found all of this new.

I decided to explore. I strolled down the Great Lawn at the entrance of campus, past the beautiful stone replica of a Boccioni sculpture, past games of Frisbee and students who lay reading in the grass. On the bridge between campus and town, I paused for a few moments to watch the glassy currents. The air was clean and free; drinking it in, I began to lose myself in the idea that I belonged here.

The blocks along Main Street were unlike the sprawling out-skirts of River Bend I'd seen from the train and on the short drive up the hill to Ms. Rivera's house, where I would live for the next year in a studio apartment over her garage. There were pedestri-ans, cafés, a post office, a florist, a pizzeria, and a knitting bou-tique. White and yellow flowers—Florence school colors—hung in baskets from the street lamps. The outlying parts of town were populated by subdivisions, strip malls, and gas stations. I'd even spotted a tractor dealership, the first I'd ever laid eyes on. But Main Street was idyllic. I liked it immediately and didn't care if it was a façade that stretched only a few blocks. I stopped in front of a coffee shop and, after peering in the window, stepped inside.

It was well after the lunch rush and the place was almost deserted. A pair sat talking at a window table; a few singles sat alone, their heads bowed over books and newspapers. Dvorak's String Quartet no. 9, op. 34, streamed like thick ribbons from the speakers. I noticed the two rows of track lighting aimed at a raised platform in one corner of the room and walked toward the small stage, eying the microphone stand and stool pushed to one side, the black curtain draped over an opening in the wall.

I stopped just short of stepping up onto the platform. There, I turned to take in the view of the room, imagining it full of faces turned toward me, their attentive features barely visible through the glare of the lights.

I became aware of the guy standing behind the counter after it was too late. Not that he'd caught me doing something truly embarrassing—I wasn't *up on the stage* lip-synching with my eyes closed—but I must have seemed wholly lost in a daydream. He was smiling.

"Oh, hi." My cheeks burned. "I didn't see anyone there."

"I hope you weren't waiting long." He had a dish towel draped over one shoulder.

"Not at all. I just wandered in and…I was just looking around."

He smiled. "Let me know if you need anything." I ordered an iced coffee and watched him hum along with the strings as he prepared the beverage, angling his head slightly in anticipation of a crescendo. Something about his presence made me smile. I thought of the many times Jasmine, my roommate in New York, and I had played "Gay, Straight, or Taken" with guys we noticed, and tried to guess what she might say now. His green-eyed warmth and freewheeling grin struck me as genuine, rather than put on. Gay, I thought. Definitely gay. But Jasmine was always better than me at guessing. The thought of laughing with my friends put me at ease and, without realizing it, the fingers of my left hand began to press into my palm, whitening the knuckles in rhythm with the music.

"Do you go to school here?" I asked, pulling my hand away self-consciously. Even though the calluses had softened over the spring and summer, I still occasionally experienced the eerie sensation of phantom violin strings whispering at my fingertips.

"I'm a senior. Three years down, one to go. But who's counting?"

"Don't you like it here?"

"Absolutely. I love it. Sometimes I think it'd be easy to stay forever. Which is why I have to leave as soon as I can. If something seems too good to be true, it probably is, right? So, you're new here."

"Is it obvious?"

He smiled. "You're wearing the only set of platform sandals ever to walk across these floors. At least since I've been here. I love it." Gay, definitely. "I'm Jamie."

"Haile," I said. I'm not sure when I decided that it would be the name—the only name—I used when I got to Florence. Before this moment, I guess I still thought of it only as my stage name.

"Where are you from?" Jamie said.

"New York." I don't know why this felt like a white lie. Maybe because I sensed the weight of what this answer couldn't explain. It made me think of how Mother always told people we were from New York even though we've lived across the river in Hoboken ever since the divorce and our hasty retreat from San Francisco. The truth was that before I'd left Juilliard to go on tour with the Atlantic Quartet, I *had* been living in New York, sharing a small two-bedroom with Jasmine in the West Sixties. Technically, I still shared the apartment with Jasmine because Mother continued to pay my half of the rent—all part of her plan to make it as easy as possible for me to decide at the last minute not to go away to Florence.

"Manhattan?" Jamie's eyes lit up. "That's where I'm headed as soon as I graduate. You know, you look exactly the way I imagine a New Yorker should. I have this fantasy—it's ridiculous, I know—that the streets are filled with smart and pretty people all talking about interesting things." I felt myself flush a little. "Why did you come *here*?"

"To finish my degree." Another white lie, another response that grossly underexplained the situation. "You like classical music?" I asked, changing the subject before he had a chance to ask what my major was.

"I can't imagine the world without violins and cellos." He paused over the register where he'd been counting my change, head tilted, apparently moved by the music.

I said nothing.

"I just discovered this quartet from Rio. They spent the last year recording every quartet Dvorak ever wrote. The best thing about working here is that I have time to listen to them all."

"When you move to the city I could put you in touch with some of my friends. I think you'd like them. Do you have friends there?"

"Sure." He grinned. "Well, I don't know them yet, but I can't wait to meet them."

Was he serious? "Aren't you even a little scared, moving to the city without knowing anyone?"

"Come on. Aren't *you* scared, coming here?"

I thought about lying again, but couldn't think of a believable alternative to the truth. "Terrified," I said and felt a little better.

"Look at you. You don't have a thing to worry about."

I thanked him for the coffee and promised to stop by again. "By the way, is there ever live music in here?" It was the question I'd been thinking about since the moment I walked in.

"Sure. Schedule's on the bulletin board. A few local bands are playing in the next couple of weeks, and we have an open mic night the last Tuesday of every month. I wouldn't recommend that. It's worse than it sounds. You should check with Patrick. He's the owner. He's out for the afternoon, but if you bring him a CD I'm sure he'll have a listen. What kind of stuff do you play?"

"Oh, I...I didn't mean for myself..." I trailed off, blushing. Was I that transparent? Jamie only smiled with a knowing—and somehow comforting—twinkle in his eye.

SCENE: INTERIOR. AUDITORIUM. DAY.

IAN is wearing a bright blue polo shirt. The syllabus on his desk says "Art History: fall semester." The PROFESSOR is lecturing on stage. Ian yawns and turns around in his seat to look for the clock on the wall. Instead, he notices a girl in the next row staring at him. They briefly lock eyes. Ian turns back around.

Haile, caught in the act of composing

I made the exciting discovery, while browsing news sites online before class, that our professor had authored a piece for *The Daily Beast* on the subject of art's meaning to society. The short bio at the end of the column read, *Mr. Acton Gilles is a professor at Florence University and the author of the forthcoming book* The Search for Meaning, *to be published by Harvard University Press next month.* The auditorium had filled rapidly and then kept filling, forcing nearly a dozen students into the aisles and against the back wall, where they double-checked their class schedules with rattled expressions. The room buzzed in anticipation of Professor Gilles, eager to witness this academic celebrity in the flesh.

I was scribbling a reminder in my songwriting sketchbook to look up Gilles's new book when laughter erupted from a section far in the back of the room. I turned around in my seat as four guys in baggy clothes and baseball caps shuffled loudly into the last available seats. According to the awed and geeky-looking guy beside me, the new arrivals were so-and-so and such-and-such on the football team. I rolled my eyes. For a city girl who had been consumed with music all of her life, I'd never had any interest in sports, and didn't see a reason to start now. What was the big deal with these guys? I didn't get it. Our attention was suddenly drawn forward when a door swung open at the side of the stage.

As if he'd planned his entrance for maximum effect, Professor Acton Gilles breezed into view from stage left at the exact minute class was scheduled to begin. The auditorium acknowledged his arrival by abruptly ceasing all conversation, which, the moment before, had risen to a volume rivaling that of the trading floor of the New York Stock Exchange. My first impression of Professor Gilles was that he was disarmingly attractive. His face was clean-shaven and sculpted with handsome lines, and he appeared more physically active than his age—I assumed he was nearing fifty—might have predicted. If he had many wrinkles they weren't visible from the third row. The only evidence of physical insecurity was atop his head, where his hair had receded only slightly but couldn't possibly have sprouted out of his scalp in the rich black color that was on display for the first day of class.

I became horrified by what entered my head next. With regrettable vividness I could see him pressing me gently onto a couch, his shirt fully opened and sleeves rolled up, his touch daring but gentle. And then the thought turned revolting as I realized there were probably dozens of other awestruck girls around me imagining a similar scene. I could never go through with that. Not even for a grade. I hoped he had a lovely wife to whom he was happily and faithfully married.

"Ladies and gentlemen," Professor Gilles began, appearing to bask a little in the remarkable attendance, "this will not be a typical art history course. In fact, if we are successful, this will not be a typical college course at all. I have convinced the dean—who, for better or worse, happens to be my wife—to give me creative liberties in the design of the curriculum. This will be neither a survey of art nor of history. You will not be required to memorize slides. You will, however, be required to think for yourselves."

Gilles strolled out from behind the podium and resumed his introduction as he paced confidently across the front of the stage, hands clasped behind his back.

"As noted on your syllabus, the subtitle of this course is 'The Search for Meaning.' That is exactly what we will be doing this semester. In our search, we will study art, which you will see is nothing more than depictions of life: of reality, joy, pain, triumph, tragedy, and every shade of emotion in between. This art, this lens through which we might better see the world, has been given to us by our ancestors stretching back twenty-five hundred years. We will avoid examining any one period too closely and will instead view the whole body of human work as the connecting tissue between our existence and its meaning.

"In short, this course is an experiment. It is nonrefundable and I assure you that you will get out of it only what you put into it—plus the grade I decide to give you." A few chuckles rolled through the audience as the lights dimmed and a projector at the back of the room flickered to life. "We'll begin by referencing one of the earliest experiments. Can someone tell me what is happening in this slide?"

A girl in the second row was the first to raise her hand.

"That is Adam and Eve in the Garden of Eden."

"Ah, the smart ones can always be counted upon to sit in front. Let's see, you've got the characters and their setting dead correct. But what are they doing?"

"She's taking the forbidden fruit, the apple," said a male student in the first row, dangling the thought cautiously as if it were his interpretation of something more abstract, like a Pollock.

Professor Gilles stood back and stared at the image for several moments.

"Interesting. What makes you say the fruit is forbidden?"

The young man shrunk a few inches in his chair. "The Bible?"

"The Bible. You mean the artist here is banking on his viewer's literacy?"

"I guess. I mean, everyone's heard of Adam and Eve. Even if they haven't read the Bible."

"I see. What else is happening?"

"It looks like the guy is after some forbidden fruit of his own, if you know what I mean, right?"

Laughter seized the room and heads turned toward the source of the comment. It was one of the football players.

"I see we have a spokesperson for the back of the room. Mr...?" Professor Gilles waited for the student-athlete's name.

"Goodman, sir. Jesse Goodman. But the guys call me Pile Driver."

"I find that entirely believable," Professor Gilles said. Goodman was a large, round white guy with a shaved head. "Well, Mr. Goodman, you make an excellent point. Do you also read the Bible?"

"Yes, sir. I got the fear of God in me. I read the Good Book every now and then. But that ain't where I got my idea here. The guy in the picture just looks like he wants to get a piece, is all."

More laughter.

"You're referring to Adam's eyes, I assume." Professor Gilles stopped himself and held up a finger. "Let me rephrase the question. What is the real sin being depicted here?"

"Knowledge!" someone called out.

Gilles's eyes lit up. "Close. Knowledge, represented by the apple, is the symbolic object taken from the Garden of Eden. But what is the human force that drives Eve and Adam, and I hope all of you, toward knowledge?" The room fell silent in thought. "I'll give you a hint. It has nothing to do with getting a good grade."

"Curiosity," someone wagered, quietly.

"What?" Gilles said, tasting victory.

"Curiosity."

"You are absolutely correct. Curiosity. The temptation behind the forbidden fruit. And see where it's gotten us?" Gilles chuckled aloud. "The title of this picture is *The Fall of Man*." He returned to the podium to check his notes. "Can anyone name the artist?"

"Is it Michelangelo?"

"No."

"Bosch?"

"Nope."

"It's Cranach."

"Good guess. But again, no. I suppose that through a process of elimination we might as a class eventually happen upon the correct answer, but I've only got you for a semester so I'll just tell you. The artist is a man named Albrecht Dürer. *The Fall of Man* is actually an etching on metal, not a painting." Gilles suddenly gave the podium a loud smack with his open hand. "No, no, no! Put down your pens and pencils. They will not think for you and I will not tolerate incessant note taking every time a proper noun slips out of my mouth. You'll hear plenty about Dürer, enough anyway that you won't need a flash card to remember him."

I already had reason to remember him. The day before, on my way back from the coffee shop, I'd noticed an inscription at the base of the statue on the Great Lawn. The statue was a stone replica of a Boccioni I'd seen at MoMA. It depicted a muscular figure in motion, a man in midstride who appeared to have been turned to stone and left there for ages while the wind carved ripples, like a sand dune's, on his powerful legs and body. Etched on a plaque at its base were the words: *"I hold that the perfection of form and beauty is contained in the sum of all men." – Albrecht Dürer.*

"Now, you're forgiven for not immediately pegging Dürer as the artist. Hundreds of major artists have depicted Adam and Eve in some form or another. I've chosen Dürer's version to illustrate two points about the meaning of art. The first is the power of universal emotions. This cannot be overestimated. Whether something strikes in you the fear of God or sparks an erotic fantasy, or both, you can bet that someone else has already felt the same emotion, even if they had no way of articulating it. We are individuals, and as such, we are not automatically connected to one another by emotions. But because we tend to find comfort in being connected, we use art to make these connections. By replicating emotions, art makes the private universal."

I'd first noticed the guy in the row in front of me, three seats to the left, when I was reading the paper before class. I watched him wander in by himself. He was clean-cut and wore a blue polo shirt. Wore it well, actually. His arms were visible below his sleeves and though they were a little pale, they appeared toned without being too heavily muscled, which is gross. When I realized that he appeared to be interested in the lecture, too, his appeal only grew. I developed a habit of looking down at him each time Professor Gilles paced to stage right, naturally placing the back of his head in my direct line of sight.

Suddenly, he turned in his seat and looked back in my direction. His eyes, the color of his blue shirt, were all I saw before my own eyes darted back to the stage. Had my staring drawn his attention or had he noticed me on his own? When I dared to look again he was still facing in my direction but pretended to look past me, as if at something else. I knew that trick.

We spent the period looking at slides of paintings and etchings and sculptures with titles like *Adam and Eve, The Garden of Eden, Original Sin,* and *The Temptation,* while Professor Gilles pointed out their similarities and differences. When the TA snapped off the projector and the lights came up, not a single person was asleep.

"You have one simple homework assignment," Professor Gilles said before dismissing us. "You are to go to the library— wait! Pens down! Holy smokes. You people are unbelievable. You, miss, what did you just write down in your notebook?"

I felt my cheeks flush as the full focus of the auditorium became fixed on me, including, I guessed, the guy I'd noticed a few minutes earlier, whom I was now too mortified to look at. At first, the only thing I could do was move my hand over the page to cover my writing and then hope to wait out the moment. Unfortunately, the professor's question was not rhetorical. I was expected to say something. The whole class was waiting.

"Um, it says, 'Art History homework, Aug 29. Go to the library—'"

Gilles shook his head. "If I do anything in this class it will be to break you all of the habit of writing down what you *think* is important before you even listen to what I've said. Now, before next class you need to go to the library. I've assembled a packet of reference materials, slides, and articles for further reading. The copy center should have them put together by now. If you forget what I've just said, perhaps you can borrow notes from this earnest young lady. She seems determined to transcribe every word of my instructions."

I *had* resumed frantic activity in my sketchbook, but nothing of what I wrote had anything to do with the homework. I wasn't about to explain to Professor Gilles in front of the whole class that an idea, the basis for a new song, had blossomed my head.

Find me in the Garden of Eden. If you want to tempt me, just open my eyes.

Casey Boyd is pissing in a cup for the NCAA while some dude watches (kinda weird)

Casey Boyd joined the group "The BCS blows…playoff system anyone?"

Casey Boyd wrote on **Jerrell Allen**'s wall: "did you see the spread? wtf?"

Haile, looking for a key change

The library, where I was expected after class, was a four-story conglomeration of concrete, granite, brick, wood paneling, and glass surrounded on three sides by fifty-year-old oak trees. Its fourth and best face, if more is better, was thrust in the direction of the Great Lawn and featured stone gargoyles at either end of an ornate frieze perched atop six marble pillars. From without, the building appeared to employ more architectural themes than it held printed ideas within its thousands of volumes. Which is to say, I found it a bit tacky. It was believed, Ms. Rivera had half-joked when she first walked me around campus, to be the only building in history to present gargoyles, domed skylights, and multilevel Frank Lloyd Wright-ish reading rooms as architectural companions. No one contended that the architect, if in fact there had been only one mind behind all of this, had pulled it off. But there was something fitting about the building's message, an unneat and disorganized outer shell that contained biographies of Gandhi and the Marquis de Sade, the collected works of both Ayn Rand and Immanuel Kant, the Bible, and novels by Janet Evanovich and Dostoevsky, all under the same strange roof.

The main lobby was an oversized, echoing room, a grand cavern of space whose only real purpose was to display portraits of each Florence president stretching back to Albert Gilles, Professor Gilles's grandfather, who founded the school in 1950. I paused in the lobby to glance up at the late first Gilles, portrayed as if preoccupied with an ambitious thought. A plaque beneath the portrait claimed that Albert Gilles had sat for the painting in the final year of his life, and if that was true, the cause of death must have been an accident or a sudden fall from good health, because the man in the portrait appeared much too young and lively to be on his last leg. I wondered if Professor Gilles hoped to get his picture up there too someday, as president of the university, or if he'd decided it was best to steer clear of the path that had led both his father and grandfather up the hierarchy of the school and then abruptly to their demises.

On either side of the portraits, archways opened to a common area that contained the main information desk and a cluster of computers used to search the library's holdings. Beside a bank of elevators, the main staircase ascended through the ceiling to the stacks.

"Can I help you?" The girl behind the desk acknowledged me without looking up. Hoops the size of onion rings dangled from her ears and her black, tightly pulled-back hair gleamed with product. She was healthy-looking, displaying more curves than ribs and daunting breasts that were too large to envy. Most importantly, she wore it all well—that is to say she wore it confidently, in a way that said she didn't give a damn what you thought unless you liked what you saw.

"I'm looking for Ms. West."

"She's in a meeting."

"I'm Haile. I'm supposed to start work here today." The girl finally turned her eyes up from the papers she'd been stapling to look me over.

"Haile," she repeated uncertainly. She checked a note on the desk beside the computer. "Nancy told me the new girl's name was Haven Libby."

"It is. I just—I go by Haile."

Part of the deal with my scholarship is that I work ten hours a week. I was given the option of working either at the library or for a professor in my major. (A third option was to work for the athletic department, though I'd immediately ruled that out.) I figured I'd have plenty of time with the music faculty so I opted for the quiet, productive, book-walled peace of the library.

"Well, Haile, there ain't nothing to do out there. You on this side of the counter now." I went around the opening in the circular desk and slid my book bag under the counter. "I'm Eva. Grab a stapler and help me speed up this nonsense."

"I just came from this class," I said, taking a stack of the Art History packets.

"I can't believe after three years they still have me doing mindless shit like this. It seems to me, if you're going to have a copy center making this stuff all day, you ought to have a staple center, too."

"You've been here three years?"

"It supplements my financial aid. Most of the time you don't have to do anything so it ain't so bad. You new, or what?"

I nodded, angling the corner of the first packet into the path of the waiting staple.

"What are you studying?" she asked.

"Music."

"Mmm-hmm. See. No offense, but I don't see why anybody got to go to school to study music. You can get all the musical education you need out of everyday life without paying thirty-five grand a year. But that's your business. What kind of music?"

"Uh, everything, I guess. The school is starting a new program. It's supposed to give me a lot of flexibility as a songwriter." I hated talking about this. Eva probably thought of me as I thought of people who say they're trying to get into writing or acting. But it wasn't like that. Even though I wasn't famous yet, I knew I was talented and this is what I really wanted to do. But people never judge you on what *you* think you're capable of. They only judge you on what you have and haven't already done.

"I'm prelaw," she said a little bitterly. "Basically, I just study all the time."

"You like it here?"

"You mean, do I fit in? Mmm-hmm. I know. I haven't actually checked with the admissions office but I think I'm the only black girl here that's not on a sports team."

"So why did you pick Florence?"

Eva rolled her eyes. "It was my safety school. My father's choice. But when the song and dance with all the admissions departments stopped, the only seat left was this place. Apparently, the quotas for inner-city black girls had already been filled at the Ivy League institutions. That's just fine. They've got to preserve whatever it is they think they got going for them."

"Come on. Racism? At academic institutions in America?"

Eva eyed me carefully out of the corner of her eye. And then a smile broke out on her face. "Ooo, girl. See, I'm likin' you already. People 'round here think of this valley as paradise. But those people are white and they got it put in each others' heads that attending a reputable university out in the country is some exotic American rite of passage, a nice break from their stressful life in the suburbs. Mmm-hmm. Puh-leeze. You white, but you a woman, right? There's more women than men goin' to college across the country and we still a minority somehow. Figure that out. But don't try to call 'em on it. Na-uh. That's the last thing you want to do 'round here."

I'd almost finished with my half of the packets and I took a few of hers, since her talking, which I was enjoying, seemed to slow her stapling.

"There was a student 'bout ten years ago who got beat. Put him right in the hospital. Poor kid decided to kill himself a week later. The school didn't stand up for that boy or discipline any suspects. What *did* the school do? Nothin'. My damn safety school."

"Who did it?"

"That's the worst part. It happened in the woods by where these baseball or football players lived. But they couldn't figure which one of them bastards was involved so the whole thing just went away."

"Why did they beat him?"

"Girl, does it matter?"

"No, of course not. I meant, something like that doesn't just happen."

"They thought he was gay, I guess."

"That happened here?" I asked, baffled. To me, Florence still retained the glossy, youthful innocence of the admissions brochures I'd fantasized over. Eva just nodded.

We were almost done stapling the packets and it occurred to me that soon my classmates would start appearing to pick them up. It probably wasn't cool to work in the library but I was okay with that. I'm not overly concerned with coolness. But was it *un*cool to such a degree that I'd find myself trapped in some loser category that would be impossible to break free of, no matter what redeeming qualities I could later demonstrate? I definitely wanted to avoid that. It was a relief to be paired with Eva (who *was* cool, right?). Maybe we weren't friends yet, but at least I had one more person on campus whom I could talk to and who seemed to enjoy talking to me.

I was caught up in Eva's colorful introduction to Florence when we were interrupted by three guys wandering in through the front doors. We heard them first—they were laughing loudly about something—and when they came into view I recognized them immediately. It was Pile Driver: the beefy, bald, white, God-fearing football player from Art History. His witless laugh echoed without shame through the marble room. He always seemed to be laughing about something. I guess for him ignorance wasn't just bliss—it was hilarious. The joker who had inspired this particular outburst was a black guy in sunglasses, whose red and white baseball cap rested on his head so that the bill not only teetered upward, but was skewed off center. The third guy, the tallest, was the only one who seemed to realize they were in a library and made a vain effort to shush his buddies. He also had a baseball cap, though he wore it straight, with the bill low over his eyes. The hat was navy blue and bore a compass emblem with an *S* in the middle of it.

"Y'all lost?" Eva asked. I reached for three Art History packets on the counter, praying that none of the football players would recognize me from class. When they approached the desk, the black guy pulled off his sunglasses.

"Eva? *Damn.* How you been? They got you *workin'* up in here?"

"Someone's got to," Eva said. She tried to look busy stapling, but all of the packets were already assembled, so she pretended to shuffle them as if they needed to be in a special order. "Y'all got booster clubs, money from our student fees, and God knows what else to take care of you, but there just isn't the same kind of free ride system set up for black girls with no athletic ability. And why should there be? Where's the profit for anyone in that?"

"*Damn!* Girl's got op*ini*ons. I like that."

"Seriously. You lost?"

"Hell, no. The fellas and I just dropped in to read some books." This provoked more laughter from Pile Driver. The other guy remained silent. By the way he looked down quickly when I glanced at him, I thought he might have been looking at me.

"Bullshit, Darius," Eva said. I admired the way she acted around them, like they weren't any big deal.

"Okay," Darius threw his arms up in surrender. "Maybe some other time. We got practice now. But we ain't here to cause no trouble. Honest. See, we're in this art class and we s'posed to pick up some packets or something."

"Here," I said, sliding the packets forward.

"There's a dollar-ten copy fee. Each," Eva said.

"See. Wasn't that easy?" the player said, fishing for the change and then leaning over the counter to look into Eva's downcast eyes. When she didn't respond, he put his money on the counter and smiled at me. "Thank you, miss. I'm Darius."

"Haile."

"That's a pretty name, Haile. Like Halle Berry?"

"No. Haile. Just Haile."

"Well, Haile, these are my fellas, Jesse and Casey." They both put bills on the counter. Eva gave them change. Jesse grinned at me widely, grossly misreading the effect his status as a football player had on me. At that particular moment, I actually wondered if they called him Pile Driver because he'd been hit on the head with one or if his social tone-deafness was simply a gift from God. The other guy, Casey, only looked at me quietly from beneath the bill of his hat. When I looked back at him, he nodded hello.

Eva didn't look up until they'd turned their backs to leave. I could see in the way she looked after him that her indifference to Darius had been an act.

"Oh, I almost forgot." Darius swung around and jogged back to the desk. "It ain't none of my business, but are you still seeing that guy you was with for a while last year?"

I thought Eva was going to remind him that, as he'd just mentioned, it wasn't any of his business. But she folded her arms across her prodigious chest and looked him up and down. "No. He moved to D.C. To work for a senator."

"Perfect. Then you should come to the party after Saturday's game."

Eva eyed him disapprovingly. "Just like that, huh?"

"It can be however you want it to be."

"I think I'm really busy on Saturday."

Darius smiled. "Ha! See. I knew you'd want to come. See you there, then? It's at DeAndre and Orlando's place. On West Drive." Darius jogged back to his friends while Eva stood with a hand on her hip, shaking her head.

"You're not going to the party?" I asked when we were alone.

"Oh, hell yeah, I'm going. And you're coming with me."

"Now you're crazy."

"Girl, you got something better to do? That's what I thought. You've got to *meet* people. And that is the football team. This time of year they're like the most sought-after guys on campus."

"They didn't seem like my type."

"That ain't the point. Besides, you already got a head start. That cute white boy had his eye on you."

"God, I feel like I'm in grade school."

"Oh, get over yourself. You got to start somewhere," she said, and had a point. I *did* want to meet people. But let's be serious. Was a house full of people who chose to associate with Pile Driver the best place to meet a guy? I realized that all of the scenarios in which I'd imagined myself meeting a guy at Florence had one thing in common: they took place in either a classroom or the library. He'd be studying nearby and say something smart and funny at just the right moment and we'd fall into conversation; or, he'd have followed me from class and would pretend it was only a coincidence that we'd run into each other at the search desk. (This sounds creepy—it was sweeter the way it played out in my mind.) Or, we'd be going for the same book at exactly the same time and laugh about it when we met in a narrow aisle between bookshelves.

More classmates started to drift in looking for their reading packets. I had to wait until the very end of the day, however, before the guy in the blue polo shirt finally made his appearance. Suddenly, I wanted to disappear, even though I'd secretly hung around longer than was required just to see him. As he approached the counter, I busied myself by clicking refresh over and over on the library's search page while squinting my eyes at the screen as if concentrating very hard on something interesting. If he remembered me from class, he gave no sign. Instead, he inquired about the packet in a bored tone and offered polite thanks as he stuffed it into his bag and left.

I ended my first full day as a Florence student by walking back to Shostakovich Hall to meet Ms. Rivera for a ride home. After a few blocks she pulled over to the curb, where her husband waited for her. Dan Brooks slid into the passenger seat, and she leaned over so he could kiss him on the forehead.

"How was practice?" Ms. Rivera asked.

"Good as could be expected with these people running around." He nodded at a group of padded football players coming off the practice field. They seemed to be everywhere. "You'd think they were getting ready for the Super Bowl."

"Is the football team here good?" I asked cautiously, hoping my ignorance of all things competitive and athletic hadn't been revealed in one simple sentence.

"They ought to be better, the way they're treated like gods. They made it to the national championship game a few years ago, but I don't think they're even ranked this year," he explained. I didn't say anything because I didn't know what "ranked" meant. "The tennis team, on the other hand, gets no recognition around here, even though we're one of the top twenty-five programs in the country."

"Oh, no. Now you've got him going," said Ms. Rivera. "Buckle up."

"I don't follow sports," I said. "But I could get into tennis. I like their outfits."

"My kind of sports fan," Ms. Rivera agreed, smiling at her husband as if they shared an inside joke on the subject. "At least they've built tennis a new facility in the last ten years. The music program is almost perfectly neglected. All they want is for Florence University to be the best. The best at everything. Well, unless sports are 'everything,' they need to back that ambition up with a little cash. And give me—not some committee—the freedom to spend it. Instead, it's just football, football, football. Maybe during concerts at the theater we should start wearing last year's football helmets—'cause you know they've got new ones—just in case the roof collapses."

Even Dan had to chuckle at this. It occurred to me how we must look, the three of us together in Ms. Rivera's car comparing stories about the first day of school. Like a family. I thought for a moment that when I got back to my apartment I would call my mother and tell her about my day. But when I was sitting on my bed with the phone in my hand, I decided against it. I'd managed to get myself here and to finish my first real day of classes in a good mood. I was too proud to give her the opportunity to ruin that.

SCENE: INTERIOR. LIVING ROOM. DAY.

Close-up of the television. The football game is on. Pull back to see IAN on the couch doing homework. A roar rises up from the crowd and Ian glances up. Onscreen, one of the Florence receivers holds the ball triumphantly in the end zone. Ian sits up, his interest piqued. He stares at the player onscreen. The camera cuts away just before we're able to see the name on the player's jersey.

Haile samples some hip-hop

"Hold on." Eva urged her breasts upward while attempting to contain them within her overburdened tube top—contradictory ambitions. She looked, well, ready. I was afraid to say for what. "Mmm-hmm, that's right. Let's go."

As we clicked up the porch steps, I noticed that the heels of her slide sandals were at least an inch higher than mine. I had to admit that despite the precarious matter of her breasts, the ensemble she'd put together for the party was a success. It was appropriate—for her, anyway—and made no attempt to conceal what others might. What you saw was what you got. This was a *woman*, let there be no confusion about that. A woman who was ready for action.

I was ready to turn around and go home, but now that I'd been pushed this far, a small part of me wished I'd tried harder than tugging on a pair of plain white jeans and red V-neck shirt. Since partying wasn't something I planned on making a habit of, I could've at least given it one fair shot.

Once inside, I could tell within the first few seconds that the party was unlike anything I'd ever experienced. In the dining room, six gargantuan men, black and Samoan, were seated around a table, three with petite, heavily made-up girls on their laps. It seemed impossible that the massive, overdeveloped bodies of these men in fact represented college students who had come into the world at approximately the same time as I.

Eva led us from room to room, making her boobs-first entrances with a swaggering confidence while I shuffled invisibly behind. I envied her self-assurance. Everywhere I turned I saw huge men. Even the guys not endowed with unusual height or width wielded thick, seemingly indestructible bodies and bulging, veiny limbs. I wanted desperately to be home in my bed reading a book or listening to music. But I'd come with Eva and it seemed unfair to turn immediately to my deep well of prepared excuses for leaving. I just needed to relax and buy some time before I could cut out.

I distracted myself by listening to the hip-hop music drifting at a surprisingly reasonable volume from speakers attached to a computer in the corner. The basement beneath us thumped with louder dance music, buzzing in pulses through the walls and floor. In the crowded walk-through kitchen at the back of the house, the counter was littered with bottles of liquor, empty beer cans, bags of ice, and leaning stacks of plastic cups.

And there, suddenly, was Darius.

"*Damn.* Now here's some fine ladies." Although I assumed he'd initially been referring to the both of us, it was Eva's hand he grabbed to lead her out into the backyard. Any hope I'd had that our finding him might improve my enjoyment of the evening quickly evaporated. Taking a few steps in their direction, I considered whether it was worse to tag along unwanted or to stand alone like a friendless loser. When I saw that there were a few dozen other people who had spilled out into the backyard,

I decided to give it one more shot before accepting I'd been ditched for good.

Darius and Eva were in a group of people I didn't recognize. I loitered nearby, just outside their circle, feeling as though I stuck out even though I don't think anyone even noticed me.

"I'm Mercedes," a girl said to Darius, leaning into him despite Eva's presence at his side. Mercedes was wearing a cheerleading sweater and could not have been anything but a freshman.

"I bet you are," Darius said, tipping his sunglasses down to get a better view and adding that she looked like a smooth ride.

Eva didn't seem at all jealous or disappointed, and for a second I wondered whether she secretly viewed the evening in the sporting way Darius did. In any case, she was in her element and I was sinking away. I didn't feel ugly beside her, just plain and unnecessary. Why had she invited me to the party? I was white, unathletic, female, and friendless, and although none of these qualities had ever seriously bothered me before, this was the first time in my life that they happened to constitute almost precisely the opposite of everyone surrounding me. Of the men, I was grossly intimidated; and of the few other girls, there were none who I could imagine befriending, even under such desperate circumstances. The first sign that this party was a bad idea should have been that Eva had spent three years at Florence and yet she apparently didn't have anyone better to invite than me, who she'd known for less than a week.

Tonight, I realized stupidly, had never been about Eva and me going to a party together. It hadn't even been about me making a new friend. This was about Eva. Specifically, Eva having me there so she wouldn't look sad and lonely in the short time it would take her to find Darius or some other suitable football player who would be a sure thing for the night. Finally, it struck me that no one would even notice if I just left.

No sooner had I made my way inside the back door than I saw him coming through the kitchen. He wasn't wearing the blue shirt—of course, he wasn't; that had been two days ago—but there was no doubt it was him. I'd kept my eyes out for him on campus, hoping maybe we'd share another class or that I'd catch a glimpse of him coming out of one of the residence halls, even though I knew the latter was unlikely. The dorms are occupied mostly by freshmen; everyone else lives in houses or apartments off campus. The party, though, was the last place I expected him to be. A gathering of jocks didn't seem like his type of crowd. Of course, it wasn't my crowd either. Immediately, I concluded that our meeting here was fateful.

He didn't see me at first. He was looking around as if searching for someone else. But at the exact moment my heart began to sink with the possibility that he would walk right by, he turned and stopped midstride. He registered my presence as if by accident, looked away, and then his eyes darted back. Finally, I saw in them recognition.

"Hey, you're the girl from the library."

"Yeah," I said. "Some people call me Haile, though." He nodded and slid over next to me with his back against the wall.

"Haile. Like Halley's Comet?" he said, rhyming it with "daily."

"No, like 'Haile,' " I said, rhyming it with "alley." "But the spelling is like Haile Selassie." I don't know why I said it. No one, not even Jasmine, had pressed me about where I'd come up with the name.

"Haile Selassie," he repeated, as if the name was only half-familiar. He glanced over my shoulder.

"The former king of Ethiopia," I said.

"Right. Your parents into reggae or something?"

"I'm impressed you'd know that." Then I laughed and quickly apologized when he looked confused. "It's not you. You'd have to know my parents. Forget it."

"Cool. I'm Ian." I saw him look past me again and couldn't resist turning to see what behind me was so interesting. But there were only a guy and a girl talking at the top of the basement stairs. Was I boring him already?

"I guess we keep running into each other," I said.

"What? Oh, right. You must be new. You'll see. It's a small world around here."

"I noticed. But what I meant was that this is the last place I would have expected to see you."

He shrugged. "You mean like it's a sign or something. 'It is written.'" He said the last part in a voice not his own, as if quoting something. "Trust me, I don't think it's written." When he saw that I hadn't the faintest idea what he was talking about, he jerked his head back to study me. "You know, *Lawrence of Arabia*? 'It is written.' 'Nothing is written.'"

"Sorry, I don't—"

"You've never seen it? It's a movie. And here I thought a girl like you, who takes art history and works in a library, would be a little more cultured."

"Cultured?"

"Sure. Films are only the most important art form of our era."

"You can't be serious." I had to laugh.

"You disagree. What, artwise, is more important to society than movies?"

"Music."

"What, are you some kind of musician?"

"Yes, in fact, I am."

"See, then you're biased."

"Are you some kind of filmmaker?"

"No, but maybe I should be. That's it. I'm changing my major tomorrow."

"What was your major today?"

He said something but I missed part of it because someone squeezing through the crowd bumped me forward. I had to put my hand on Ian's chest to catch myself. When I clumsily apologized and took a step back, we ended up closer than we'd been standing before. "I didn't hear. You said environmental sciences?"

He smiled. "No. I said I haven't decided."

"What year are you?"

"Senior."

"An undecided senior. I like that," I said.

"Really? You should talk to my parents. They don't seem as fond of my academic promiscuity."

"Where are they? Your parents?"

"Seattle."

"Really? I'm originally from San Francisco." I don't know why I said it like that, as if we had something in common just because our hometowns touched the same ocean. I had to drive to Seattle once for a recital and it took about twelve hours. It felt even longer because I was in the car with my parents who, in retrospect, had probably already begun exploring the possibility of divorce. "How does one qualify as a senior without declaring a major?"

"I'm an athlete," he said as though this took care of certain things.

I had imagined him in such a different light since first setting eyes on him in Art History that it hadn't even occurred to me, even seeing him at this party, that he was a football player.

"Of course," I said. "Exceptions must be made."

"That was sarcastic, wasn't it?"

"Sorry. I didn't mean to—I think I'm just at the wrong party. But maybe you can help me with something. Why are so many of you athlete types drawn to Art History? I thought it was one of the hardest classes to get into."

"Is it? I don't know. The rumor is, Professor Gilles likes student-athletes. And we get to register for classes a few weeks before everyone else. What?"

"It just seems unfair. Why all the special treatment?"

"Maybe it's because we're dumb. We need all the help we can get." He smiled. Were we flirting?

"Then, assuming Professor Gilles grades on a curve, I have nothing to worry about." This came out a little harsher than I'd intended and he took the upper road by saying nothing and looking past me again, over my shoulder. "Sorry. It's just that I don't know what I'm doing here. I came with this girl, Eva. But she's already run off with someone."

"Forget it. I don't really belong here, either."

"What do you mean by—?"

"Never mind. To answer your original question, my major is econ. Technically, to be NCAA-eligible we have to declare a major and maintain a 2.0 GPA. But I'll probably change it again. I don't know what I want to do."

"Besides make films."

"Yeah, right. I think I gave that up just after I gave up my plans to be an astronaut."

"And what about being a professional athlete?"

He shrugged. "Naw. I got out of football too early and got into tennis too late."

"Wait. You're on the *tennis* team? So you don't play football?"

"I don't think I've ever heard it phrased as a compliment before."

I was beside myself with relief. "That's so funny. I live with your coach. Dan, right? I mean, I live in a studio over his garage. He's married to the music professor who convinced me to come to Florence. Dan's a nice guy."

"Yeah, I'm lucky. If he hadn't married—what's her name?"

"Ms. Rivera. Jen."

"Right. If he hadn't married Ms. Rivera and settled down here, I think he would have gone back to coaching in the pros. Do you want another drink?"

I agreed to a rum and Coke without mentioning the fact that it would be my first beverage of the night and that I'd been on my way out before he'd stopped me.

"Did you say you were recruited by Rivera? Are there scholarships for that?" he said when he returned. I nodded. "You play a particular instrument, or what?"

"The keyboard mostly," I said. And then, because I still didn't trust that there were people out there, even strangers, who didn't automatically identify me as a violinist, I moved quickly to change the subject. "How did you end up in Art History?"

With a sly smile he acknowledged my evasion of the topic of myself.

"Destiny, I guess. If I'm going to be a filmmaker I must have known subconsciously that I'd need an understanding of the lower art forms that came before mine."

"Like music?"

"I wasn't going to single anything out."

"You know what I think? I think you should watch fewer movies and read more books," I suggested.

"What for? Novels are dead. It's the twenty-first century. Has there ever been such a time in Western civilization when the visual was as important as the written word?"

I reached for a flirtatious, sarcastic reply—we *were* flirting, I was sure of it now—but came up short. Then I remembered reading something in an article in the Art History packet.

"The Renaissance."

"That was before film," Ian said dismissively.

"You think culture today is more important than the Renaissance? Because of *film*?"

"Absolutely."

"You're discounting a lot of accomplishments. A lot of great artists."

"Not discounting them," Ian said. "I'm just saying that the movement is bigger than the people it produces. Do you think Michelangelo would be a painter and sculptor if he were alive today?"

"He might be. What's your point?"

"My point is, he would be a filmmaker."

"I bet we'd have better films to watch."

Ian smiled, something he did often. Each time, it rendered me a little more helpless.

"Did I just win this argument?" he said.

"Were we arguing?"

"No," he said, suddenly distracted. The couple talking behind me broke up and the guy squeezed passed me into the kitchen. After his back disappeared into the crowd, Ian turned back to face me. "If we were arguing, more people would be paying attention to us. I think we were just being the lamest people at this party. No more talk about school."

"But we weren't talking about school. We were talking about you giving up your passion for filmmaking to major in economics, which you couldn't care less about."

"Here, you should meet someone." Ian grabbed my arm and turned me toward a person coming in from the backyard. "This is my—" Ian started, but an uproar from a group of guys on the porch drowned him out.

"He's your what—?" I already recognized him by his blue baseball cap. He was one of the football players, the quiet one who kept looking at me when he came into the library with Darius.

"He's my best friend," Ian said. "We went to high school together. Case, this is Haile. Haile, Casey. He's the best wide receiver on the football team."

"I don't know anything about football," I said, shrugging unapologetically. "Was there a game today or something?"

"Yeah," Casey said. He gave Ian a look, like *Is she for real?* "The first game of the season."

"Did you win?" It was all I could think of to say. My cheeks were getting hot again and suddenly I remembered all the reasons I never wanted to come to this party in the first place. For a while, talking to Ian, I'd somehow tricked myself into believing I'd been chatting pleasantly over coffee with a new friend.

"Yes," Casey said before he was pulled away by a shorter guy, who said Casey should come quickly because something was happening.

I talked with Ian for a while longer and realized after he got us drinks a second time that he was drunk. "I feel like I'm talking a lot," he said at one point. "I don't usually do that."

I looked at him, expecting eye contact, but he was looking down into his empty cup.

"Look. I should go," I said. *No, I shouldn't. No, I shouldn't. No, I shouldn't.* "But I guess I'll see you around."

He shrugged. " 'It is written.' "

"What?" I said, and then realized he was teasing me. God, that smile! It was unfair. I walked away knowing that that smile would be stuck in my head, haunting me all weekend until I could see him again in class Monday.

It took me a while to find Eva and tell her I was heading home. Because I'd stayed so long and actually had a decent time, I'd returned to the belief that maybe we could be friends after all. She wasn't in the living room, where a dozen football players had gathered around the television, and there weren't many people in the basement. I finally found her sitting on Darius's lap on a patio bench out back. She waved me over as soon as she saw me.

"You're not leaving. No way are you leaving."

"Yes, I am. I've got some things to do in the morning."

"The morning? It's the weekend, o-kaay!" Obviously she'd been drinking, but I still believed she was genuinely sad to see me go.

"I'll see you next week," I said.

She waved me off with a hand. "I'll let you go this once, but I'm gonna teach you how to have fun, girl."

"When you teachin' *me* how to have fun, baby?" I heard Darius say as I walked away.

"You better quit all that carryin' on. You'll get your fun."

Casey Boyd one game down, eleven to go. Syracuse 24, Florence 34

Casey Boyd posted a video: "Highlight reel from the Florence home opener"

Casey Boyd wrote on **Ian Everett**'s wall: "You're coming tonight. I better see you there."

There is always a party after our first home game and the party is always better when we win. We'd volunteered DeAndre and Orlando's house because they had a basement for loud dance music and a backyard where revelers could spill in and out without disrupting the relative peace of West Drive. Not that we had to be too worried about the cops. Chance Paddock, River Bend's sheriff, was a former Florence nose tackle who'd stuck around town too long after he graduated—and graduating had taken long enough. He remained loyal to the team and did his part to call off his boys whenever they were summoned by neighbors or campus security to break up a post-game celebration.

We celebrated victory the old-fashioned way: beer and girls, though it seemed there might be an excess of the former (if there is any such thing), and a shortage of the latter (which, unfortunately, there almost always is). The usual cheerleaders and volleyball players were present, as were a handful of softball players who, judging by their skimpy outfits, appeared desperate to prove by the end of the night that they weren't lesbians. Standing in the backyard with my beer and my friends, I felt lucky. Lucky to have my life. And lucky to have Krista, who had left a message on my phone to say she'd be at the party later. This was it, wasn't it? To be playing football, to have a girlfriend, to be on track for med school. Wasn't this what all of America dreamed of, even if the cold shoulder of reality often forced them to settle for less?

When I first saw the girl from the library, she was standing alone inside the back door. Though entirely committed to Krista, I'm biologically permitted to look at other girls. I'm a guy. Studies have been conducted and evolution has confirmed the simple fact that survival of the fittest does not favor the monogamous. Objectively, Krista is smokin' hot—a round, tight ass; long, wavy, blonde hair; a cute, deceptively innocent Midwestern face; and medium breasts that bounce gloriously when unconstricted. My interest in the library girl was a mystery to me, which only made her that much more appealing. She looked bored with the party, even a little disgusted. She wasn't exactly hot—when you saw her, you didn't automatically picture her topless—but nor was she not hot. Her frame was small, almost fragile-looking, but this was countered by her confident posture. Her clothes favored fashion over sex appeal, which made her stand out at this party. She had wavy, black hair you could spot across a room and large brown eyes that tended to look away too quickly. I decided she was *secretly* hot. A secret she may have been keeping even from herself.

When I caught sight of her again, it was just as Krista ran up to greet me with a long, congratulatory kiss. She leaned in toward my ear, pressing the warm side of her face to mine and whispering with hot breath that we would celebrate "just the two of us" a little later. And over her shoulder was the library girl, in the exact same spot she'd been earlier. But now she was talking to

Ian. The typical girl at a party like this is one who feels grateful to be there and wants nothing more than the opportunity to tell her girlfriends that she'd slept with a football player. This girl was different. And something about Ian set him apart from the rest of us and made me think he just might be the only guy at this party who had a chance.

Haile.

Her name was Haile. I handled this new word in my head as if it were a dangerous piece of intelligence. Ian introduced us and Haile acted oblivious to the football game. I'd caught seven of seven passes for eighty-six yards and four first downs. And Haile didn't even know that we'd won. *That* was sexy. I tried to learn more about her, but the whole time I was afraid Krista would appear and kiss me and stand against my body clutching my upper arm with both hands the way she does sometimes. More than anything, I didn't want Haile to see that.

"Shit, dude. Where've you been? You have to see this." T-Smalls pulled me away, which was probably for the best. I was an intruder on Haile and Ian's conversation and didn't want to be accused of interfering if he was going to hit that.

When I caught up with T-Smalls, he'd stopped in the front room. A dozen guys were clumped around the television watching what I thought at first was the local news, because the picture on screen was of Coach Draper. But the sports ticker running along the bottom was as unmistakable as the four-letter ESPN logo in the top corner of the screen. The UW-Notre Dame game, ESPN's late Saturday offering, was at halftime, and the anchor sat clean-cut and straight-backed behind his desk as if speaking from the bridge of the sporting universe's mother ship. Something was wrong. Subtracting for commercials and first-half highlights, there could only have been a few extra minutes to summarize the day's top stories from around the entire world of sports. What could ESPN possibly have to say in these precious few minutes about Coach Draper?

Reading from a bulletin just handed to him, the anchor queued up a replay of Coach Draper's post-game press conference. When the tape rolled, Draper was sitting comfortably at the microphone taking questions from the unseen press corps. Seeing him there, featured on the national feed, gave an extra, satisfying weight to our win. It made it tempting to think that the rest of the country believed what we believed: This year the Achaeans were back. We were for real. Coach looked his usual self—stern, in control, disheveled and sunburned, perfectly unaware of his appearance. At first, the reporters had standard requests for Draper to comment on certain pivotal plays and his overall impression of our performance. He spoke slowly, taking care with his words and managing to say almost nothing in a great deal of time. Then a reporter asked a rare yes or no question.

"Coach, were you in contact with DeMarious Williams as early as his sophomore year of high school?" DeMarious Williams had been a star running back for Florence a few years before I got here, back when Florence was a perennial contender for a national championship. Williams now played in the NFL. Draper leaned forward and squinted into the lights. There was something wrong about the way he was squinting. Was it a stare-down, an attempt to intimidate the inquiring journalist? Was it anger or fear in those narrow slits of eyes, or merely innocent confusion? The journalist repeated his question, encouraged by the tension that suddenly had silenced the room.

"Three phone calls were made from your office to the Williams residence in 2001, when DeMarious Williams was a high school junior. Can you explain those calls?"

"Excuse me?" said Coach Draper, cocking his head as if he didn't understand.

"Did you make contact with DeMarious Williams in violation of NCAA recruiting rules?"

"Stop. I heard you." Draper tortured the room with another long silence. "I make a lot of recruiting calls. I can't recall when a particular call took place years ago."

"Coach, DeMarious Williams was the most sought-after high school player in the last decade. He was certainly the best player ever to wear an Achaean uniform. Surely, you remember your first efforts to contact him. Did you speak to him before his senior year of high school?"

Again, silence. Then a simple, "I don't know."

When our sports information director stepped out of the shadows with the panicked goal of guiding the press conference back on track, she appeared to have aged five years. "Any other questions about today's game?"

There were plenty of other questions, and all of them were about Coach's recruiting calls. "Coach, when did you first talk to DeMarious Williams about playing for Florence University?" "Coach, have you called other players before they were NCAA-eligible?" "Coach, has the NCAA been in contact with you about these calls?"

After what felt like a half hour but was probably around thirty seconds, Coach stood up and walked out without mumbling another word.

ESPN cut abruptly to an aerial shot of Husky Stadium where the second half of the UW-Notre Dame game was getting underway. The score was tied, seven-seven. UW—where Ian's dad is the head coach—is where I'd always wanted to play. But they didn't offer me a scholarship. It was Florence, on its way down in the rankings while UW was on the way up, that had been the only Division I program willing to give me a shot. I'd repaid them, I thought, with my hard work, earning a starting position and playing each down with the expectation that we could always improve. Here we were, at the threshold of what I knew could be our best season ever.

And now this.

SCENE: INTERIOR. HOUSE. NIGHT.

Every room is filled wall to wall with students drinking, talking, and dancing. Loud
hip-hop music spills into the yard and
street. IAN presses through the crowd by
himself, his eyes darting around as if he's
looking for someone.

I'd been at the party an hour and hadn't seen him. But it was early, I told myself. People were still arriving. I pushed through the kitchen toward the backyard. Like all football parties I'd been to, this was nothing like the wannabe fraternity parties on University Street. From what I'd witnessed, the whole point of those gatherings was to concoct new methods for white guys to consume perilous amounts of alcohol, usually via methods that combined ghastly punch, coils of plastic tubing, headstands, absinthe-laced Jell-O, hastily carved ice chutes, partial nudity, and games with cards or coins or ping-pong balls. The objective was to drink drink drink and on a good night maybe fuck if someone else has been drinking enough, too.

The premise of a football party was fundamentally different. The atmosphere was more subdued. There were close to equal parts white and black athletes, plus another third Hispanic and

Samoan. The kind of turnout most campus minority groups could only dream of. They drank and listened to music. A few of them smoked. Most of them were trying to get laid, an activity they pursued free of the unbecoming urgency of the hopeless. They were the kings of campus and they knew it.

I saw him by the back door. He was standing with a girl on the landing atop the basement stairs. His hair was cut to a length that called for little fuss and he'd obliged that fact modestly by working in only enough gel to pat down the sides and brush the front off his forehead. Pausing on the landing would have been awkward, so I turned toward the door with plans to do a quick circuit around the backyard and then return to—

To what? I hadn't a clue.

It was then that I recognized the girl standing alone against the wall. She looked exactly the way I'd seen her in the library: studious and shy.

"You're the girl from the library," I said.

I positioned myself so I could watch him over her shoulder without being too obvious. Nate Orton. That was his name. Nate Orton Nate Orton Nate Orton Nate. I'd first noticed him in the weight room last year but he hadn't been a starter and I'd never learned his name. Until today, when I'd looked for him on the TV broadcast of the game. Now he was right in front of me. Close enough to feel me staring. Time passed. I talked forever to the library girl. More time passed and he never looked in my direction. Not once. He just stood there talking to this tall volleyball girl, seeming neither bored by her nor eager to take advantage of her obvious interest in him. He never touched her. Not once. I definitely noticed that. Maybe he had a girlfriend somewhere. Or maybe maybe maybe maybe maybe. Eye contact would have gone a long way. I really could have used a little eye contact. He was close enough to feel me staring and I pleaded with my eyes for him to turn around and give me just one Look.

My hope swelled as he parted ways with the tall volleyball girl and angled toward us. I would have been close enough to see the color of his eyes had he not kept them pointed at his shoes. The last I saw him that night was a view from behind as he disappeared into the kitchen with his slightly tapered back and wide shoulders humbly concealed within a faded blue tee shirt and his low-cut jeans hanging loosely from his hips, their bottoms collected in frayed bunches around the heels of his shoes.

The library girl's name was Haile and I found myself a little drawn into her helpless flirtations. I liked her and I told her so, and in retrospect, I probably should have been more aware that I was misleading her.

And I introduced her to Case. This may appear to have been a ploy on my part. It *was* a ploy. But not the obvious one. There was a part of me that felt duty-bound to suggest to Case that he could do better than Krista. The less noble, more accurate reason was that I wanted Case to see *me* with Haile. I wanted him to see the way she was looking at me. Let him believe from that what he may.

In any case, the first time the three of us found ourselves standing together in a small triangle braced against the crowd, we each held in our heads a different idea of what was really happening between us. And we were all wrong.

After Haile left, I found myself in the kitchen mixing another drink and wondering if Nate Orton was still around. Orton Nate Orton Nate Orton Nate Orton Nate Orton Nate Orton Nate Orton Nate Orton Nate Orton Nate Orton. When a group of football players rushed by, I followed them into the living room. They had fallen silent around the television. My eyes found Case and

I could see the setback on his face. I was about to ask him what had happened but then I caught the tail end of the head football coach's press conference and no explanation was necessary.

The screen returned to live footage of the Washington–Notre Dame game and there was Dad on the sideline in a windbreaker with his head clasped in a headset. His eyes scoured the field around him. Those eyes that saw everything. Mom would be in the stands at this very moment wearing her Huskies sweatshirt, her face locked in a tireless smile. She always claimed not to care if or how she was mentioned in the media, but I knew it was always in the back of her mind that the cameras often panned to her in the season-ticket seats. It happened more than you'd think. The television networks can't help themselves, plugging this idea that there is a relationship between football and American family values. Let's remember that my parents are perfect. They're perfect in the most conventional sense. The kind of familial perfection that less innocent families scowl at with envy but never actually go too far out of their way to emulate. I remembered that my sister, Nikki, was driving over from Spokane for the game, which meant all the cooperative Everett family members were there in the stands on proud display. Everyone except for me. I didn't even watch Dad's games on TV anymore.

I told Case I was heading out back to take a piss and he followed. The spot to relieve oneself was in the shrubbery that ran along the shed at the far corner of the backyard. When we came around the bushes, Pile Driver was zipping up and swaying slightly to some current in his head.

"Nice dick," Case said.

"You're not the first to notice," Pile Driver said. He didn't seem in a hurry to leave. He drained the beer he'd brought with him and crushed the can between his meaty hands before chucking it into the hedge.

"Did you see Coach's press conference?" Case said. He had his head thrown back, eyes to the stars.

"Fuck 'em, dude. That ain't right, embarrassing the guy like that. What do they think they're gonna do? Get him fired because of some ancient history? Everyone makes recruiting calls. It's horseshit. Coach ain't done nothin' wrong."

"Hope you're right."

Case started to piss, aiming his stream high into the dense plant structure so that it diffused through the leaves and stems and finally pattered silently to the soil. A few feet away I directed my own stream into a frothy puddle at the base of the hedge. The possibility that a person might end up in this bush on account of roughhousing or passing out seemed considerable and on the outside chance it could be me I preferred in advance not to find each leaf sprinkled with urine as if covered in morning dew.

"It'll blow over," Pile Driver said. "I mean, if the N-C-double-fucking-A wants to do an investigation, we got his back, right?"

"Let's hope it doesn't come to that."

"Whatever. See you homos later."

Pile Driver stumbled away.

"How do you put up with that guy?" I said.

"He's a good guy at heart. He's had a rough life," Case said.

"He's a mess," I said.

Case shrugged as if the burden of Jesse Goodman was easier just to shoulder than to sort out.

When I left an hour later to walk home, a guy was pacing the sidewalk in front of the house, looking for his car. "Porsche!" he kept yelling. "Where is she? Porsche!" I watched unnoticed as he slapped the hood of a parked Honda in frustration. I considered advising him not to drive. As it turned out, Porsche wasn't a car at all, but, rather, a cheerleader named Mercedes. "Ah, shit!" the guy said when the girl appeared and corrected him. "I could have sworn it was Porsche. You got a friend named Porsche?" He thought this was hilarious and though she didn't laugh, she didn't seem to mind either. She was still getting lucky, if you could call it that.

As I walked home, I imagined running into Nate Orton on the deserted streets. He would say, "Hey man, why'd you leave so early? I was hoping to get a chance to talk to you about something." And I'd reassure him that everything was okay and he could tell me anything he wanted. But then I remembered I was drunk and I'd wasted enough of my time tonight. Besides, I needed to have a good tennis practice in the morning and I knew I'd hate myself if I was dragging my feet on the court on account of a night like this.

Haile in A minor

I was nine when my parents first took me to a concert. I resisted dressing up, something I did only for church, which we rarely attended. My mother lured me into the car by convincing me that dressing up meant we were going to do something special. Even under the most comfortable circumstances, I wasn't very good at sitting still for long, and for the concert she had insisted I wear a plaid skirt that made me scratch my thighs whenever I thought no one was watching. At the theater, I wiggled in my seat and stared up at the high, ornate ceiling, entertaining myself as the rows around us filled with elderly patrons.

When the lights dimmed, I strained to see what would happen next. Four musicians appeared clutching long, razor-thin bows and beautiful, polished wooden string instruments. The cello seemed about the right size, but the two violins looked too small for their respective humans and my eyes widened at the size of the bass. We had seats near the front and I remember thinking that the musicians seemed so tall up on that stage.

There was a moment after they were all seated, just before they began to play, when an electric silence fell over the room: I could sense that something was about to happen but could not fathom what it might look or sound like. I think this was the first moment of real, grown-up curiosity I ever experienced. And then, in unison, they drew their bows across the strings and the first sounds touched me. My legs, which were not yet long enough to reach the floor, suddenly stopped swinging. I had of course heard classical music in my parents' home, but it had only been background music to me, one of the many adult things—like cooking, or my father's business calls, or the *Wall Street Journal* that was delivered each day—that I'd never bothered to absorb into my world.

Experiencing this music in person was an altogether different story. At the first low, quivering tone from the cello I felt something shift within me. And when the violinist danced her long fingers in a precise, sliding jump up into a higher octave, my heart did a little leap in my small chest. I was too young to identify passion, too naïve to recognize seduction, too innocent to understand what it meant to have an obsession. But it had begun.

The way I remember it, I was transfixed by the performance from the first note to last. But that memory isn't entirely accurate. There was at least one moment—I recall this almost like a separate memory, as if my mind had filed it elsewhere—where I must have taken my eyes away from the stage to look up at my mother. I remember this because when I looked at her she was not looking at the musicians. She was looking at me. Something about the piqued amusement in her eyes made me feel as though she'd been watching me for some time. What I had no way of knowing then was that that look represented the birth of an indestructible force that would steer the direction of my life.

SCENE: INTERIOR. BATHROOM. EVENING.

IAN stands shirtless in front of the mirror. He appraises himself head-on and then
in profile, puffing out his chest. He picks up
an electric shaver and looks at it. He eyes
himself again in the mirror. Then he turns
the shaver on. He winces at the loud buzzing
noise it makes.

Casey Boyd is in a relationship with **Krista Marshall**
Casey Boyd is taking things 4 downs at a time
Casey Boyd is 40 effin' min on hold with the dealer after losing his car keys! F@#K

Ian sat across from me with a sweating pint glass, alternating his attention between the competing televisions mounted on the wall. We were at Third Base, the better-than-decent sports bar off Main Street. Admirably, the Florence baseball club's decade-long slump hadn't sunk the bar's ambition to single-handedly wear out every pun that linked baseball with drinking and eating greasy bar food. Playing darts or pool in the flickering glow of televisions, students could still drink Relief Pitchers to wash down their Base-Clearing Hot Wings, Dugout Potato Skins, and Hey-Batta-Batta Beer-battered Fish Sticks.

"He left without a word to the team?" Ian asked.

"Coach Evans told us Draper resigned, and that was it. The NCAA is investigating everything and they could take away wins and scholarships from us. So I think the AD wants to make a big change, to show we're serious about the rules or whatever. I feel bad for the guy. I mean, he fucked up, I know, but that was a long time ago. Anyway, he's a good coach."

We sat in the glow of a Mariners game—safe to say, we were the only Ms fans in the place. When we were little, Ian and I would get to the ballpark early and climb the upper deck of Safeco Field and stand on top of everything. During night games, the sun set over the sound in the west and the rows of seats sloped steeply down in the east toward the tiny, famous players and the precise diamond inlaid within the glowing green field. Overhead, the bellies of huge Boeing planes roared heavy and graceful, close enough that I thought if one of the pros were to climb up there with us, he'd be able to peg one with a baseball.

"Now what happens?" Ian said.

"Coach Evans is taking over. But I heard they're interviewing other candidates, too. Probably just a formality. I don't think they're stupid enough to try to bring in someone new mid-season. Evans hasn't been a coordinator very long, but at least he knows the system. I just hope they name him head coach sooner than later so we can move on. Some of the guys are freaking out. Draper recruited them, you know? And now he left 'em hanging."

Ian nodded and glanced casually over at the television, as if the thing to do here was to monitor the game rather than watch it. After three years of little interaction between us, he was still familiar to me. We'd been too young back in Seattle for us to share memories of closing down sports bars and stumbling back to homes where hangovers, not parents, awaited our return. But little had changed, only now it was drink- and smoke-stale air that filled the margins around our language of baseball, football, girls, movies, and school.

There was no way of getting around the fact that the last time I watched late-summer baseball with Ian was in the hospital. There was no way not to be aware that she passed away four years ago today. I didn't expect him to, but I wondered if Ian remembered. The weight of such an anniversary is lost on those who haven't lived through the death of someone close. Certain tributes are no longer difficult—visiting her gravestone or looking at pictures—the traditional nods of support between survivors. They get easier over time. But worst is the part that can't be shared. The constant feeling that something is out of place. The sway of moods. The inability to concentrate, which causes dropped balls at practice and lost car keys. August 28 is no longer just a day in August. It's a wall of time, sometimes stretching a week on either side, that hijacks my personality. Thank God, or whomever, for football. I'll get through this week, the week of September 3, as I have for the past four years: four downs at a time.

At the commercial break I checked the other TVs. An ESPN reporter was speaking from Seattle where one of the big college football matchups of the weekend—USC at Washington—would be played. The screen showed a few clips of a UW practice.

"How're your parents?" I said. Ian looked over his shoulder and acknowledged the footage of his father—roaming the field amongst his players—with a roll of his eyes.

"The same. Only more so."

"Man, I wanted to play for your dad so bad. I remember how careful I was with my U-dub application. I didn't want to mess anything up. Then it turned out I wasn't a good enough player anyway."

"You're good enough now. He should have seen that."

In the media, Coach Mike Everett was known as a family man, the kind you always see portrayed with his wife and kids at their charming lakeside house. But the clues I picked up from Ian projected a darker image, not necessarily of his father, but of the space between them.

"Something going on between you two?"

"Nothing specific."

"Have your parents seen you play?"

"Tennis? Nope. Never missed a single football game, though. Not that I'm encouraging them to visit. I think my mom wants to move back East. She's been working on my dad. They both grew up in upstate New York and always planned to come back. This is where they met."

Ian turned his attention back to the game. I let the subject expire.

"I'm glad you met Krista," I said.

"How long have you two been together?"

"Since last spring." I paused. "I won't ask what you think."

Ian and Krista are not going to get along, I can sense it. All summer I had this picture of the three of us having fun together, but already I can see that they rub each other the wrong way.

"I think you're lucky," Ian said.

"Is that a fact?"

"Don't you think so?"

"Come on. You'll find a girl."

"That's not what I meant. You're lucky to have someone already. Looking gets old."

"It's one of those things. It happens when you're not expecting it."

"Trust me, I'm not expecting it."

"What about the girl in Art History? You two hit it off."

Ian said nothing, and I took this to mean he was more interested in Haile than I thought. I'd give him two weeks before they hook up. He has that look to him that I know girls like. It's the only thing I've noticed that's changed about him. He looks more—I don't know—aware of himself.

"Hey, isn't that Krista?"

I turned around to see her by the door, hugging herself with her arms while she searched the bar with her green eyes. They lit up when they found mine. Six months of the horniest years of my life, and this girl still did it for me every time. Nothing to do with her, but as she started toward us I almost wished she hadn't come. Ian and I used to have so much fun bullshitting with each other and watching baseball games and suddenly having Krista here didn't seem like the appropriate setting to try get our three-pronged friendship back on track.

"Hey guys. Afa said you might be here."

"Hey," Ian said without looking away from the game. Krista climbed onto a vacant stool, gave me a kiss, and started immediately to talk.

"All the girls arrived today. We just had a dinner with everyone—girls only. You should see some of these new girls. They look so lost and wouldn't stop asking questions about their classes and shit. I can't believe I was ever that clueless." She didn't seem to expect a response or mind that Ian and I were presently more interested in a pitch count two thousand miles away. She just needed to be talking. I admit, it doesn't usually bother me when we're alone. But with Ian there it seemed intrusive. She paused to take the first sip of the beer the bartender had put in front of her. "Wow, you guys are exciting."

I was about to respond when the DH, Juarez, connected with a pitch. "He got alla that one," Ian said, downing his beer as Juarez trotted businesslike around the bases. A graphic popped up to tell us that Juarez had set a Major League record for RBI facing any one opposing pitcher. "Imagine being the guy who has to sit in a truck computing all these random stats," Ian said.

"It's all computerized," I started to explain, but stopped. The thing was, I'd more than imagined it. Even though I was premed, next to playing in the NFL I couldn't think of a better job than computing and interpreting major league sports statistics.

"What's RBIs?" Krista said, more to Ian, I knew, since she never would have asked a question like that if he weren't there. I wondered if she wasn't as desperate for Ian to like her as I was.

"It's RB*I*," I said. "Runs batted in. The plural is already in the R." Ian and Krista looked at each other as if I were the one who had said something wrong. Whatever. "Let's go. It's getting late."

It was actually only eleven and we'd barely finished two beers, but I was suddenly anxious for the day's end. While we got ready for bed, Krista was the only one who spoke. Some of her new housemates were really cool and some of them were kind of bitchy but she thought that was only because they were jealous of her because she had a real boyfriend and was so happy and centered as a person because she's in a long-term relationship...

This went on and on and while her carefree voice was soothing, a part of me wished that she wouldn't stay over every night. Some nights I'd rather just sit alone and play my guitar. I think I heard her say how liberating it was to know she was safely with the guy she wanted to marry, but I was too tired to think about what that meant. Maybe, in a way, she and Ian were right. I was lucky to have found someone and I shouldn't take that for granted.

When I took off my shirt she said "oooohh" in her sex voice. Her sex voice is lower and almost musical, and when she uses it she tries to keep her lips parted seductively. I've explained to her that it's her body that's sexy and not this little act, but she always does it anyway. She put her hands on my chest and kissed me. I didn't want her to ask me if something was wrong so I kissed her back in a gentle way that I hoped suggested I was tired. But, even exhausted, the body obediently pumps blood when presented with this fairly basic set of circumstances. By the time she discovered that I was half hard, I knew it would be easier just to go through with it than to talk about why I'd rather not.

This was how September 3 would end.

Haile strikes a chord

On an overcast afternoon, I shuffled out of the library at six, bidding goodnight to Eva and Ms. West, our supervisor, and hurrying home on foot.

Ms. Rivera lives only a mile from campus, high enough on the low-sloping hillside to provide a sprawling view of the valley cradling university and town. The setting was to me unreal. Of the two neighbors in immediate proximity, one residence crouched far in the distance, hardly visible across the rolling terrain. The other property was obstructed completely by a stretch of spruce and oak trees running the length of the driveway.

Ms. Rivera's house, white as a freshly painted picket fence and accented with bursts of yellow blooming from flower boxes beneath each window, had been constructed around a massive brick chimney that jutted from the peak of the roof. The fireplace and chimney were the oldest in the valley, Ms. Rivera had explained in a way that suggested most people found the tidbit fascinating. Though the original farmhouse had been unlivable when she first fell in love with the idea of a home on this hillside, she purchased the condemned building anyway, and then scooped up the surrounding land, plot by plot, as she could afford it. It was her current husband, acquired last of all in these trans-actions, who insisted on tearing down the old farmhouse, save for the chimney, and building a new home in its place. This mas-sive renovation also included the conversion of the loft above the detached garage into the apartment I now called home.

For a girl who had lived only in city apartments, this allot-ment of forty acres to a single couple on faculty salaries seemed implausible. But as it turned out, Ms. Rivera and her husband were not wealthy. They were simply patient and mindful of their priorities. I found it difficult at first to see what they found so appealing about living in the middle of nowhere. But now I saw it. *Space* was the true universal luxury, and the joke was on all the city people who jockeyed to spend millions for a few bed-rooms on Fifth Avenue or Central Park West while the supposed simple folk in the backcountry wound up with picturesque acres to spare.

I stood in Ms. Rivera's living room, uncertain whether I'd been invited to dinner as a student or a boarder—or what the differ-ence might mean. Mr. Brooks was out of town for the weekend with the tennis team (which meant Ian was gone as well) and Ms. Rivera had suggested the two of us should have dinner together.

"You listen to music here?" I asked before she could invite me to sit down. The living room was formed on one side by windows overlooking the property. The other walls were lined with book-shelves and rows of CDs and records. There were a few pieces of bare antique furniture but the main feature was a large armchair placed in the center of the room. It faced two upright speakers, each as tall as a man, which stood away from the wall.

"Yes. In the mornings. The fog at dawn settles over the prop-erty and I'm left alone with my coffee and my extraordinarily expensive sound system. And all this music." All the majors were present—Bach and Handel, Mozart, Beethoven, Chopin, Brahms, Dvorak, Stravinsky, Shostakovich—with some of the minors mixed in. I ran a finger along the spines, stopping at a recording of Beethoven's Opus 18.

Without thinking, I said, "They're in chronological order, by composition."

Ms. Rivera allowed a long beat of silence.

"That's a sharp observation."

"Why do you arrange them that way?"

She studied me for several moments as if in a new light. My heart raced and I wondered if I'd inadvertently crossed back over the line I'd drawn between my Florence self and my pre-Florence self. Would I now have to explain everything to her? But then she started talking and the moment passed.

"Musical geniuses are human, too. Lest we forget, they are influenced by their contemporaries, by the politics and religions of their day, as well as by their predecessors and the versions of history that were taught to them. Arranging the pieces chronologically puts them in the context of their day rather than comparing them against the composer's entire body of work. But if we talked music theory all night I'd feel like a terrible host. The food's almost ready. Do you prefer red or white wine?"

"Oh, no, thank you."

"Miss Haile, I met you in a bar—you were performing, remember? That place was drenched in smoke and booze—and I won't believe for a minute that you simply prefer not to enjoy a drink or two with dinner."

We hadn't actually met in a bar, at least I hadn't thought of it that way. True, the café in Hyannis had a bar and people often smoked at their tables, but I think I'd allowed myself to imagine the setting as something quainter, more like a picturesque, seaside jazz venue than the open-air watering hole that tourists used it for. On an evening last spring, Ms. Rivera had approached me after one of my sets—she happened to be visiting friends on the Cape—and wanted to know if I was in school. I deflected the question, but she persisted, explaining that she taught at Florence and thought that the music program there was something I might be interested in. At the time, I politely assured her that I was moving back to the city at the end of the summer. That was all I said, leaving unmentioned my plans to return to Juilliard, which is where I'd have ended up had she not given me her business card before she disappeared. For several days, I thought about her business card in the pocket of my unwashed jeans before I retrieved it and made my first visit to Florence's Web site.

"Well—"

"It's not a test, if that's what you're afraid of. Better an artist develop a healthy relationship with drink before she goes in search of a needy one."

"I don't know a thing about wine."

"If you like string quartets, you'll like wine," she said, retrieving an open bottle and tipping it over a glass. Ms. Rivera was pretty and younger-looking than I remembered from our first brief meeting. There was more than a nod to her Puerto Rican descent in her heavily lashed brown eyes and the straight black hair that framed her face and was pulled up in back to reveal her slender neck. Her skin, apparently unaged by the sun, looked as if it would retain the rich, unblemished color of coffee ice cream even if she spent a decade above the Arctic Circle. "Any deep appreciation for wine begins with red. There's more to contemplate."

"It's good," I said politely.

"It's perfectly decent. For dinner I have a bottle of something special."

We sat in the living room while something oniony and garlicky simmered in the kitchen. The smells were warm and blended with the dusky view and the thin-stemmed wine glasses and the popping fire in the old fireplace and the oak-dust aroma of antique furniture.

"You're not a vegetarian, are you?" she asked. "I could separate the chorizo."

"No, thank you. Everything smells wonderful."

"Let's eat. We're having chorizo and pasta and wedges of iceberg lettuce with my special homemade bleu cheese dressing."

Ms. Rivera had set a small table in front of the fireplace with cloth napkins and silver that had been used more than it had been shined. It was sweet and cozy to think of Ms. Rivera and Mr. Brooks sitting here on an everyday evening with their bleu cheese salad and the valley's oldest hearth and a conversation about the events of the day. Their marriage had a touch more of the practical than the passionate. Not practical in a financial sense, but practical emotionally. I could see that Ms. Rivera and Mr. Brooks loved each other, but it was not the head-over-heels crazy love I expected to find. They didn't seem to love each other as much as they loved this, living together like this. They were two people inclined to simple happiness, who got along well, and didn't want to be alone. I'd never imagined that sort of life could be romantic until I saw their little dining table set up by the fireplace.

"I'm afraid I can't tell much difference," I said when we sat for dinner and got around to the bottle of something special. This wine was inkier than our previous glasses, and with my first small sip it felt as if more was in my mouth than I had put there.

"Sure you can. It's no different than two string quartets. They may tackle the same piece of music but they each tease out of it their own personality. It's the same with grapes. This wine is a huge, deep merlot from Washington. Let me see." She put a sip in her mouth and held it there a moment. "Hmm. Try to taste black cherry. It also has some sort of spice combination right at the front of the tongue, like mint and cinnamon." This ritual excited her. I took another sip but all I could think of was that it felt silky, like it was going to turn my tongue purple. "Merlots—particularly this one—are bold, confident, and loud, like, say, the Emerson Quartet. The vintage matters too, of course. But with some wineries, as with some quartets, the performance is always a good value."

I'd seen the Emersons four times in concert. The sound they carved out of those strings made you feel as if you could hear the vibrations in each tense particle, as if the pitch-perfect sheepskin was about to explode on every note.

"Merlot can be a bit much," she continued. "Pinots from France are my favorite. A good Burgundy is as experienced and unpretentious as the Borodin Quartet."

"I guess you don't drink wine from boxes. I'd love to hear your musical analogy for that stuff."

"Oh, dear. That popular stuff that comes in the jugs and boxes and rakes in the most money and is still stuck in your head the next morning? I guess that's like Andrew Lloyd Webber."

The food was good and I told her it was amazing because I would have told her it was good even if it was bad. A smooth red sauce thickened by Parmesan and tossed with sautéed vegetables and tubular noodles whose Italian name I get mixed up with the bow ties and corkscrews. The spicy chorizo wet my tear ducts every few bites.

"Where is the tennis team this weekend?" I asked, though I already knew the answer. I'd had the urge all evening to mention Ian and kept bringing up topics that might present me with an opportunity. Half the fun of secret infatuations was finding a way to talk about them.

"At Brown. First tournament of the year."

"Does Mr. Brooks discuss his players with you?"

"Not terribly often. I hear about who wins and who's injured and so forth. And we have them all over for dinner before the more important tournaments at the end of the season. They act like a big family, cousins or something. Did you ever play a sport?"

"No. Not like that. Yoga and jogging on the treadmill are pretty solitary activities. Do you ever go watch them play?"

"Sure. Always the home matches. Once I went along to a tournament in Florida."

The disc in the CD player changed and I recognized the first soulful notes of a track by the Traci Rice Trio. "You like Traci Rice?" I said, excited. "I've been listening to her nonstop lately."

"I do," Ms. Rivera said, patting her mouth with the napkin. "They're coming, you know. We're trying to pin down a date in November."

"I'm *there*. They're incredible live. What wine are they like?" I said, holding up my glass.

"Hmm. Traci Rice. Reliable, earthy tones. A Chianti, I suppose. On the one hand perfect for everyday consumption with dinner, yet best enjoyed with good company for a special occasion. They can bring an evening to life."

"Cheers," I said, and Ms. Rivera refreshed our glasses.

"I can't quite figure out the boundaries of your interests," Ms. Rivera said. "I had no idea you were so knowledgeable about classical music. Do you play other instruments besides the piano?"

The alcohol had dulled my usually sharp defenses, but in a split second the thin veil of wine-flavored confidence was torn away and my anxiety returned like a spear driving through my chest. I tried to shrug casually and piece together a response in line with the simplicity of Ms. Rivera's question. But before I could stop them, I felt my eyes shift. I was incapable of pretending this was something minor. What I finally said felt like the seven-word version of my life story.

"My mother enrolled me in violin lessons."

"Do you still play?"

"Not much." I felt a sudden temptation to tell Ms. Rivera the truth—everything. But I could tell from the lump blossoming in the back of my throat that I wouldn't be able to make it through the whole story. "She pushed me kind of hard," I said, regretting it immediately. *Had* she pushed me too hard? Did it matter? "I was ready for a break."

Ms. Rivera was quiet for a moment, watching me over the rim of her glass. "Well, my violin is in the studio out there under your apartment. You're free to use it anytime. I'd love to hear you play, when you're ready."

So that I wouldn't seem desperate to change the subject, I waited a few moments before I said, "Did you used to perform?"

"When I was your age, it was what I wanted to do most."

"Do you mind my asking why you stopped?"

"Yes, but since it's a fair question, I'll answer it."

"I'm sorry."

"Nonsense. It's an important lesson. I stopped because I couldn't handle the rejection. Through my high school teacher in Miami I got an audition at Juilliard. It was what I'd always wanted. To go to Juilliard and then to travel the world performing." She laughed, but it wasn't a laugh of joy or irony. It was harsh, like a cold judgment. Suddenly I knew where her story was headed and I wasn't sure I wanted to hear it. I couldn't swallow. The flesh around my tonsils had gone bone dry. "I flew up to New York for the audition. I was brave. I played Chopin until my knuckles hurt and my heart wept. But it wasn't good enough. That's it. There's no horror story about stage fright and icy sweats. The audition went perfectly and it wasn't good enough. I took it personally, I'm afraid. I believed if my best wasn't good enough to get into Juilliard I must have been fooling myself all along. So I ran away. I went into hiding, from myself."

"Where did you go?"

"I came here," she said. "Did you ever play hide and seek? Coming here was much like scattering off to hide, crawling into what appears to be the first dark hole you find, only to discover it's actually an opening to a place you never knew existed. Eventually, I came back to music and it felt right again. I guess you could say I came here for the wrong reasons and stayed for the right ones. But how is it that we're always talking about me? You're the natural performer."

"I don't know."

"You have a gift, Haile. You know we have our concert at the end of the semester. But have you thought of playing a few gigs in the meantime?"

I knew I was blushing. Could she tell how much I'd already thought about this? I felt as transparent as my wine glass.

"I guess I have. I mean, I think I could get better at it with more practice."

"Put a set list together. Set something up."

When I walked across the driveway to my apartment, it was raining soft, pattering drops that kicked up the smells of the earth. I could drink a whole bottle of wine if it smelled like that rain smell. It must have been late but I was full of energy and optimism. I entered Ms. Rivera's studio without even going upstairs for my notebook. I found pages of scratch paper and a dull pencil on the desk and sat down at the keyboard, playing and writing, exploring and stretching, laughing and singing. I stayed up for hours and discovered more music than I had in a month.

I felt as if I was on my way.

I was Haile. I was really becoming her.

SCENE: INTERIOR. TENNIS COURT. DAY.

IAN, wearing short tennis shorts and a headband, glares over the net in concentration.
He bounces the ball twice against the ground
and then pulls his racquet back, preparing
to serve.

I figured I could move through the semi-finals in straight sets. Four sets tops, if my opponent had really improved his serve over the summer. So the fifth set was frustrating territory when I found myself down 4-1 two hours after stepping onto the court.

My opponent was a tall, hairy scruff from Penn State, all elbows and knees, wearing a tie-dyed bandana saturated with sweat. He was a fine tennis player. But the fact was, he wasn't beating me. I was beating myself. The ball and my racquet met again and again on inconsistent terms, mostly resulting in heavy, dead shots that came flying back at me out of reach. Whenever I struck the ball my wrist had that buoyant feeling you get when you lift an object that's lighter than it looks. This grew frustrating and I didn't handle it well. Instead of taking a few deep breaths, I swung harder and harder, putting my anger behind shots that sent the fuzzy little bastard sailing high over the baseline. To acknowledge my distress I shouted a combination of curse words and other unintelligible syllables, mostly in general disgust but once at the chair umpire. That was a mistake—both his call (that ball was *in*) and my reaction to it. But neither the call nor my temper had any hope of being reversed.

I managed to hold serve late in the set and trailed only 5-4, but match point was swiftly upon us. When I spliced a crafty drop shot that, despite all my hand-eye calculations, dropped on *my* side of the net, I exploded. How I'd managed to wait until the bitter end to break my racquet was the only measure of restraint I demonstrated all morning.

Coach Brooks told me to take a walk when I came off the court. He usually encouraged emotional play from his athletes but I could see that even he suspected this was something else. When I returned from a few minutes of fresh air, we sat together on the bottom bleacher as the next match got underway.

"Any idea what happened out there?"

"Yeah. I was a fucking mess."

"That was a side effect. A very lively and disruptive one. What I meant was, where did it come from?"

"I lost concentration," I said.

"No. You *weren't* concentrating. There's a difference. Concentration isn't lost or found. It's either done or not done."

"I just didn't have it today."

"Not good enough. Today was the match. You can't postpone matches for your better days. You know better than that."

I nodded.

"What is it? Yesterday you're on fire; today you're down. Something's up."

I leaned back against the bleachers and watched a volley play out on the court. Coach Brooks tried again after a few minutes, this time taking a little heat off his tone.

"Is everything all right?"

"Are we still talking about tennis?"

"Don't have to be."

A long pause rose up between us. He waited.

"Never mind," I said. "I'll think it over."

"All right. You're off the hook today. But, Ian? If something's on your mind, you can't just run from it. Some things don't just go away. We'll sort everything out next week, how's that sound? Now go watch your teammates."

On the ride home, I lay in the back of the van with a full seat to myself. Coach Brooks was driving. Two underclassmen, Cameron and Gretchen, were exploring their budding romance in the seat in front of me.

Somewhere between the New York state line and River Bend, my cell started buzzing in my pocket. I reached to dig it out, figuring there were two possibilities of who might be calling. One was Case, though I knew he'd barely returned to campus from their losing road game and was probably in no mood to chat.

The other was my mother. Before I could decide whether I was in the mood to talk to her, I saw that the incoming call was actually from my father's cell phone. The likeliest excuse for this occasion was that my parents must have followed the tournament results online and Mom had forced him to call and tell me to keep my head up. You know—father to son, coach to coach's son. The other possibility was that someone had died. I'm telling you, Dad doesn't call on his own volition. Mom calls. She calls all the time, maybe three times a week, and every once in a while she forces the phone into Dad's hands so we can say a few things to each other about the Mariners, Seahawks, or Pacific Northwest vs. Northeastern weather patterns.

During football season my senior year of high school, I started making decisions about my future that darkened the mood around my parents' house. I wanted to move East for college. I wanted to try something new. I didn't want to play football anymore. My relationship with Dad had always been a close one, but the truth was that it was never something we had to work at. We both loved football and we both excelled at it. But when the untested foundations of our relationship began to break down on account of my decision to give up football, his displeasure distilled quickly to a chilly silence with only a brief detour into anger. This was ultimately tempered by my agreeing to go to Florence, which is my parents' alma mater and lies within driving distance of scores of relatives. But the wedge had been driven between us. If only he was a fraction as capable of analyzing his family as he was a football game.

The turning point in our spiraling relationship was the Sean Wilkins porn incident. Sean Wilkins was a point guard on the high school basketball team, a sheer-talent kid who knew he could get a long ways just by coasting. With his athletic body and clear skin, he had more time to worry about being cool than most high school sufferers could afford. Midway through our senior year, Sean came over on a Friday night to play pool and swig from a bottle of vodka we'd stashed under the couch. Sean didn't intimidate me as he did others. We were quarterback and point guard—the leaders of two separately prospering cliques. And yet, we talked about what anyone else would have talked about. We talked a lot about girls we wanted to bang and how much better life could get by going away to college.

When I came back from a piss break feeling light and wavy from the drink, I found Sean had discovered my new laptop. The computer was an early Christmas gift from my parents, intended to help me organize my college applications online. In the ninety seconds he was alone, Sean had come across a Web site called Sweet Teen Sluts. I'd seen these sites before but never had the guts to get past the first page, where they tell you to enter if you're over eighteen or else to get lost. I always figured entering would require some form of additional proof of age and that—what did I know?—there was probably some way for the computer to alert the authorities of my intrusion as a minor. Another concern was the incurable flashing pop-ups that materialized when you ran searches for phrases like "hot nude women" and "boobs free pictures." What was to stop them from popping up again if my mom searched for breast cancer or some other seemingly benign trigger?

The warning on the home page of Sweet Teen Sluts did not faze Sean, who was as seventeen as I was. Not only did he enter the site, which offered a free tour littered with uncensored stills of improbable breasts and glistening pink vaginas spread open with fingers, but he had purchased rights to a password at $6.95 a month that allowed unlimited access to galleries and videos and chat rooms that I was sure had the ability to corrupt my new computer. "The money's totally worth it," he explained when he detected my shock, which was least of all for the price.

The pool game meanwhile went unfinished. We'd made more progress on the bottle of booze but that, too, suddenly took a back seat to the new world opened before me. A video was streaming on the screen: two girls who were neither sweet nor teens but wore a lot of makeup just in case it was their faces you were interested in. An unattractive, long-haired man played the role of the carpenter who'd come to install shelving on the wrong day, happened upon the ladies, and was obliged to join in. Without shame, Sean looked for and found evidence of my erection. Then he showed me his own condition through his jeans. "You got any lotion for this?" he asked. Just like that. Even if Lotion For This was an everyday occurrence, I'd never dreamed it was something two guys would acknowledge openly, as if the problem was a loose outlet cover and it was simply a Phillips head that was needed.

I got the lotion from the bottom of a drawer by my bed (of course I had Lotion For This) and Sean turned off the light over the pool game and set the laptop on the coffee table. We sat at opposite ends of the couch with our eyes on the screen and our hands rubbing ourselves through our jeans.

I was suddenly a little intimidated by Sean Wilkins. I was most afraid to act in any way that might sour Sean's opinion of me, so I simply followed his lead while trying desperately not to betray any sign of reluctance or eagerness. When a new scene started with a new set of girls and he unzipped and pulled out his dick, I did the same. I don't remember wanting to look but I remember seeing it. It was larger than I expected, the flesh darker. He squeezed a drop of lotion the size of a Hershey's kiss from the bottle and rubbed it between his fingers and palm. At his first lubricated stroke, he moaned once very quietly in a way that made me feel as if I'd intruded on an intimate moment. By the time I'd spread a cool layer of lotion over my own dick, Sean was work- ing his jeans down his legs with his dry hand until the waist was around his ankles. I began to feel more confident that Sean didn't suspect me of wanting to look at him. Or didn't care. This made me want to look at him more. He was totally caught up in the girls on screen and what he was doing with his hand and being drunk and horny and hot and the best basketball player in the school. I barely looked at the video once but I couldn't bring myself to look directly at him again either. I thought about girls mostly, girls from school and what it would be like to have sex with them. But I'd thought about all of that before and my body had never felt like this. Something about Sean being there was different and complicated and far out of reach of my understanding.

My folks were in bed, but of course it turned out that Dad was unable to sleep and had gone in search of a TV to watch game film on that wouldn't disturb Mom. When he walked in and turned on the light, he froze and said, "What is this?" It was clearly a rhetorical question. Sean said, "Ah shit." As quickly as he had come, my father turned around, video tape in hand, and went back upstairs. You can't blame him for that. There was nothing more to be said. But there was something about his silence in the weeks afterward that made me feel as if he'd handled it badly. I can't imagine what he might have done or said to make it better. God knows I was plenty happy to have nothing said about it at all. But Dad has never dealt well with matters unrelated to football and I felt as if I'd exposed him somehow. When I told him three weeks later that I didn't want to play football anymore and that I wanted to go to a school on the other side of the country, he must have been disappointed and angry. On the outside, he was only silent.

When I listened to Dad's message there was no sign of anything out of the ordinary. His voiced sounded relieved to have gotten my voicemail. He said he was calling to touch base and say hello and good job in the tennis match and that he had some exciting news to share. I couldn't hear Mom but I knew she'd been standing there with him. He had that tone of voice that implied *I'm doing this because it's easier to call and get it over with than it is to deal with her nagging.*

I laid my head back and stared at the roof of the van, trying not to relive those final months of my senior year of high school. It's funny how the mind works. A year earlier, I hadn't had a clue of how to characterize these feelings. And suddenly I felt like I wanted to explain them to someone. I don't know how I decided it, but lying in the back of the van, I made up my mind that Haile Laine, the girl in my art history class, would be the first person I would tell. I thought it would be safe with her. It wouldn't get back to anyone in the athletics department. And so what if it did? I was planning to leave for film school in a few months. Soon I would be in New York or Los Angeles and there would be no reason to hide anything.

Casey Boyd is sampling the population and graphing a normal distribution

Casey Boyd posted a final score: Florence 10, Louisville 31

Casey Boyd became a fan of Guitar Hero

"Look at these homos. What is it they're all reading the same papers for? There ain't a decent sports section between 'em." The auditorium was about half full, mostly with students reading *The New York Times* or *Wall Street Journal* until Professor Gilles showed up. Pile Driver scratched his fleshy head. "So, how we doing this Homecoming thing?"

I shrugged.

"What?"

"I don't know. Maybe we shouldn't."

"Don't be a fag. We have to."

As an underclassman, I'd gone along with the tradition. It had only recently occurred to me that someone *made it happen*, that a tradition like that didn't just carry on under its own momentum. "Look, if it happens, fine, but I don't want to be responsible."

"What'd the first guy say when he stepped onto the moon? 'If not here, where? If not us, who?' "

"There are so many things wrong with what you just said."

"We have to do this, man. It's tradition."

"What are you looking at me for? If it happens it happens." I was annoyed with Pile Driver, but mostly because he had a point. A thought waved in my head like a banner: if I was really a leader on the team, didn't it fall on me to take charge? Kyle, our QB, wasn't a natural leader when it came to dealing with the team off the field.

From our seats at the outer reaches of the room, I watched Ian and Haile find their places in the third row. Her hair was pulled to the side and draped over one shoulder, leaving the cream-colored flesh of her neck exposed above the collar of her red shirt. Had I seen her wearing anything other than red? It made me think of lips. Her lips.

Professor Gilles began class with the announcement that the book he'd penned, the inspiration for this very class, had landed recently in bookstores. He held up a copy for our benefit. "I'll be discussing and signing books in the theater next Tuesday—a literary to-do, for those of you who like that sort of thing. I'm under no illusion that the majority of you are thinking at all past this weekend's Homecoming festivities, but Tuesday will come nonetheless, and there I'll be if you should care to drop by."

"Do we get extra credit if we come?"

Gilles squinted in our direction, cupping a hand above his eyes. "Ah, the Illiterati." The class erupted in laughter.

The corners of Pile Driver's big, proud, stupid Texas smile fell to a flat look of confusion. He turned to me to see what was so funny, but I'd slid down in my seat as if we were about to glide under a low bridge. "No, Mr. Goodman. There is no extra credit in this class. I believe in second chances, but not in planning them out before you've wasted your first. If any of you are as anxious as Mr. Goodman is to prove yourself, today is your lucky day. You have an assignment. *This* is something you'll want to write down."

The sound of a hundred pen caps and notebooks replaced the laughing eyes that had been aimed in our direction.

"Two months from today you will each turn in a piece of original artwork. You may paint, draw, etch, or sculpt. Video and photography submissions, however, are not permitted—not because they are not art, but because a camera does too much of the work for the purposes of this lesson. I prefer that you choose a human subject and that you place your subject in a context that has symbolic or thematic meaning, like the examples of famous works we've studied in this class. Expose your imagination. Don't fear vulnerability. Be adventurous. Art is most exciting when it breaks new ground.

"The grading for this assignment is very straightforward. The first third of your grade will depend on whether or not you complete the assignment. The second third of your grade will reflect the level of effort you put into your artwork. This mark will be at my sole discretion and my only contribution to your grade. The final third will be the impact of your piece as judged by your classmates. Impact and meaning are everything. Your artistic ability is of minimal importance."

Gilles paused at the edge of the stage as if remembering one last thing.

"In addition to a grade, the top two pieces, as judged by your peers, will be put on display in the museum for the rest of the semester. As for your apprehensions about exposing artistic flaws, and to preserve objectivity in the judging, your art will remain anonymous. You will turn it in to my TA, who will be the only person with access to the master sheet until grading has been completed. Any questions?"

There were a lot of questions about grading, which Professor Gilles waved aside.

"We'll not waste any more time on the petty issue of grades. Try for once, ladies and gentlemen, to do the assignment, rather than the requirements for the grade. Nothing important in this world is measured by grades. Intelligence, character, integrity, success, happiness—do you want these things, or do you want to struggle with the arbitrary difference between an A minus and a B plus?"

"This is crazy. Can't we just take a quiz or something?" Pile Driver said as we gathered our books at the end of class.

"Didn't you fail the last quiz?"

"Whatever. I thought we were dropping this class."

"We're not dropping the class," I said, my eyes on the third row.

"I got to get out of this class, man," Pile Driver insisted as we walked to practice. "It's the gayest shit I've ever seen. Who wants to look at statues of naked dudes three days a week?"

"There are women, too," I pointed out, remembering the extended discussion Professor Gilles had led about the *Venus de Milo*.

"They're all fat."

I could have pointed out that Pile Driver was in no great position to judge others for their figures, but I didn't.

"You know what I'll do? I'll get a tutor. Way I see it, if a class is gonna fuck ya over you might as well have pretty little tutor come to do the business."

"There you go," I said, unsure whether I was more embarrassed for him or for me for putting up with him.

~ ~ ~

Practice was cut short for the announcement.

Coach Evans wasn't in the training room where we all gathered to hear the news. Some of the guys joked nervously to lighten the air. A circle of players at the front of the room prayed. I spotted Nato sitting on the floor by himself, stretching. Nato and I had been getting the same number of reps in practice and it wasn't clear that the new coaching situation was going to fall to my advantage. If I wanted to play in the NFL, I needed to be more than just one of the top receivers coming out of Florence University. It's not like we were a top-ranked team at the moment. To stand out, I had to be the best. And in a head-to-head comparison with Nato, I hadn't yet proved that I stood out. On the field we were equals.

Chamique Robinson, the athletics director, entered and the room immediately fell silent.

"Gentlemen. I'm about to go into a press conference to announce the official hiring of a new head coach. There will be more details forthcoming but I felt I owed it to you to fill you in on the decision before it was released to the media."

What she said next did not fall under any of the options I had considered possible.

Haile, *crescendo*

All air is clearer than in the humid, grimy city, but the autumn air in River Bend was something you really noticed, like a crystal wine glass without fingerprints. The afternoon sun came in warm beats on our arms and necks. There were exactly three clouds in the distant sky.

Ian looked around and said, deadpan, "Shitty day, huh?"

After class, he'd invited me to lunch. Not invited. He'd said he was going to the student union cafeteria in a way that suggested I could come along. After we ate, I suggested in the same way that I was going for a walk. And here we were.

"What were you doing in New York?" he asked as we walked. The campus paths seemed so different to me now from how I'd first seen them, arriving alone weeks earlier. The buildings and sidewalks and lawns felt more familiar now, more like an environment where I belonged than one I happened to be passing through.

"I was studying music," I said.

"I'm no expert on the music scene but it seems like maybe a step down to come here from New York." We were only a few hours from the city, but he said *here* as if maybe we were standing in northern Siberia. "What kind of music?"

"Mostly classical."

"A bit of the old Ludwig Van, huh?" he said.

"What?"

"*A Clockwork Orange*? The movie? Alex likes Beethoven."

"Sorry, haven't seen it." Ian shook his head as if I'd just told him I grew up abused and parentless. We walked a few steps while I devised a way to change the subject. "Can I ask you a personal question?"

"If you have to ask that before you ask it's usually a good sign that you shouldn't ask. But go ahead."

"How long has it been since your last girlfriend?" An awkward look came onto his face, part embarrassment, part fright, and I saw right away how dumb I'd been. "Or, I mean—what I meant was, if you don't have one now."

"No, no. Not now. Actually. Well, let's see. My last girlfriend was sophomore year. She was supposed to come home with me for Thanksgiving—my parents' idea—but as soon as we bought the tickets I knew I couldn't go through with it. I broke up with her a week before the holiday and went home alone."

"I'll keep that in mind," I said.

Ian didn't say anything. We walked down the Great Lawn past the Boccioni statue and over the bridge to the coffee shop on Main Street.

"When are you going to bring us a tape?" Jamie said when we were paying for our coffee. It was something he nagged me about every time he saw me. I felt my face flush and hoped Ian hadn't caught me gazing over at the small corner stage.

"Forget it."

"A tape?" Ian said.

"Jamie has the crazy idea that I'm going to record a few songs and let him pass them on to his boss."

"It's not a crazy idea," Jamie said. "What are you afraid of?" I flashed him a look of caution but he forged on. "You know, fear never made anyone special. It's a perfectly unremarkable emotion and should be given no credence."

"You record your own songs?" Ian said. I was a little hurt that this had never occurred to him. There had been so many times when I'd wanted to talk to him about music—so many times I'd imagined us talking—that I occasionally almost forgot that none of these conversations had actually taken place.

"The whole thing was Jamie's idea," I said. "The songs—never mind. They aren't even done yet."

Jamie smiled and shrugged and reminded me that I knew where to find him when I changed my mind.

"You know him?" Ian asked when we were outside.

"Sure. I guess you could say he was my first friend at Florence. I met him the second day I was here. He's a sweetie."

Ian only nodded. We set out in the direction of campus. Ian's phone rang as we were walking over the bridge.

"That's so weird," he said, putting it back in his pocket after glancing at the screen. "My dad never calls. And now he's called twice in two days."

"Are you close with your parents?"

Ian looked at me as if I'd said something funny.

"Mike Everett. You have no idea who he is, do you?"

"Should I?"

"No, you're my new best friend. My dad coaches football at the University of Washington. In certain circles he's a big deal, I guess. We had a little falling out over me giving up football."

I got the impression that Ian wanted me to believe that he didn't like his parents. But I didn't. I could tell he regretted something about his distance from them.

"Well, if it helps, I think you made the right decision. That sport is so...mindlessly barbaric. No offense to your dad."

"Let's go this way," Ian said when we got to the fork in the road before campus. We turned down a dirt path that disappeared into the woods ahead.

"I started reading Professor Gilles's book over the weekend," I said. "It's interesting. Better than his lectures, even. It makes you notice how art connects our inner lives and informs our identities. Which I already knew, I guess, because of music, but I'd never seen it put so clearly like that. There was this passage I read last night that—never mind, I won't try to explain it. Just read the book if you get a chance. Maybe when you're done watching every movie ever made."

"I don't watch *every* movie. Just the good ones."

"How do you know if a movie is good or bad if you haven't seen it?"

"You take a calculated risk."

"What's your favorite movie? No. That's a boring question. If you were to require me to watch one movie, what would it be?"

"This sounds like a test."

"Innocent question, I promise."

"I would require that you watch more than one movie. But if you've never seen *Lawrence of Arabia*, I think you should watch that."

"Why?"

He shrugged, but then seemed to think about it. "T.E. Lawrence, he could have lived out the war safely in Cairo but he chose to return to the desert. Maybe he did it for the thrill. Maybe he was a masochist. Who knows?"

"What are you saying?"

"Nothing. Just that it's a movie that should be seen." Ian smiled. "Innocent, I promise."

"What is this place?"

We'd arrived at a tree-walled clearing at the edge of the river. The water was flat and wide, moving slowly, like lava. This was the first time I'd been level with the water, rather than safely above it on the bridge or enjoying the sight of its winding path along the bottom of the valley from afar. I shivered at the way the motion affected my bearings. It felt in odd moments as if we were on a barge chugging upstream.

Nearby, a small, crumbling building had been claimed by the undergrowth, like ancient ruins explored by underage drinkers instead of archaeologists. A single stone wall remained intact and in it a high window frame cradled a mass of wilted glass.

"I've heard about this place," I said.

"Heard about it?"

"Eva said this used to be a church. It burned down."

"Looks that way," Ian said. "I like coming here. It's peaceful."

"It was a suicide—a student. It's a horrible story. He lit the church on fire and hanged himself from the balcony as it burned."

Ian nodded slightly. His eyes had gone stony. Behind them, his mind had drifted far away. He climbed down into the church's foundation. I watched him bend over to pick up an empty bottle and toss it into the woods, almost as if he was straightening up the place. When it landed in the brush, it clinked against what sounded like an entire pile of discarded bottles. Ian looked up at the scarred and dilapidated church wall as if the body was still hanging there. I couldn't get a good read on the moment— I felt strangely as if I was intruding on something—so I let it pass.

"Well, the clearing is beautiful," I said. Branches of shadow sectioned the ground around us. The leaves were green and dancing in the trees, dancing like a chorus line that timed its kicks with the breeze, unaware that in two weeks they would face the beginning of the end of their leaf lives. Or maybe they *were* aware and awaited their journey with eagerness. From a leaf's perspective, maybe this was the pinnacle of life, waiting and waiting for the sign, for the first chill, and then bursting with color. You toss away your green jacket like a grasshopper leaping off a flame and then you flare and twirl on the breeze that has no beat, dancing the last dance, no longer an arms-linked chorus line but a clear-blue-day storm raining crispy licks of fire to the ground.

"We should go swimming," Ian said. He'd climbed up out of the foundation and was standing beside me.

"In the river?"

"Yeah. I've done it before."

I didn't even consider the possibility that he was serious. "Isn't it cold?"

"Sometimes. Today is nice. Still early in the fall."

"Right. I don't think so."

"C'mon. Even if it's cold, it's okay. It's a rush. It clears your mind."

"I doubt it."

When I realized he was serious about swimming, and after I'd convinced him that I was serious about *not* swimming, he shrugged and then we walked back along the dirt road toward campus. It was almost dusk and I wanted him to say we should get dinner together. But he had been less talkative since the church clearing and when it came time to decide what was next, he said he should go home to do some homework.

SCENE: EXTERIOR. WOODS BEHIND IAN'S HOUSE.
DUSK.

A twig cracks underfoot as IAN walks through
the woods. The trail is narrow. Ian is alone,
hands in his pockets, eyes pointed at the
muddy earth.

I took the back way home—the popular shortcut through the
woods behind the baseball stadium. Before our backyard becomes
visible through the trees there is a low spot in the trail that retains
moisture year-round, creating a miniature mud bog discolored by
a natural mineral deposit. For a few yards in every direction the
soggy earth is stained the reddish orange of a turning leaf. Two
logs had been laid across the spot for easy crossing, and in the
quiet evening, my steps over the makeshift bridge made a quiet
sucking noise.

I hated my cowardice. The moment to confide in Haile had
come but the words had not. They just sat there, obvious but
impossible, like a puddle that is too wide to leap. Several times,
I'd tried to steer the conversation but it never went far enough
in the right direction. I hadn't wanted to leave the conversation
unfinished, but the longer I waited the more certain I became that

I wouldn't tell her. I felt now like I did after losing a bad tennis match, exhausted and heavy with regret.

I could see from the backyard that no one else was home. I stomped the orange mud off my shoes at the door and threw my backpack on the couch. Dinner was reheated pizza while the ESPN crew counted down to Monday Night Football out in the living room. I could hear the TV from the kitchen, a football player saying *um* and *you know* too often, stumbling through an interview about growing up in a gang. I considered going over to Third Base to watch the game with friends but I was in more of a mood to celebrate my loneliness.

After the pizza I read a little from a textbook called *Globalization: Expanding Opportunities in a Shrinking World* with the welcome distraction of the TV running in the background.

...John Clayton spoke earlier today with NFL commissioner Roger Goodell. We'll hear what he had to say next...

The top of the hour was marked with a summary of the day's important stories. The Yankees and Braves could clinch the playoffs with respective wins tonight. The Forty-Niners' quarterback would be out for three weeks with a shoulder injury. And then came breaking news.

...And finally, a surprising resolution has been reached in the controversy over Florence University's head football coach. Florence Athletic Director Chamique Robinson announced at a press conference this afternoon that University of Washington head coach Mike Everett was leaving the Huskies to coach at Florence, his alma mater. Robinson acknowledged the midseason hire was unusual, but said it was a natural fit for the team. Everett played receiver for the Achaeans in the early '70s and was instrumental in the school's first national championship. Speaking from Seattle, where he'd been a fixture on the Huskies' coaching staff for eleven years, Everett fol-

lowed Ms. Robinson's press conference with his own comments. "I've never felt more at home on a football field than I did during the years I wore the Achaean uniform. It's been a dream of mine to return. I'm proud of the great program I've helped build at Washington, but an opportunity like this only comes around once in a lifetime." Coach Everett also said in his remarks that the decision was made in part for family reasons. His son is a senior at Florence University and both he and his wife are from nearby upstate New York. He will join the team in River Bend later this week as it prepares to face NC State in Saturday's Homecoming game.

I felt the lump of the cell phone in my pocket. I don't remember reaching for it but I must have done so because I remember the messages. There was a text message from Casey that said, "Did you know about this? Great news. We're at Third Base. Come over." There was a voicemail from my father. Dad said he had exciting news. He'd been trying to contact me and it couldn't wait anymore. He added that, obviously, he'd wanted to talk about it in person first but now he had to go ahead and accept the job.

I'm telling you it was a moment of hatred. How had I not been consulted? Okay, I hadn't answered my phone, and I'd ignored his messages. Fine. What about the voicemail he'd left yesterday? What were these messages about "touching base" and having something exciting to tell me, as if they were getting a new barbeque grill or a flat-screen television? What about e-mail? Christ, you could probably find someone to deliver a goddamn telegram if you tried. If I'd been given a chance—even a day's notice—maybe I could have got through to them that this was a terrible idea.

But now it was hopeless. Here was my father on national television saying it was a wonderful opportunity for his family. Wasn't I part of the fucking family? This absolutely was not wonderful. It was a disaster. I decided to go to Third Base after all and then decided again not to. Was there a right thing to do in this situation? Was I really expected to do it? My film school plans were changing quickly. New York wouldn't do anymore. Not far enough away. Now it had to be L.A. The opposite fucking coast of the continent. USC, UCLA, UC Irvine—Compton Fucking Community College, for all I cared. In the heartbreaking history of young, ambitious, delusional people moving to Hollywood to make it big, there had never been anyone as motivated as I was to get started.

I wanted to see Haile. I wanted to go back to earlier this afternoon, to a time when I was ignorant of my faraway parents because they were indefinitely far away. I wanted to be walking with Haile, comparing movies she hadn't watched and books I hadn't read. I wanted to sit in the coffee shop or fling flat rocks over the river until I got one to skip up onto the far bank. Anything but this.

Suddenly I remembered the art project. An idea had come to me that afternoon as I stood with Haile in the clearing by the church. The thought had materialized in my head; it had simply appeared there without any warning or any map of the connecting logic that had ushered it forward. Professor Gilles had shown us a picture on the first day of Art History class. *The Fall of Man*. I'd imagined that picture with me in it—only, I wasn't in the Garden of Eden. I was right there in the clearing beside the devastated church.

The art assignment for Gilles's class wasn't due for a month, which meant I really didn't need to think about it for at least three weeks. But the inspiration presented itself with urgency. I went up to my room and shut the door. I got out a sheet of paper and a pencil and studied the picture of Dürer's *The Fall of Man* from

Professor Gilles's Art History packet. Then I pulled my shirt over my head and stood at the full-length mirror behind the closet door. I tried to picture the lines of my body not as muscles but as pencil strokes. It might work. With the same sensation as jumping into cold water, I removed the rest of my clothes and found a pencil. The blank page waited, cream-white and agendaless. My mind held only a vague idea of what the final result should look like. I hesitated, daunted by the uncertainty of where to start. Maybe the first line wouldn't matter. Who thinks of the first brush stroke when they look at a painting?

I touched lead to paper and with rising goose bumps drew the line of my shoulder the way I saw it in the mirror.

Casey Boyd changed his profile picture

Casey Boyd wrote on **Afa Mokofisi**'s wall: "you ate all the eggs! that was like 10 eggs"

Casey Boyd is going for it on 4th down

"I'll have those." There was a label but I couldn't bring myself to say the word. Instinct warned me not to attempt it, promising that my brain and tongue couldn't quite get together on this one. It didn't matter what they were called anyway. They looked nice and that was enough.

"You want the chrysanthemums, sir? Or the roses?"

This is why guys don't buy flowers. We literally don't know what the fuck we're doing. I didn't think I wanted the roses. Roses mean something too specific. Something about love. I only wanted to say that I was in a good mood and was willing to go out of my way to share it. Honestly, I wasn't even trying to get laid here.

"Those there. The yellow ones."

I'd set out with the belief that the gesture mattered most. Wasn't it something, romantically speaking, to show up with flowers for no reason at all? After practice, I crossed the bridge to the floral stand adjacent to the bookstore on Main Street. It was the kind of place that sold gum, newspapers, and candy in addition to pre-made Get Well Soon and Happy Birthday arrangements that fogged the display refrigerator's glass door. The woman lifted my selection from a rack of bouquets. She was grumpy and overweight and said *sir* in a tone that suggested something was my fault. A true martyr to her own life. I paid her and drove home with Krista's bouquet of blooming, unpronounceable flowers.

I was in a chest-soaring good mood. Twice the opportunity to play for Coach Everett had narrowly evaded me—first after high school and then again before I transferred to Florence—and now in my senior year when I'd given up on the idea, it was finally coming true.

The news was welcomed less enthusiastically by others. Jerrell, who was the closest to Coach Evans and had expected him to be named head coach, was bitterly crushed. Ian was strangely distraught, seemingly paralyzed by the idea of living in the same town as his parents again. Even Afa, who'd been recruited personally by Draper, was in a low mood. Hanging around our house had become a grim affair.

My plan was to go home, change, and then deliver the flowers before I met the guys at Third Base. But Krista was waiting for me when I got home.

"Just who I wanted to see. These are for you."

She laughed. "Sometimes you can be so corny."

"I was only in a good mood. Look, practice didn't go so well today. I've got to go do some stuff with the team tonight."

"What about dinner? I can't eat flowers."

"We can do dinner a different night. This is important." I went upstairs and began to undress for a shower. She followed.

"I know what this means. What you really want is to be talked out of going out with the guys." Here her voice dropped into the sing-songy range. "Why don't you lie down for minute and see how you feel." I already had my shirt off and now she had her hand at the band of my sweats.

"I'm serious, Krista. I can't. It's been a tough week. They need me right now. And I'm really not in the mood anyway."

"That's not what it looks like."

I brushed her hand away from my crotch, which had, in spite of my best intentions, swollen conspicuously. "Don't flatter yourself. It's basically an automatic reaction."

"Like buying flowers when you have to let someone down."

"Stop it. I'm not going to fight with you and I'm not going to give in to this guilt trip. Please leave. Or stay. I don't care, but I have to go."

She stayed, putting on quite a show of pouting on the bed. But when I got back from the shower she was gone. I thought she'd taken the flowers with her until I found them in a pitcher with water on the kitchen table beside a note. "Go fuck yourself."

~ ~ ~

Main Street glowed with cones of orange light. The afternoon had been overcast and I could still sense the clouds there, hovering tightly in the blackness above the street lamps. It was an imposing sky, the sort of low ceiling that made you walk with your head down, lost in your own thoughts. I was crossing the street for the bar's entrance when a sharp whisper gave me a start.

"Boyd!"

I jerked my head up, self-conscious of how I'd drifted so far inside myself and how foolish I must have looked coming back out. I heard my name again and strained to locate the source. I'd assumed the patrol car at the curb was empty, but from the way the street lamps reflected I could now see that the front window was open. A hand came out of the shadows, not visibly attached to a body, and waved me over.

"Hey, Sheriff Paddock. I didn't see you there." He actually wore the hat, a brown park ranger thing. With his mustache, he looked like he'd just walked out of an old western.

"I've got the key for you."

"The key?" I assumed he was speaking figuratively, the key to winning the Homecoming game, that sort of thing. But then he held up his thumb and index finger and the light glinted off a shiny object between them. "What's this?"

"Your way into the stadium."

"The stadium. What do I need that for?"

Paddock smiled. "That's my boy. Goodman said you were the boss. Look, I'll be keeping my boys away from campus tomorrow 'round ten. You guys should have plenty of time." I stepped away from the car when he turned the ignition. "If I don't see you before, good luck Saturday. Got the whole town behind you. Plow 'em down." He rolled forward and cruised slowly up Main Street, monitoring the Wednesday night peace.

I slipped the key into my pocket and turned toward the bar.

During the season we usually went to Third Base on Wednesdays because it was the best night to avoid crowds. Besides, what else were we doing on a Wednesday night anyway? Homework was best faced on Monday or Tuesday, if at all. By Wednesday we could think only of the upcoming game, especially on Homecoming week.

A skinny kid slipping what had to be a fake I.D. back into his wallet studied me when I stepped up to the bar.

"Hey, you're Casey Boyd?"

"Yeah," I said, not as surprised as he was. Sometimes being recognized made me feel ridiculous. There's just something weird about the look people get in their eyes—and I'm talking total strangers—like they think they know you when all they really know is that your face goes with your name.

"Good luck Saturday."

I said thanks and ordered a Starting Pitcher of pilsner.

Most of the guys had already arrived, and the sight of a good-sized chunk of the football team seated at a table in the back had drawn a small crowd of girls. I slid onto a stool near Nato and Pile Driver. Within about a minute, it became clear that the innocent-faced girl between me and Nato had taken to him. Pile Driver, sitting across from us, had picked up on their flirtations and felt it was important that Nato fuck this girl tonight. The girl had straight, chardonnay hair around a pretty face, with a mousy nose and almost no eyebrows. They were having a conversation about where they were from, about how she'd never been to Virginia but he had been to Ohio. Whenever the girl turned to say something to one of her friends standing in the pack behind us, Pile Driver would lean in to pat Nato on the shoulder and say "Atta boy" and ask him if he needed a condom. This was the kind of thing you tolerated from Pile Driver. Nobody bothered to point out that, out of all of them, Nato would probably stand the best chance of getting laid and Pile Driver would need the most assistance—or luck or alcohol or whatever it is that permits obnoxious and unattractive people to have intercourse.

The key sat in my pocket like a bullet. I didn't really want anything to do with the Homecoming ritual, but as the night wore on I began to think that maybe the team needed it. Whether we won together or lost together, we thrived on togetherness, and I felt that that bond had become fragile. I imagined the key in my pocket had been passed down through generations of Florence

Achaeans football teams and that maybe there was no coincidence that it had landed in my pocket.

"Okay guys," I said when the girls finally moved on. "We have
to do this thing." There were eight, maybe ten guys within ear-
shot, and they all paused their private conversations. "T-Smalls
and 'Rell, you go to the liquor store. We'll all chip in. The rest of
you get the word out, but keep it down. We meet in the home-side
locker room at 10:00 p.m. tomorrow. Everyone should be there,
but freshmen and transfers don't have a choice. It's mandatory."

When I stopped talking, there was an eerie silence, a small,
crack-like gap in time that seemed to fill rapidly with doubt as
it split open. I felt smaller than I'd ever been. The guy posing as
me a moment ago, the guy with the will to step forward and the
words to command, had vanished. I no longer had any desire to
be in charge. All I wanted was to sit back and be told what to do
like everyone else.

And then everyone nodded in unanimous agreement and the
gap was gone. The Homecoming tradition would go forward as it
always had because someone was making it happen.

~ ~ ~

In high school, most nights before games Ian and I would order
pizza and play catch in the yard, rehearsing trick plays that our
coach would never sanction in a game. Ian won't play catch with
me anymore. I asked a few times but he said he was too busy
with other things. I think that has less to do with me than with
the mysterious aversion to football he's developed since high
school.

I'd had enough beer to feel antsy. It would have been good
to play some catch. But when I got home from Third Base, Ian

wasn't there. I'd printed off the box scores from NC State's previous games and decided to study my match-ups. I couldn't concentrate. I watched SportsCenter and played my guitar for a while
and finally went to bed alone, which reminded me of Krista. I
wanted her here—not enough to call her but enough that I didn't
feel guilty for the sudden desire to solve this restlessness on my
own. I pulled back the covers and freed myself of my boxer shorts.
I pictured Krista, just to keep things uncomplicated. Tomorrow, I
told myself, I'd talk to her and everything would be fine.

Half the rush of an orgasm is the vulnerability, the hanging it
all out there, not just arching your back and flexing your thighs
but letting your mind go as well. Non-Krista thoughts emerged
and then grew difficult to ignore. I don't know if the buildup to
a good orgasm causes you to temporarily lose your mind or if
it *comes from* losing your mind. Either way, the untamed parts
of your brain strain desperately to contribute. And fuck it, why
ignore them?

Legs spread, back arched, I gave in to the sight of Haile. She
was coming down the steps the way I'd seen her once outside
class, the sunlight filling her dress, searing into my mind her delicate silhouette underneath.

The guilt afterward was bad. I wiped up the mess with a dirty
shirt from my laundry, wanting to believe that the image of Haile
that had flashed across my mind at just the wrong moment was
a meaningless fluke rather than a larger problem that probably
couldn't be resolved by something as simple as an orgasm.

SCENE: INTERIOR & EXTERIOR. IAN'S CAR. NIGHT.

IAN, driving to loud, angry music, slows as
he approaches Main Street. A sign for The
Attic comes into view. He rolls past it once
and loops around the block. He eyes himself
in the rearview mirror and adjusts his hair.

The house looked exactly as it had on ESPN. They'd arrived the
previous morning and met the first moving truck, which was being
unloaded in the background by a crew of Starving Students as Dad
strolled down the flawless green lawn to oblige the waiting press.
There was someone from the Associated Press, a large man from
the *Seattle Times* who was here to cover Dad's midseason betrayal
in the eyes of Huskies fans, a crew from the ESPN affiliate, and a
gaggle of the local hawks who wouldn't bother driving up the river
to check on whether the landfill was dumping waste into the water
but had staked out their new neighbor's driveway because this was
a worthy story. This was good stuff. This was football.

Onscreen behind my father, our rec-room couch wobbled
across the porch between two khaki-clad movers who fed it in
jerks through the front door like it was going into a wood chipper.
One of the papers had actually lauded Dad's family man–ness,
pointing out that the move brought him nearer to his son and

other extended family. This implied that his son was somehow in favor of the move. Which is untrue. I didn't want this. And here was the couch I watched television on for each of my adolescent summers—watched television on and napped on and jerked off on. Here it was all the way across the country turning up in the background of a special ESPN segment. It was surreal. My brain telescoped noxiously, like when you aim a camera at a screen that's hooked up to the camera. The output is the input and the result is a picture that doesn't make any sense.

The house was part of the contract Dad signed with the university. Mom had given me the address but I didn't look at the numbers as I drove up the quiet street. I recognized it from the television segment: L-shaped, two broad stories of brick, white siding, green trim, and the long porch stretched out like a welcome mat. There were no reporters out front now. I'd come after dinner because Mom had said apologetically that the kitchen was in boxes in the living room. They met me in slippers on the porch.

"Welcome home," Dad said, ridiculously.

Mom hugged me too tightly and though I knew she was the most excited to see me I could tell it had all happened too fast. She had an uprooted, exhausted look and it terrified me to see how much she had wanted—*needed*—to see me.

"You want the ten-cent tour?" she said. "You'll get your money back since it's such a mess."

They led me on a path through boxes and plastic-wrapped furniture and bare hallways, stopping in each room to explain in too much detail what it would look like when they were done. Only two rooms, the master bedroom and Dad's study, were functional at this early stage. In the study, I recognized his shoebox of loose coins, the shelves of binders that held his playbooks, the television already wired to watch game film. He was a man who placed a high value on routine. There was no greater symbol of this than his Zippo lighter, which I spotted on the corner of his desk. I reached out and gave it a light spin on the hard surface. Mom shook her head.

"Oh, that damn thing. Last week he went through a whole canister of lighter fuel in one night and I had to rummage through boxes to find another one."

The Zippo was heavy and shiny, the kind villains and bad-asses flick open in dark alleys in the movies so you can see their face in the shadows. My grandfather gave Dad the lighter on his eighteenth birthday even though Dad told him he didn't smoke on account of staying fit for football. "Well, you can't play football forever, can ya?" Grandpa said. Grandpa figured Dad would go off to college at Florence like everyone else they knew, but he'd eventually find his way back to Smalltown USA to build roads, houses, and strip malls. Grandpa knew little about football. Maybe real men played it, maybe they didn't. But every man he knew smoked. To my knowledge, Dad had never lit anything with the lighter, but he always had it with him in the study. You could tell how much thinking he'd done by checking the fuel level.

"We're handling fine," Mom said.

We were back in the front room. Dad stood behind Mom rubbing her shoulders and Mom started to cry. We looked at each other helplessly, Dad and I, his eyes popping a little before he realized the best thing to do was keep rubbing her shoulders and stroking her hair.

"Sorry," she said. "I'm just tired. It's been an emotional week."

In Dad's mind, in his vision of how all this would go, he'd apparently overlooked the finer family details, the emotional minutiae of leaving your house and moving friendless to a small town two thousand miles away. It had not fully occurred to him that other lives beyond his own would be altered. He'd thought only of football, only of that part of the challenge. Not the other human challenges, which, to anyone else, would be obvious.

And where were the hungry reporters now? I know from experience that they were off writing about their model Everett family. Well, these were the only Everetts I knew: a workaholic father, a suddenly lonely and overly emotional mother, a daughter who'd gone off to college and found Jesus, and a son with a secret that couldn't possibly improve any part of this situation.

"I have to go," I said.

Dad had already gone off to look at video of his new team. Mom looked disappointed. She thought I'd meant that I needed to get back to do homework or go to bed, when what I'd actually meant was that I needed to leave River Bend.

"I should go," I said, letting her think what she wanted. Now wasn't the time to get into it. "Why don't we have lunch sometime next week?"

"I would love that." Her lower lip quivered. "Oh, I just can't stand not having my kitchen, my house."

"It'll get easier," I lied.

On the road with the music up loud, I thought this was no way to end the evening. It was only one evening but it felt like something larger was slipping away. I wanted to counter this sensation by doing something drastic, something dangerous, something extreme. Steering the car off the road, for example. I came to Main Street and slowed as the road narrowed for the rows of parallel-parked cars. The dance club above the coffee shop—The Attic—was right there on the corner. It was Thursday. Everyone knew what Thursday at The Attic was. I drove by once without stopping and then turned to circle around the block.

Haile, linked forever to her past

You'll go far in this world.

This was the most common phrase I heard as a young teenager. After concerts, during rehearsals, in hotels and taxi cabs, at private dinners where I was the only guest under thirty-five; from instructors, music critics, friends of my mother, strangers on planes; in Italian, German, French, Norwegian, Spanish, and Japanese. It was all, of course, because of the violin. *You'll go far in this world*. It started when I was ten years old: neck kinked, bow drawn, left hand trembling over the strings, going far in the world.

I hated my mother for not letting me discover it on my own.

Casey Boyd is making it happen
Casey Boyd is attending "Homecoming pep rally: Florence vs. NC State"
Casey Boyd was tagged in an album

At ten, we were sitting in the locker room beneath the stadium.

Typically, we came here only on game days and on the Fridays before game days. The room had a way of grouping us—receivers with receivers, linemen with linemen, special teams guys filling in the gaps, kickers in the corner. On Saturday, when Coach walked in to give his pregame address he was likely to find us more or less in the same places we'd retreated to now.

But there were no coaches tonight.

"All right, ladies," I said when everyone was accounted for.

We corralled the first-year guys, the freshmen and transfers, into the common area by the white board. Pile Driver flicked the lights. T-Smalls hollered and beat the walls, harmless as always but out of his mind jacked up as if he'd snorted coke instead of swallowing a few beers like the rest of us. The first-years still hadn't earned the use of their lockers. Tonight was their chance.

My mouth was dry. My voice sounded to me as if it was coming from somewhere else. It rang and echoed through the locker room like a cheap played-back recording of itself.

"Time to drop trou. Let's go. You're gonna meet us over in the visiting team locker room. Nobody gets in unless you're butt-ass naked."

There was a rumor that a player a few years before us had refused to take part. A month later he transferred to another school. No one wanted to be that guy. In the last three years, I'd seen straight-A students skip evening classes, men drop dates with chicks they could have bagged, and Mormons shoot alcohol. We'd all done it, so these freshmen would do it, too.

We left the first-years to undress and went down the hall and waited. I sent a few guys out to the field to pour the shots. It took the first of the wise first-years only two minutes to come to the realization that there was no way out of this and that it was better just to get it over with as painlessly as possible. They came down the hallway and through the door naked as the day they were born, only bigger and hairier, dicks wagging pendulously, and we corralled them up to the wall beside the entrance to the showers, where six electric razors waited. A few tried to enter the room still clad in their undershorts and they weren't allowed in until everything was removed. Some had to be dragged or carried or pushed. Everyone laughed.

"There are two ways to do everything. The easy way and the hard way. Take your pick: Either you're shaving 'em yourself or we'll make your teammates do it for you."

Contrary to the looks on their faces, we were serious.

One of the first-year cornerbacks, Cornelius Hathaway, held a shaver T-Smalls had given him. Pile Driver smacked him on the shoulder. "Are you shaving your own dick or Walker's?" Hathaway steered the shaver jokingly toward Walker's midsection, and Walker scooted away ass-first, promising Hathaway that he'd lose his arm to the elbow if he so much as looked at his dick again. Everyone laughed. Hathaway looked at the shaver and then grinned as if to say *You bastards* and then flicked it on. He drew it once, a little experimentally, through the dense bush above his dick and the upperclassmen cheered him on as if he was chugging a beer. The other freshmen looked aghast and then complacent and then most of them shrugged, accepting their fate.

It was easier for everyone after that first cut. People fall back on different strategies to endure humiliation. Some went for speed in a mad rush to get it over with. They ran the buzzing jaws around their vitals as if every second mattered, quantity not quality, trying to outrun reality. Others were flat out insecure, terrified yet cooperative because they were even more afraid of not belonging. No one wants to be that guy. They found that it helped to make fun of the next guy's dick or body fat or hair or alleged sexual orientation. Some people looked for the high road, feigning comfort and playing along. They let others shave them while they barked, "That ain't symmetrical," or, "You missed a spot under my sack."

Everyone laughed. This was rich. Imagine how these guys were going to explain their new look to their girlfriends without giving away our secret ritual.

Everything was under control until one of the freshmen tackles refused to do it. He was a quiet kid, tough as hell in workouts, and never looked you in the eye except on the field across the line of scrimmage in that heartbeat before the ball was snapped. I admit he'd gotten into my head a few times. His name was Hyde, Paul Hyde, and I didn't know a thing about him, where he came from, if he had both parents, if they were rich or poor. But I understood him on the field and I understood him here. He probably didn't even mind the shaving, but rebelling against it was his way of rising above the humiliation, challenging us to face it with him, to see who would blink first.

We pinned him down. That was the way it worked. Four of us upperclassmen, each taming a limb, while another freshmen began running the buzzer through his pubes, cutting them loose onto his stomach and the floor tiles between his legs.

Guys were using the showers to rinse off the loose hairs and T-Smalls was splashing water from a bucket that he found God knows where across the deck, herding the mess toward the shower drains. The drains had begun to clog with wet mounds—black hair, red hair, brown hair, blond hair, tight curls, loose curls—all tangled together. This was one of the subtleties of the prank, to leave two soggy patches in the showers for the visiting rivals to tiptoe around.

I could sense the situation beginning to get away from us. The ritual, remember, was bigger than me. I didn't start anything. It had a momentum of its own that carried on around me. But in my gut, in the honest part of the pit, I knew that one of us could have regained control. We were only pretending. Individuals pretend to be in control, mobs pretend to be out of control. Here was a room of courage-drunk young men, half of them naked, the other half remembering how they once had been here too, reminded of that feeling of getting through it, maybe thinking it seemed a little more real now than they remembered. Everyone laughed. Here were the kings of campus ascending their throne. How did you think we got there?

I could have stopped it all. There are gut feelings and there's the honest pit, and each of us knows the difference. They would have listened to anyone. They were desperate for a leader. I could have given the word that it was time to move it out to the field. I could have said we'd all had enough.

Instead, I got down on the floor and sat on this kid Hyde's leg, clasping one hand over his fleshy thigh, the other on his turf-scraped shin. The other freshman was working—buzz buzz—with the razor not far from my head. Buzz buzz, but now I was close enough to hear the individual hairs being cut, a slick ticking sound beneath the drone. It felt indecent to watch. I looked down at the floor, following the grout lines between tiles as they converged on their vanishing point, a tiny grid mosaic with dizzying monotony.

My eyes were fixed on the revolting sight of the drains when it happened. I was holding this big freshman tackle's leg down—he'd stopped kicking now, he'd given in to the futility of it—I was holding his leg, gripping his meaty flesh sparsely sprouted with wiry black thigh hairs, my face turned away from the razor job and staring at the clogging drains, when I started to wretch. Without warning, my stomach took a vicious turn. It felt like a slipknot coming free and then, starting in my gut and climbing up my chest, my esophagus felt like a beer bottle that's been popped on top by someone else's bottle, the kind of d-bag prank that causes the contents to bubble over volcanically, faster than you're expecting.

My throat opened but nothing came out.

"You all right, man?" Pile Driver said.

I swallowed hard and tried to play off the gagging as a random coughing fit. I had to get up and find a water fountain. As soon as I released pressure on the leg, it swung free, kicking wildly. Hyde took a good swipe at my hip, pounding it once with his heel. Pile Driver, who had been assigned to the other leg, was knocked harmlessly aside. Hyde was lucky the razor was pulled away in time. Now he was free, with more than 90 percent of his bush clipped away, which suddenly seemed good enough and everyone clamored to their feet.

"Watch it, asshole," Pile Driver said. "You see anyone else flipping out?"

"Fuck you. Maybe I got sick of your fat head that close to my dick."

The part no one had thought about was that it wasn't only the naked first-years who had insecurities in play. So when Pile Driver sucker-punched Hyde in the gut it seemed to come out of nowhere. I suppose it was to remind Hyde of his place, upperclassman to freshman, as if the nakedness hadn't been enough.

Nato was the only one to react. He stepped up and shoved Pile Driver, who had a good eighty pounds on him, into the wall. "Not cool, dude. Knock it off." Pile Diver glared at Nato and then pushed him back. His eyes darted around as if looking for support. But it was Pile Driver's turn to be humiliated. He'd gone too far. If it had been anyone other than Nato, there probably would have been a fight. But Nato stepped back and let Pile Driver huff and puff a little, looking like he might take a swing, until T-Smalls and Afa stepped in to separate them.

"You okay, man?" Nato was standing in front of Hyde, and I'll never forget the faces of the guys around him. Bare-assed freshmen and intoxicated upperclassmen alike, all looking at Nato with respect. My fingers dug into my palm for an instant, and then the wave of jealousy passed as quickly as it had come.

The rest was easy. The freshman ran out through a gauntlet of teammates and then everyone met at the fifty-yard line and did a shot of tequila. We were all equals now, and the freshmen were allowed back into the home locker room where their clothes were waiting in their lockers. Starting with Saturday's Homecoming game, they would be able to use their lockers like the rest of us.

The team dispersed from the parking lot except for a group of eight guys that I told to meet at the bed of T-Smalls's truck. T-Smalls and me, Nato, Kyle, and four freshmen. T-Smalls carried the grocery bag and we set out to pick our target. It needed to be prominent. Last year the Achaean bust outside the stadium's main gate had been hit. The year before that it had been the Florence University sign that greets people coming over one of the bridges from town.

It was Nato's idea to do the statue, the running figure at the base of the Great Lawn.

"Are you sure?" Kyle said. This was why he'd never be a real leader. "It's kinda out in the open. Anyone could see us."

From the grocery bag, T-Smalls handed out the spray paint— NC State red and white—a carton of eggs and rolls of toilet paper. Not terribly original, but it was tradition. The idea was to create the impression that the opposing team had come into our house and disrespected us, rallying our fans and players with vengeance. By game time we'd be ready to tear their heads off.

I rattled the ball around in the can as I circled the stone figure. I took aim and white molecules leaped hissing from the can. Nato swirled red streaks on the statue's head like a shiny helmet and the excess rolled off like blood. Todd smashed an egg in the statue's face and Kyle looked around for campus security. We handed off the supplies and turned the freshmen loose, patting their backs and feeling good about the stories we'd have to tell our grandchildren.

Everyone laughed.

SCENE: INTERIOR. THE ATTIC NIGHTCLUB. NIGHT.

The club throbs with electronic dance music
and strobe lights. IAN, sitting alone at the
bar, turns away when he spots someone walking toward him. But it's too late. He's been
recognized.

The Attic was above the coffee shop but the entrance was around
the corner off of Main Street. I'd been to The Attic on other nights
but never on a Thursday. Tonight I'd walked on the far side of the
street first, casually reconnoitering. Outside the propped-open
door, a bouncer sat on a stool cast in red from an overhead lamp.
Two skinny guys wearing tight tee shirts, their short hair chun-
ked and twisted, scampered quickly around the corner and disappeared safely past the bouncer and into the red glow.

    I stood with my back against the wall, listening to my breath
and waiting for courage. I could hear the faint bass beat of dance
music. My heart was beating five times as fast. When I was sure
no one was watching I crossed the street, showed my ID to the
bouncer, and I was inside.

    The Attic was livelier and smokier when commandeered by
a gay crowd. Gays seemed to smoke like the characters in old

movies—a lot and as if someone were watching. The music was building up, doubling rhythm every four measures, outlasting your expectations for when it would climax, and then it dropped a beat and unleashed its full theme, a euphoric, chest-deep trance that brought hands skyward on the dance floor.

In talking myself into going to The Attic on a Thursday, I'd chosen to ignore the certainty of recognizing someone from school. River Bend is a small town and Florence's student body is a cozy thirteen thousand. I'd been standing against the bar for only a few minutes when I spotted a guy from one of my classes last year. We'd never so much as acknowledged each other before but now he came over. He was wearing a clingy, bright red tee shirt that said My Body is a Wonderland.

"You had Haverman's Finance 310 last semester, right?"

"Uh, yeah," I said.

"Thought you looked familiar. Wait, I know what it is. Aren't you some kind of athlete or something?"

Fuck.

"No. Must be someone else."

"Hey, bro, it's cool. I'm in this house on University Street and none of the guys know about me. I don't come here often."

"Me neither."

"I'm Jordan," he said.

"I'm Dave," I lied.

I wanted to get away but I had no one else to talk to and this was a room in which it felt unwise to stand alone for too long. Jordan said he was going out for a smoke and asked me if I wanted to come. When I declined, he shrugged and looked rejected, as if I'd turned down more than a cigarette.

I was suddenly sitting alone. A few older guys sat apart from each other at the bar, each separately looking in my direction. It creeped me out the way they just stared at me instead of talking to one another, so I got up and started toward the dance floor.

Then I saw him. He was sitting on a stool at the other end of the bar and I wouldn't even have noticed had he not been looking at me. Thankful to have found a friendly face, I made my way through the crowd hoping I would come up with something to say.

"Hey."

"Hey."

"It's Jamie, right? I'm Ian."

I always noticed him at the coffee shop when he was working but I never really thought about him later. At most, we'd had three conversations, each having to do with my usual order—iced coffee, no room.

"Are you studying film?" he said.

"What?"

"When you come in to study you're always reading books about film."

"Yeah, sort of studying. I want to go to film school."

"Have you applied yet?"

"Working on that now."

He was wearing a green tee shirt that said Pedro's Taco Stand in lettering arched around a sombrero. Maybe it was his relative normalness against The Attic's over-fashioned Thursday crowd, but I thought he was attractive in a way I hadn't noticed before.

"Are you surprised to see me here?" I said.

"Not really. I kind of figured it out."

"What does that mean?"

"Relax, it's a compliment. It means I was paying attention."

"Sorry, I'm not good at this."

"See, like that. The way you're always looking around. You're too aware of everything. Straight guys aren't like that."

Jamie said he had moved from the Midwest to get away from his parents. He worked in the coffee shop to supplement the loans that were paying his tuition. He liked art and music. Everyone says they like art and everyone likes music but he managed to convey an uncommon appreciation for it, which I understood because everyone likes movies but not the way I do. Jamie liked all types of music but didn't try too hard to impress me by dropping the names of obscure, cutting-edge indie groups. He said he had a passion for classical music, which was cool, I guess. We spent an hour talking and he introduced me to some of his friends, who were hilarious even though they made me feel uncomfortable, and then it got much later than I realized.

"Well, Ian. If you haven't left for Hollywood by next week, you should stop by."

"Yeah," I said. "I'll see you around."

~ ~ ~

Coach had said the van would be leaving at eight, which left me five hours from the time I departed The Attic to get home and accomplish some sleep. The cul-de-sac was full and I had to park a block away from the house. I felt light and full of life walking the quiet streets at this rebellious hour and it hit me suddenly, with a force that stopped me in the middle of the road and made me look around, that it was somewhere around here that the gay student had been attacked. The most popular version of the story was that they'd dragged him down the trail to the low, muddy spot in the woods behind our house. If he'd been coming home from The Attic, he would have come this way. He would have been feeling just about the way I did right now.

Up in my room, I shoved clothes for the road trip into a duffel bag so I wouldn't have to do any thinking in the morning. Then I stripped down to my boxers and went to brush my teeth. I got to the bathroom as Casey was coming out of his room.

"Where've you been?"

"Out."

I stuck the brush in my mouth and Casey staggered into the bathroom behind me and stood sleepily over the toilet. It seemed to take him the full length of his piss to process the word.

"Out," he said. "What time is it? It's like three-thirty."

I spit and rinsed my mouth with some water from my cupped hand. He looked at me.

"You okay?" he said.

"Yeah. Just a little tired. I'll get some sleep in the van tomorrow."

"Were you with Haile?"

"No, I went to see my parents."

I realized too late that I should have said yes, I'd been with Haile. It would have been more plausible than the partial truth about my parents. Casey must have suspected there were a few hours unaccounted for in my alibi, but he didn't press me.

"How are they? I mean, I saw your dad at practice, but how's your mom?"

"They're fine. Really fucking terrific."

"Dude, did you shave your chest?"

"So what?"

"That's just weird."

"You should try it sometime."

"Right. I'll think about that."

"No, really."

"Why?"

"Obviously, it looks better."

I flexed and made a meathead grimace in the mirror.

"Whatever, dude," Casey said.

"I bet Krista would like it."

I thought I heard him mutter that that was just what he needed, but he was too far down the hall to be sure.

I set my alarm and pulled back the bed sheets. I kicked off my boxer shorts, cut out the light, and climbed onto the bed, sliding naked between the sheets. I imagined what Jamie looked like without his shirt but I could not picture him naked. He was not athletic but slightly muscle-toned, as if maybe he put in irregular appearances at the gym. I tried to imagine what it would be like to kiss him. My hand moved beneath the sheets. The orgasm was intense and privately dramatic, like smashing a bottle against a wall: the sudden surging pleasure, the resulting mess, a guilty glance around to be sure no one had seen. And the slightly empty what-now?-that-didn't-really-solve-anything feeling.

Haile, one note too many

I was at the piano in one of the practice rooms in Shostakov-ich Hall, fleshing out a new composition, when Kimberly Park tapped on the thick, soundproof glass.

From the eight other music students in my program, I was different, a ninth wheel. And not only because I lived in a loft over Ms. Rivera's garage. There were four guys and four girls. Save for slight exceptions, the girls gravitated toward chamber music compositions, the guys toward jazz, except for the two fragile boys, one dark and serious, the other hyper and flam-boyant, who spent their independent studies arranging and composing orchestrations for stage musicals. I fear we formed something of a clique. A few had dated each other, a few lived together, a few had backstabbed others for unoriginal reasons rooted in jealousy and insecurity. They came from places like Denver and Charlottesville and Toronto and Minneapolis. All seemed to know little about anything but their musical notes and instruments and the history of the great composers who had become great before them without the benefit of a univer-sity degree like the one we were pursuing. They spoke of them-selves and The Program in a swell-headed fashion, as if we were a society of Nobel Prize–winners and not a socially marginalized breed of music geeks.

"Sorry to interrupt," Kimberly said. She was apologetic. I don't mean right there in the practice room, I mean always. She has the inaccessible personality of a genius, and I mean that in the best way, even though I'm not sure she really is a genius. She's a good musician, one of the jazz students, and the worst thing that could be said about her compositions is that they're experimental, which, in certain jazz circles, is more or less a compliment. Apart from her music, however, she lacks conviction and boldness, and in conversation she conveys an awkward nothingness beyond her fear that she is getting in the way.

"It's nothing," I said. "One of my new songs. But I'm stuck. I probably need a distraction."

Lately I'd been conscious of a need to tell stories with my music. Stories that appealed to universal emotions, like what Professor Gilles talked about in class. Which reminded me: I still had no idea what I was going to draw for Gilles's art project. I wondered what Ian was going to do, if he would even take the assignment seriously.

Kimberly said she and a few of our classmates were rehearsing one of her compositions and she wanted me to sit in on a part because someone else hadn't shown up. Of course I would, I told her. This was the beauty of the program. We wrote music and had it played on the spot and made changes if necessary. The learning was instantaneous. I assumed she wanted me to play keyboard. None of my classmates had seen me play anything else. But when we got to the rehearsal room I saw that Ms. Rivera was there. And then I saw the violin.

The look on my face must have frightened poor Kimberly because she flashed a worried glance at Ms. Rivera and said, "You can play? It's not so hard. It's nothing. It's just a simple part I added last minute, to hold things together."

She handed me the sheet music. I stared at the winged and barred notes climbing up and down the staff. I thumbed the fingertips of my left hand as I looked at the page. The hand had begun to feel more and more vulnerable as the calluses on each fingertip gradually softened. It was a sensation I'd chosen to ignore. Now it occurred to me that this was the longest my fingers had gone in ten years without working the steel strings of a violin.

Ms. Rivera watched from the back of the room. Ted Horvich blew spit out of his trumpet. The others were looking over their respective parts. *There's no reason I can't do this*, I told myself. Even if I didn't want to, going along with it seemed easier than declining. After all, this was not a sold-out Walt Disney Concert Hall. There were no salivating critics sitting in the front row. I was only standing in at a student rehearsal.

I grabbed the neck, fit the chin rest, and set my fingers. The motions felt strangely automatic, as if the instrument was attached to me by an extra joint, like a limb I depended upon.

I made the first mistake in the thirteenth measure—a mental error, my fingers were solid—and I realized I was nervous. Kimberly smiled to reassure me from behind her stand-up bass. She played the bass athletically, it being her equal in size, plucking and slapping the strings with full arm motions as her music left the page and came alive for the first time. There were five of us, Kimberly and me, Ted on his horn, Adrienne on keyboard, and Jamal holding forth on the drums. I began to relax and understand the music. The part for the violin required long, sustained notes that ebbed and flowed modestly in the background as a way of thickening the sound and bridging the other musicians' solos. It was a swinging jazz tune, highlighted by the trumpet's flair, hollowed out with drop beats, and made gritty with muscled slaps from the bass and sharp scratches from the drums. The cohesion came, almost accidentally, from the remedial violin part.

Kimberly stopped us at a section that was, in her mind, not working.

"From eighty-six, please," she said, and we played it again. She stopped us and scrunched her face. "I don't know quite what I'm looking for."

"What if it goes just bass and drums there?" said Ted. Jamal, eager for a solo, beat out a few sample measures.

"No, no. It's been building. Can't you feel that? Dropping to bass and drums would kill it." Kimberly let the bass down onto a chair like an unconscious lover and stepped over to the keyboard to plunk out a few potential solutions. "Almost. Do you get what I'm going for?" She was using major chords to simulate the other instruments. "It's been building in a way, underneath. Something fighting to get out. The keyboard, maybe. I don't know if the keyboard can soar properly."

"Play it again," Ms. Rivera said from her inconspicuous perch in the back of the room. She liked this. She liked to see her students on the brink. This is where the real learning began.

We did it again and as Kimberly raised her hand to stop us, again at the same place, I went down to A instead of F. The note trespassed into the silence and I pulled back the bow.

From the back of the room, Ms. Rivera looked up.

"That's it!" Kimberly said. "What was that?"

"I'm sorry. I didn't mean to—"

"No, don't say anything. Do it again. Only, keep going. Play it out. Can you try that?"

"I'll try," I said. I'm not sure she really wanted me to do this.

The violin can soar. It can build up inside of me, underneath everything, like it had in Kimberly's song. She had felt it fighting to get out without knowing what it was. I knew. I'd carried it everywhere with me. From the A, I slid up the fingerboard and Kimberly's hidden melody emerged, surging through the bluesy scales she'd built in pieces broken up with the percussive drop beats, climbing and falling with a thick-sweet caramel tone. I hadn't been looking at the page and didn't notice the room growing blurry. The moment expired when I felt the tears on my cheek and my bow clattered to the floor at the foot of my music stand.

"Wait. Where is that?" Ms. Rivera was rummaging through the sheets in front of her, looking for the violin part. "Where did that come from?"

Kimberly did not need to say that those notes were not ones she'd written. "You can really play," she said softly.

I apologized and ran from the room before they could see my tears. I felt trapped, like a captive bird that sees light through an escape hole over and over again, only to have it slammed shut.

I hated her for not letting me discover it on my own.

"What's wrong, sweetie?" Ms. Rivera found me in the hall.

"I'm sorry," I tried to say, but it was lost in a succession of gulping sobs. "I can't."

"Honey, what happened?"

"I can't." I said it over and over. "Not the violin."

"I don't understand. I meant it as a small challenge. I had no idea that you—" She was laughing. "You never said anything. I mean, Jesus, *that* was amazing. How come you didn't tell me?"

"I can't..."

Ms. Rivera wouldn't allow me return to practice. She said I'd given enough for one day. I collected my notebook and tape recorder and stepped from the halls of airtight practice rooms out into the afternoon, feeling released, empty of tears and thoughts and important ideas. I strolled past the theater and down the Great Lawn. A man in coveralls looked up and smiled at me from where he was scrubbing white paint off the Boccioni statue. The vandalism had been front-page news in the campus paper, not, I suspected, because it was shameful vandalism, but because it was somehow related to the football team.

The water under the bridge was gunmetal gray, reflecting the slate clouds overhead. The afternoon felt perfect for hunkering down with a book, but I headed first to the movie rental store where I borrowed *Lawrence of Arabia*, and then on to the coffee shop to read because I wanted to get through as much of Professor Gilles's book as possible before his reading on Tuesday.

SCENE: INTERIOR. IAN's BEDROOM. DAY.

Short montage of IAN at his computer filling
out an online application for film school.
He reaches a screen with a button that says,
"Click once to submit your application." He
drags the cursor over the button. He stares
at the screen.

Haile and the unexpected key change

"Can you believe this?"

"It's nothing. They do it every year," Ian said.

"Is that supposed to make it okay?"

"It's a tradition."

The toilet paper and eggs had been cleaned up, but the maintenance crew had failed to scrub away all the paint from the statue. Ian seemed unoffended. Actually, he seemed as if he wasn't listening. "What do you want to do?"

"Let's walk," he said.

I'd assumed, when Ian called me, that he had something in mind. The way he'd said it on the phone—*We should talk. Tonight.*—made me think about all that had gone unsaid between us. I was excited, but also nervous. Was I ready to be clear about what I wanted? I couldn't deny that we were becoming more than friends, and my feelings weren't commonplace, but it seemed trite to rush into a relationship.

We walked away from the statue and through the campus gates.

"It's cooling off," Ian said. "Feels like fall now."

"You should be a meteorologist, as fascinated as you are with the weather." Ian said nothing to this, just stared straight ahead, the distracted look of someone whose mind is doing circles around itself. Maybe I was being insensitive. "Sorry. Something's wrong. We could go get some coffee?"

"Okay," he agreed, and only then seemed to register what I'd said. "No! Let's just walk." But as we started over the bridge he suddenly said that we should sit down. There were benches at each end of the bridge and we sat facing upstream, watching the water roll slowly out of the woods and into view. The ruined church was only barely out of sight around the bend.

"Ian?"

"Okay, okay. You know the guy who works at the coffee shop? Jamie?"

"Yeah."

"We. Well. I saw him again. I mean, I met him. At The Attic on Thursday."

"Okay?"

"We're kind of…"

"Kind of what? I don't understand." And then I did. But only in a disconnected way, the way unimaginable things are understood, like your own death or the president's underwear. "Oh, my God. You're gay."

He flinched at the word, and for a moment I thought I'd gotten it all wrong. But then he nodded slowly.

"How could I be so stupid?"

"I'm sorry I couldn't tell you sooner."

Humiliation has a way of padding itself with anger, and for a few minutes I was an inconsolable bitch. Crying made it worse at first, like tossing gas on flames, but finally I settled down enough to allow a conversation to emerge.

Ian said he was sorry again about a dozen times.

"How long were you going to wait until you told me?"

"I'm telling you."

"You have no idea, do you, how cruel this seems to me?"

"I'm sorry. It's not like this is my idea of a good time."

"I know. I'm sorry, too. I just wish you could have given me a warning sign. My God, you even told me you had a girlfriend a few years ago."

"I did. That's true. We had sex four times."

"You kept track?"

"When it's four times, it's hard to lose track."

"You've told other people?"

He shook his head and for the first time I forgot about myself. He looked bad. His whole being sagged with the kind of loneliness that persists even when among friends.

"Your parents?"

"I can't even think about my parents without shaking and losing my breath."

"And they're here now, aren't they?"

"Very much so."

"Are you going to tell them?"

"I'm having lunch with my mother tomorrow. I don't know if I can do it. But I have to, don't I?"

"No. Wait a while. Or, I don't know. Sorry. I'm no help." I tried to imagine myself as a parent. I'd want to know, right? I'd want to know everything. But maybe this was one of the things mothers only *think* they want to know.

"I saw your dad in the paper. You were right. He's famous. He looks like you. Or the other way around, I guess. You have the same eyes and forehead."

"This will seriously bother him. What? What's so funny?"

"I just remembered. I watched *Lawrence of Arabia* last night. See how silly I am?"

"What did you think?"

"I thought it was long. It's beautiful, though. Your eyes are like what's-his-name's."

"Peter O'Toole. You didn't like it."

"I didn't say that. It's not a girl's movie. There are no women in it. Maybe that should have been a sign."

"They were at war in an Arab desert. It's historically accurate."

"I'm just saying."

It hit me again then, Ian's confession, all at once. This time it took the form of a heavy sadness, a loss that I was unable to quantify in words. Ian started to say something but stopped himself and we fell into a long silence. I looked around. A warm spell had lengthened the fall and the foliage kept on like a fireworks display, bursting with new and surprising color. Leaves made their way back to earth, collecting in dry, graying piles blown by groundskeepers from the walks and lawns. The leaves still clinging to branches, sparse now, flashed their yellow faces and orange undersides in the gusty breezes that would eventually pluck them away. Change rolled through me.

"Have you started your Art History project?" I asked.

"Yeah. But I'm going to throw it away and start over."

"Why? What is it? I want to see." I was suddenly, desperately curious to know what Ian had done, even though I couldn't be sure what I expected to learn from his artwork. Maybe I was looking for evidence, a clue that would explain how I'd misread him for so long.

"No. It's the equivalent of bad high school poetry. You know, something you write for yourself in a depressed state and when

you look back at it you see that you really should've kept it to
yourself."

"Maybe that's what Professor Gilles wants," I said.

"Well, he can't have that. What are you doing for the assignment?"

"No clue."

The last moments of daylight blanketed campus like flakes of
gold and the breeze off the river flicked the leaves on distant trees.

"I've never lived in a place with this many leaves. It's beautiful."

"A yellow wood," Ian said. He was looking back at the dirt
road that winds toward the church.

"What?"

"Nothing."

Then streetlights clicked on overhead and we were walled
in a cone of artificial light. The desire to flee hit me suddenly. I
had to get away from Ian. I think it was the way he said that last
"nothing," the way this reminded me that he always kept so many
things to himself. Before, this had made me more and more curious about him. But now I resented him for it, for thinking it was
fair to be closely guarded when it suited him and then suddenly—
if it suited him—to reveal something like this. His confession—or
revelation, or whatever it was for him—provided him some relief
from a private torture. This only made me angrier, as if he'd transferred his burden onto me without any concern that I too might
be living with a private burden and didn't want anything to do
with his.

I got up and left without saying good-bye.

SCENE: INTERIOR. MAIN STREET BISTRO. DAY.

IAN is sitting across from his MOM at a
small table in a crowded café.

The lunch spot on Main Street where I met Mom was popular for
its bakery and its lack of competition. It was the kind of place that
sold hearty soup-and-sandwich combos, sides of chilled pasta
salad, and burnt cappuccinos, and then dressed itself up with
cloth napkins, table coverings, and seasonal centerpieces so that
it could be called a bistro instead of a deli.

Two women no younger than eighty were speaking loudly of
the foliage at the next table. This time of year, leaf peepers came
in charter buses from the city because there was apparently nothing better to do on a weekday afternoon on the Upper East Side.
At the center of each table, dried fall flowers had been stuck in
square, glass vases filled with polished pebbles. As Mom talked,
I fidgeted with the tall vase on our table. It was a little wobbly,
though it might have been that my hands were shaking.

The fear was not only in my head. It crawled through each
of my systems—epidermal, nervous, skeletal, and digestive—
gripping me with a frightening panic. My underarms were damp
with cold spots. My lungs felt lodged at my collarbone. When I
spoke, the words came out precariously. Mom did all the talk-

ing. She had plenty to talk about. She had an insatiable interest in many practical details of my life that I hardly cared for. How I got around campus, how I signed up for classes, how—if there were five bedrooms in our house—had I ended up in my particular room? She wanted to know which was the better grocery store in town and when could she watch me play in a tournament. She talked about how they'd have to go back to Seattle a few times to sell the house and retrieve belongings they'd put into storage. I'd never felt so close to going insane, to really flipping out and swallowing my tongue and spitting out my teeth.

"Actually," I said. "There's something I wanted to talk to you about."

I felt sick. Physically askew. This was worse than I'd imagined. It felt like I'd set off through a desert like Lawrence into the Nefu, only I'd arrived at a deep chasm, an impassable cut in the earth, that had been hidden by the mirage. I stood peering dizzily over the edge. This was a bad idea. It was too far to jump. But then it seemed almost worse to turn back. I didn't *want* to go back that way. That was why I was here in the first place, wasn't it?

"I've been dating someone."

I had to clear my voice. It couldn't be trusted.

"It didn't seem important to tell you before. But I don't want to hide anything from you. And now that you're so close by you probably—"

Her cell phone started ringing and instantly her attention evaporated. She patted her coat pockets and then her pants and finally dug around in her purse before locating the blaring device.

"Oh, it's your sister." The ring tone started again from the beginning. "I guess I can call her back." Her instinct was to answer the phone. I could see it. The cell phone above all could not be ignored. I might have pointed out the absurdity of her taking a call in the middle of a conversation already in progress, no less in a restaurant, but in this case the greater part of me actually wished she'd answer the damn thing so that the present topic could be forgotten. She let it ring once more in her hand, torturing herself and the other diners, before finally silencing the phone and dropping it back into her purse.

"Sorry. I thought I turned that off. I'll just call her back later. Have you spoken to your sister lately? I worry about her."

I hadn't spoken to Nikki in a few weeks but I knew my mother was referring to her religious zeal. We were raised Catholic and Nikki went off to Gonzaga only to discover that Catholicism didn't provide enough channels through which to vigorously defend her love for the Lord. She'd fallen into a Christian campus group, Baptist, I think, where they worked together at becoming exponentially more religious by the day. Their Sunday worship was the kind where white people sang Christian pop-rock songs with their hands raised overhead, feeling God in the room. In conversations with us more secular types, she sought biblical metaphors for every aspect of our modern lives and quoted the Bible in ways that seemed intellectually lazy, if not blatantly unreasonable. Blind to her hypocrisies, she'd begun signing e-mails In His Loving Name.

"I'm sure she's fine," I said.

"She just seems to have changed so much. You never went through any drastic changes like this."

I took a drink of water, giving up for good my intended purpose for this lunch. Mom showed no sign of noticing anything was wrong.

"Did I tell you we're planning a big barbeque at the house in three weeks? It's a Sunday after a home game. Nikki might try to make it. Now, who is this girl you were telling me about? You want me to meet her?"

Shit.

"No. Not a girl." I lowered my voice. The phone call had attracted glances from nearby patrons and I felt some attention lingering around our table. The elderly tourists were discussing the whereabouts of their hats and coats as they prepared to leave.

"Uh," I said. "Actually, I've been seeing a g—"

The last syllable was canceled out by a sharp crash. In the act of rising to leave, one of the octogenarians had dragged her purse across the table. The gaudy sequined handbag struck the centerpiece, knocking over the substantial vase with a sharp clank against an empty plate and sending pebbles cascading and bouncing under chairs and tables across the width of the wood-floored dining room. Mom's face contorted but I could see her fright was entirely for the accident. She hadn't heard my confession.

Waiters responded and within minutes the room had returned to normal. Everyone but me seemed to have recovered from the shock. My chest was too tight to continue the conversation. I felt physically drained. Mom had either forgotten the subject or assumed she'd have the opportunity to meet the girl soon enough. Either way, she'd given it up for now.

Outside, we walked together for a block.

"Where's the car?" I said.

"Back the other way. I thought I'd poke around in these little shops a while. Do you have to rush off?"

"I've got practice."

"Oh, the coffee shop! Have you been in here? It's the only thing that's kept me sane this week. The coffee, I mean. It's as good as any you'll find in Seattle. Who knew, in a town this size? And the employees are so friendly. Don't you have time to come in with me? I'll get it to go."

"No." Oh, hell no. "I'm running behind as it is."

"All right. Well, thanks for the lunch date. It's so fun to be close by. You play Friday, right?"

"Mom, it's all the way down in D.C. Why don't you wait? There'll be a home tournament in a few weeks."

She paused and I knew I'd said something.

"What's wrong, Ian? You're so distant. We moved all the way out here. Don't you think I'd want to go to D.C. to watch you play?"

"D.C. isn't the point," I said too harshly. It was like a switch had been flipped. The frustration just poured out of me. "*Why* did you move here now? Did you think anything through? Me, for example. Did you think this is what I wanted? Think about it. Wasn't it enough that I came to Florence? Why did you and Dad have to move back here, too?"

She turned her face away, blinking. It would have taken less to bring her to tears but I hadn't been able to stop myself. Now she was sobbing.

"This is our family," she said. "I don't know what's gotten into everyone."

What neither of us had said was that all of this had to do with Dad. He was too busy to notice or listen, so we could only take it out on each other.

Casey Boyd posted a final score: NC State 17, Florence 14
Casey Boyd commented on **Kyle Brown**'s video: "Dude, I can't watch this anymore. The refs screwed us over. That was obviously pass interference."
Casey Boyd poked **Krista Marshall**

At Monday's team meeting the coaches devoted two hours to our Homecoming defeat, exposing with reels of video evidence the many ways we'd been outplayed. Coach Everett was particularly amazed. We'd had the game won. And then we'd gone out of our way in search of a last-minute path to defeat. He'd never seen a full squad of eleven defenders fail to make so many tackles. He'd never seen a coordinated offense so unable to move the ball in the direction of the end zone. Then he let Coach Evans have some words. We were in lousy shape, the way Evans saw it, and it showed in the fourth quarter. Were we athletes or not? He'd seen the fattest of Major League pitching staffs move faster.

After the full team meeting we broke into position meetings where we were shown, via slow-motion video and many replays, our personal contributions to the loss.

"Nate Orton. The stop-and-go move needs work," Coach Everett said. "Watch this and tell me where it is that you stop."

The tape rolled.

"There?" Nato said uncertainly. "At seven yards."

"I see seven yards but I don't see any stop. That was a stutter. You know what that was? That little noncommittal stutter you do with your feet sends a message to your defender. It's Morse code for 'I'm going deep, don't bother with this lousy move at seven yards.' If you don't actually stop, achieve a set position, and then turn as if for the ball, any cornerback worth his oats is going to see in your eyes what you're up to. Fundamentals, people. It's all very straightforward. Stop and go. Stop. And then go. There is nothing enigmatic about the route. It is exactly what it says it is. It doesn't work because it's sneaky. It works because you do it right. Get it?"

"Got it," said Nato.

Up to this point, I was feeling pretty good about myself.

"Now, Boyd." Shit. "How many men are we allowed on the football field?"

"Eleven, Coach."

"Eleven. And how many for the other team?"

"Same. Eleven."

"Eleven and eleven. Seems pretty fair, doesn't it?"

"Fair and square."

"So if we're on offense, the other team has how many people to tackle our ball carrier?"

"Eleven. In theory."

"Eleven, in theory. Unless?"

"Unless some of them are taken care of?"

"Taken care of. What is that? You sound like a mobster."

"I mean blocking."

"Blocking. I'm relieved. I thought maybe you were unaware of this football concept. Roll the tape."

The tape rolled.

"Did you get the ball on this play?"

"No."

"Were you blocking on this play?"

"Not really. No."

"Then what were you doing on the field?"

I took this to be a rhetorical question.

"Fundamentals, people. Until our side is allowed more players on the field than the other side, there can be no one standing around. You're not a receiver, Mr. Boyd. You're a receiver-blocker. Either you're getting the ball or you go hit someone, a good, clean block. Make sure he's taken care of, if you will. Get it?"

"Got it."

"If you need an example of blocking downfield, look at Nato's video. His man was taken care of."

Later we went outside on the practice field to rehearse the offense to death—our own, if necessary. I felt sharp and motivated. I was eager to prove my status as the top receiver.

"Do we have a kicker? Where's our kicker? Blakely!" Coach Everett shouted, consulting the roster on his clipboard to refresh his memory. Stuart Blakely trotted over.

"Stewy, sir."

"What?"

"They call me Stewy, sir. It's Australian for field goal." He grinned.

"Well in this case it's plain English for protecting the passer while we fake a field goal. Look at this, gentlemen." He dropped his clipboard to the ground and we crowded around. From his pants pocket he pulled out a fistful of coins and spread them over the clipboard's flat surface. "The quarters are linemen, nickels are backs, dimes are you receivers, and pennies are defenders." He shifted the coins around to demonstrate our movement on the field. My heart sank when I saw that the play was designed to culminate in a pass downfield to Nato. "Okay? Let's see it."

We broke apart and I hung back while Coach Everett scooped the change back into his pocket.

"Hey, Coach," I said. "Usually, see, I've been doing the deep middle routes on plays like this. And Nato takes the outside." My voice was low, but Nato was bent over nearby tightening his laces and he must have been able to hear me. I thought I saw him hesitate slightly, midcinch, but he said nothing. Coach didn't say anything either. "What I meant was I've been taking more of the lead routes since I've been top of the depth chart."

"Just run the play, Boyd."

I ran humiliated to my spot on the line and we ran the play. Nato caught a smooth thirty-yard pass and it looked like he'd done it a dozen times.

"Boyd!"

I jogged over to Coach Everett. "Don't ever try to get me to see something your way by telling me about it. I'm not a good listener. But I notice everything. You have to *show* me. Got it? Show me. Right now, you're not showing me that you're the number-one receiver. You're showing me that you're afraid of being number two. You go ahead and judge yourself by what you *think* you can accomplish. The way I judge you is based only on what I see." He gestured around the field at the team, our team, which had one win and two losses in the books. "This team needs people who can step up. Be a leader, Boyd."

"Coach—"

"No. Show me."

SCENE: INTERIOR. KITCHEN. NIGHT.

IAN arrives home and finds CASEY in the kitchen. He walks past, heading toward his room. But then he pauses in the hallway and returns. He sits at the table.

I came back from dinner with Jamie, his breath still tingling my lips from our parting moments in the car. Maybe it was the high from being with Jamie, or maybe it was the drinks we'd had at dinner, but whatever the cause, the urge to tell Case developed suddenly, like an itch I knew I had the power to scratch.

I walked into the kitchen and found him drinking a protein shake straight out of the blender. He said, "Hey," and then paused when he looked at me. What I was going to say must've already been there in my face. "What's up?" he said.

I sat down. My throat clenched and I worried for a moment whether any words could get through. After a few false starts, the two of us reluctantly got it out of me without either of us uttering the dreaded g-word. He seemed to play into the surprise like you do at the end of a whodunit movie when you're given a resolution that blends together the clues you had right under your nose all along. If he hadn't known, exactly, it was pretty clear he'd at least had strong subconscious suspicions.

Wrapped up in the moment was a lot of nervous babbling on my part and Case's fear of not knowing what to say, not wanting to offend or judge or encourage, and a general discomfort for the moment itself, the verbal confrontation and its bizarre necessity.

"Hey, it's your thing, man," he said. "We're cool." That was how his feelings of friendship and discomfort averaged out.

Time, which had ceased to exist the moment I walked into the kitchen, resumed apace. And a heaviness I hadn't known I was carrying dissolved within minutes, lightening my head and body.

Immediately after, Case wanted to talk about Haile, almost as if this was the larger shock for him, that there was nothing between Haile and me. I was too consumed with my own relief to pick up on what his questions about her really indicated.

Haile, *accelerando*

Eva and I arrived at the library after class to find our supervisor, Ms. West, waiting for us. "There you two are," she said. "Come with me."

She led us downstairs to the bottom floor, past aisles of study cubicles and bookshelves and down a short hallway with windowless doors. She stopped at a door bearing a simple placard that said "Archives" and waved her library staff ID card in front of a security card reader. A soft click signaled that the lock had disengaged.

The Archives Room was a poorly lit, narrow corridor lined with floor-to-ceiling shelves burdened with boxes. It smelled, not unpleasantly, of dusty book jackets. A table with a computer and three stools was pushed against the wall by the door. From a stack of a half dozen dusty file boxes on a dolly, Ms. West lifted the top box and slid it onto the table. She closed her eyes and sneezed like a poodle. She had a tiny nose, a delicate jawline under pale skin, a helmet of short brown hair, and degenerating eyes magnified by a pair of Coke-bottle lenses. Her cheeks were rosy from hoisting the box.

"I have a project for you. The Florence Archives Project obtained these boxes from the Gilles estate. Albert Gilles, the university's founder, spent the last few years of his life collecting rare books and writing in his journals. We've been itching to add these to our collection and we finally persuaded them that it was the intention of Professor Gilles's late grandfather that all of this be available to the public. It's up to you two to figure out what we have here. I want you to go through each box and catalog everything. It may take a few days. Your ID cards should work on the door." She showed us how to catalog each item or document in the computer system and then walked us over to an empty space on a shelf where the boxes should be stored once their contents had been logged. The room wasn't large, but it was jammed full of similar boxes, each with a label indicating which member of the Gilles family the possessions had come from, a date, and a few descriptive words such as "Research," "Photos," "Letters," and "Legal files."

"And I thought that damn Dewey system sucked," Eva said when Ms. West had left us. "This is more boring than alphabetizing the damn alphabet."

I laughed, but I didn't share Eva's indifference to the project. I thought it was an interesting window into the school's history.

As we worked, Eva relived for me the adventures of her most recent Saturday night, which had culminated in hours of toe-curling sex—not with Darius, she'd long ago moved on from him—but with another football player who already had a girlfriend.

"Does the girlfriend know about you and him?" I asked, carrying the first completed box to its shelf. When I bent to slide it into place I noticed several boxes on the bottom shelf were labeled "Acton Gilles," with dates stretching back over two decades. So the Archives had gotten hold of some of Professor Gilles's materials, too.

"Shit, girl was there *with* us. This was the craziest white girl I ever seen. Climbing all over me and him like we's monkey bars or sum'in."

One of Professor Gilles's boxes had three labels: "Course Notes - Art History," "Syllabi," and "Research/Writing." The box was dated ten years earlier. Maybe I should have been reluctant to go exploring in a family archives where private items undoubtedly lurked. But curiosity won out.

I slid the box onto the floor and lifted the lid. A third of the box was filled with an unorganized assortment of handwritten notes, typed outlines, bibliographies, and a typed draft of Professor Gilles's book, with notes scribbled in red ink. I flipped quickly through the pages, drawn in by the marginalia. Then I put the draft back. The other two-thirds of the box was filled with dated files containing syllabi from each year Professor Gilles had taught Art History, excluding the most recent two years, plus three-by-five photographs of previous students' Art History projects, reading lists, and other class materials.

I thought little of it when I first noticed the loose paper, a stapled and dog-eared corner poking up carelessly from between two folders. The paper caught my eye only because it stood out amidst the otherwise orderly files. I gave the corner of the pages a gentle tug to pull them free.

The pages had been folded in half before being stuffed in the box, leaving a hard crease across the middle of each page. Otherwise, they were in good condition. It appeared to be a paper written for Professor Gilles's class. The date on the cover sheet indicated it had been written ten years earlier. I stopped hearing Eva talking in the background when I got to the fourth paragraph.

The Wrath of Achilles
By Danny Cole

Art History
Professor Acton Gilles

I'm writing this in the hospital. But you must know that. You would have noticed me missing in class and then heard the rumors. Word travels fast. That's always been your biggest fear, those rumors, how fast word travels. What else do you know? Do you know how hard they beat me? Do you know about the fracture in my skull? The collapsed lung? The cracked ribs?

You don't. Because you never came.

This paper is meant to accompany my art project, which is almost complete. I will be unable to display it in class with the others. But don't worry, everyone will see it.

You once said your favorite painting was *The Wrath of Achilles* by Leon Benouville. I remember that because you also told me (I think you meant it as a joke, we were in the church, we had just made love) that I was your Achilles' heel. But you said a lot of things. You said you loved me. You said you'd leave your wife. You said you'd stop hiding who you are.

Eva was still talking—there was another party this weekend we *had* to go to—and she didn't seem to notice me hovered over the box in the back. I scanned quickly through the rest of the paper. It was three single-spaced pages devoted mostly to accusing Professor Gilles of hypocrisy for using art in class to promote self-awareness and introspection while he himself stayed married and closeted. It also appeared to accuse Gilles of a deep personal betrayal, for abandoning the paper's author when he was most vulnerable and without any other support. This had to have been the boy who'd hanged himself in the church.

I slowed when I reached the final paragraphs, feeling a chill ascend my spine.

I see now that I was a fool. Our affair was a lie. Just like the rest of your life.

Their violence could not kill me. But your betrayal has. If no one—not even you— has any interest in standing up for me, then why should I?

Consider this my art project: performance art. When they find me, I'll have a copy of this paper on me, along with every note you sent me, every artifact I have of our "love." You will not be able to deny it, though I bet you'll try. I see now that denial is so much a part of who you are. I have nothing left. But I will not go out as a willing victim. The only thing you told me that will survive as truth is this: I *am* your Achilles' heel.

"What are you doing back there?" Eva said.

"What? Nothing." With shaking hands, I shoved the paper back where I'd found it and returned the box to the shelf. Then I joined Eva at the table and tried to concentrate on the task Ms. West had assigned us.

SCENE: INTERIOR. EVERETT DINING ROOM. NIGHT.

The EVERETT FAMILY is seated around the dining room table. IAN looks at his watch as
if wondering if it's too early to excuse
himself.

We were finishing dinner around a table shrunken by the removal
of three wide leaves to match the family's reduced scale. For
two weeks the table had been buried under boxes and stacks of
wall art. They'd been eating at the smaller breakfast table off the
kitchen and some nights they ate separately, he in his study and
she in whatever room of the house needed most to be lived in.
Mom had insisted on the dining room for this meal, me being the
occasion, and I'd helped her section the long table and push the
ends together so that, as she put it, we didn't have to yell at each
other across the room.

"Does the barbeque have propane, Mike?" she said. "We
should get some extra. Where would they sell that in town?
Maybe Ian knows."

"We have plenty of propane," Dad said.

"Ready for Virginia Tech?" I asked.

"Well, we have our plane tickets. As for the football, there's
always more work to be done."

"Okay. I get it," Mom said. "The grill is your thing. I know nothing unless you tell me. And please tell me before the *day of.* I won't have time to go out at the last minute. We'll eat outside, right? I think that'd be easiest. Of course, we'll all fit inside if it rains. We'd have to, wouldn't we? And with all those relatives… oh, well. Think sunny thoughts! We can put the grownups at the long picnic table and find something smaller for the kids. Everyone can just serve themselves. We'll put all the food on the patio table and I already bought some coolers. I thought ours had come with us but I haven't seen them since the Fourth of July."

Here she paused for a bite. Both Dad and I were finished eating.

"Who's coming?" I said.

"Bill and Linda and the kids. Did you talk to your brother, Mike? Are they driving the day before, for the game? It's not a problem. We'll put them downstairs because of the kids. I'm afraid of what they might sound like to the rest of the house running back and forth on the hardwood upstairs. Becky and Doug can have the large room up there. And I thought Anne could take the futon in the sewing room. Is that what we're calling that room? No one sews," she said to me as if I suspected one of them had taken it up. "We're putting the antique machine in there and sewing room sounds better than ironing room. Maybe it could be the knitting room. Not that I do much of that either, but I could store all the yarn there. Poor Anne. She always gets the leftover beds."

I started to collect the dishes and when the table was clear I stood at the sink loading the washer. The house had been transformed, like a movie set. The furniture and wall hangings and lamps conveyed a just-set-in-place feeling, as if all the pieces could be rotated off stage at any moment. Particularly the couches and bureaus, arranged in dust-free corners and along the edges of still-centered throw rugs, seemed to hover an inch above ground, needing more time to settle in.

"Remember you have to wash those before you load them," Mom said.

She said this to me, though we all knew it was meant for Dad's ears. Like many of the more obvious factors that rendered life in River Bend inferior to Seattle, the dishwasher they'd inherited with the house left much to be desired. Apparently it also left flakes of food on the plates unless they were prerinsed.

I listened to my parents' discussion with one another and wondered if it was this painful when I wasn't around to feel the pain.

"Nikki's buying her ticket tomorrow," Mom said. "I wanted her to stay for the week but she has a church retreat in Bellingham, so she's staying only through Monday. Those are the confirmed relatives. Who am I forgetting?"

"That's sounds fine," Dad said. "I'm sorry, honey, I can't think about this right now."

"Okay, but let me know who from around here you think we should invite. What about Coach Evans? I saw his wife the other day at the cleaners. Rita. I've run into her around town a few times and she's always so friendly."

"I thought we were keeping this a family thing."

"There must be some people from the university we could invite. It would be a nice gesture."

"I can't do this right now."

Dad made a break for his study.

"Mike, I'm making an effort. We're a part of this community. Have you thought of that?"

"I'm very aware of it," Dad called back to her. "It's a community that expects their football team to win."

"And you have a family that expects a human being around the house every once in a while," Mom shot back. "I've seen you like this before. It's not healthy."

"Look," he said, stepping back into the doorway. "It'll get easier. We moved in the middle of the season. That's the reality and I'm sorry, but these social events might have to wait. We're near enough to our families now that every rendezvous with the relatives doesn't have to be a three-ring—"

"I'm gay."

She gasped. I suppose it was a gasp, anyway. I hadn't expected anything good to come out of this but it was a really awful sound she made, like something wrong had gotten in her mouth, scalding her tongue, and then lodging in her windpipe. I'm telling you, it was awful.

My words in the open air had sounded absurd and unconvincing in the way your own voice sounds in a recording. My parents might not have believed what they'd heard if the plates I was holding hadn't started to chatter. In the awful silence that followed Mom's gasp, I slid them feebly into the lower rack of the dishwasher.

"Well," Dad said. "That explains a lot."

He walked down the hall to his study, leaving me with my betrayal.

Mom was gripping the collar of her shirt with both hands and shaking her head. When her voice returned to her, what she wanted to know was whether I was sure. As if this was something anyone would prematurely confess to his mother. At least, "Are you sure?" is better than, "Well that explains a lot." *What* did he think this explained? Yes, Dad, I'm too gay to play football. That's why I quit. Is that what you think this explains? Go ahead. Think of it that way. A new page for your playbook: Ian's quarterback sneak.

She seemed surprised by her own tears, as if she hadn't wanted them to come. She held up a hand, indicating this was all too much to talk about right now, and turned to run up the stairs. I could hear her heavy footfalls overhead before the bedroom door thunked shut. I filled the dispenser cup and switched on the dishwasher.

In the driveway, behind the wheel, I looked up at the house. Upstairs the master bedroom was lit yellow by a small table lamp. The kitchen was ablaze with light but the rest of the house was dark. I could hardly look at the kitchen. I doubted I'd ever be able to enjoy an appetite in that kitchen again. Merely thinking of what I'd just done there caused my stomach to roil, the same feeling I'd had while holding the plates with the words suddenly in the open, irrevocable.

I thought I saw something. I waited several moments and then saw it again. A small flicker in one of the downstairs windows interrupted the darkness for a few seconds and then disappeared. When it returned, it held steady, a yellow flame, vertical in the still air of the house. I counted the windows, picturing the way the rooms were laid out down the hallway. It was his study. He was sitting in the dark with his lighter.

Haile, *staccato*

On the evening of Professor Gilles's reading, I climbed the steps of the King Theater and settled into an aisle seat near the back of the room. The turnout was impressive—female mostly, students and professors, wives of professors, some of them dragging along their husbands or partners for the occasion. Dozens of my female classmates filled the first rows. Mixed in with the academics were a handful of literate community members. Everyone seemed to have the book tucked underarm, eager for an autograph. Embarrassed by this herd-like behavior, I kept my copy hidden in my book bag.

I don't know whether it was Danny Cole's paper, which I had been unable to push from my mind since discovering it in the Gilles Archives, or merely my vantage point at the back of the theater, but I felt disconnected from the scene on stage. Under the lights, Gilles seemed at ease in his glory, rising to his own occasion. The whole room was on his side. Each line he uttered from the podium was met appropriately with laughter, profound silence, or generous applause. He'd reached that next level of being—*celebrity!*—where rooms can be filled without the presence of a single critic. I had been one of those admirers only

176

days earlier. But now that was impossible. Now I could only question.

"After his death, I began to pay attention to the art I'd grown up around," Gilles was saying after a long anecdote about his grandfather. "I began to examine his world. And eventually I saw that *this* was a book that needed to be written. My book, essentially, is about life. What art provides us in terms of life is far greater than the gift of knowledge we derive from science, the comfort we find in religion, or the speculation that engages us in philosophy. Art is all these things and more. Even when there are no answers elsewhere, there is still meaning in art. Art lives because we live, not because we hang it on walls or store it away in museums. It interacts with our deepest instinct and intellect and emotion, drawing us ever closer to our own meaning."

There was a period of eager and exaggerated applause through which Professor Gilles dipped his head in gratitude. Questions were encouraged and hands sprung up.

"I think it's totally amazing how you weave these incredible works of art into a narrative about everyday life," a girl near the front was saying. "How do you come up with your ideas?"

Someone else near the front wanted to know whether Gilles intended to write a novel. He thought it sounded like a wonderful idea.

Someone else thought that the way Gilles had incorporated the story of how he and his wife had met at Florence as under-grads was the sweetest thing she'd ever heard. Gilles smiled at his wife in the crowd.

They went on and on like this, probing him about his writing process (the first draft by hand, subsequent drafts on a computer), how long it had taken him (three years from conception—two for research and one for the writing), and whether there was a second book forthcoming (yes, but he hadn't started it and didn't know what topic it would address). Eventually the dean interrupted to bring the Q & A to a close so there would be enough time for people to have their books signed.

A line formed quickly at one side of the stage and Gilles, armed with a pen and a politician's smile, took his place at the table. I left before he started signing books.

The library was ten minutes from closing when I rushed through the lobby and took the stairs down to the bottom floor. A few students occupied the study cubes, their ears draped in head-phones, their eyes trained on books or glaring laptop screens, their mouths flapping open to yawn. Even on days when I didn't work in the library, I kept my ID card in my school bag. I dug it out in the hallway as I approached the Archives Room. I waved it in front of the card reader and waited, hearing my heart beat in my head. The door clicked. I turned the handle and pushed it open.

A security guard would sweep the building at closing and I had no intention of being discovered here. I patted the wall for the light switch and squinted at the sudden brightness of the naked bulbs overhead that had seemed so dim during daylight hours.

The box had not been touched since Eva and I had been in the room the day before. I pulled out the paper and unfolded its pages. *The Wrath of Achilles* by Danny Cole. Without having a plan for what I might do with it, I slid the paper into my school bag and replaced the box on the shelf with the others. Then I left, joining the thin stream of students being kicked out of the library for the night.

Casey Boyd posted a final score: Florence 42, Duke 9
Casey Boyd posted a final score: Florence 27, Wake Forest 14
Casey Boyd posted a final score: Texas A&M 10, Florence 24
Casey Boyd posted a final score: Florence 55, BYU 28

SCENE: INTERIOR. JAMIE'S BEDROOM. NIGHT.

IAN is lying on his back. JAMIE is on his side, his head propped up on his hand, looking at Ian.

"What is it?"

"Nothing."

"What were you thinking about just now?"

"Nothing."

"Liar. Tell me."

"It's nothing. It's stupid."

"I don't care."

"What time do you think it is?"

"I don't know. Late."

"I should go."

"Why?"

"Because."

"Because why?"

"I have practice early."

"I have an alarm clock. I'll get you up."

"That isn't the point."

"I know what it is."

"What?"

"You're afraid of what your roommates think."

"No."

"Ian."

"Okay, maybe a little."

"Why?"

"It just feels weird."

"What's weird?"

"Them knowing that I stayed over."

"Why?"

"I don't know. It's just weird."

"Come on. What do they *think* gay guys do?"

"I'm pretty sure they try not to think about it."

"They're your friends. They don't care."

Long pause.

"Stay. Please."

"Okay."

Long pause.

"Are you still awake?"

"Yeah."

"Can I come see you play?"

"Tennis?"

"I won't if it makes you uncomfortable."

"No, it's cool. You won't be bored?"

"Of course not. I want to see what you do."

"Okay."

"Let's make a deal."

"What deal?"

"Take me to one of your tennis matches and I'll take you to a show, one of the bands I like."

"Okay."

"Deal?"

"Deal. Do we have to shake on it?"

"I think we're past shaking."

"Yeah. I guess so."

"Ian?"

"Yeah?"

"Goodnight."

"Goodnight."

I lay awake in the dark until his breathing changed.

"Jamie? Hey. You still awake?"

He was asleep. I slid out of his bed, got dressed, and went home.

Haile's audition

Over the weekend, I had Ms. Rivera drop me off on Main Street and I walked over to the coffee shop. Jamie came out of the back with a five-pound bag of coffee and I watched him cut into the sealed package and poor half of the greasy beans into the grinder. I asked him if Patrick, the owner, was around. I expected his face to light up when he saw me, but he only paused to say that he expected the owner to arrive at any minute.

"Are you staying? I'll tell him to come find you when he gets here."

"Thanks," I said. And then, "How are you?"

"I'm okay." It sounded like just okay. I understood. Whatever stage of self-discovery Ian was going through, it was one Jamie had already endured and outgrown, and this inequity had spoiled their alliance. Ian treated their relationship experimentally while Jamie, mature beyond his age, was unfortunate enough to have fallen in love. Ian had developed a habit of breaking hearts.

"You wanna come over later?" I said. "We can drink cheap wine and listen to depressing cello music."

This forced Jamie to smile and he agreed to come over when he got off work. I sat at a table by the window and watched people wander Main Street. I couldn't help glancing over every once in a while at the stage in the corner, imagining a filled room facing me and my keyboard.

After a while, I pulled out Professor Gilles's book and opened it to the index for photos and illustrations, turning the pages until I got to the *W*s. Finding no mention of *The Wrath of Achilles*, the painting Danny had mentioned in his paper, I flipped back through the chapters I'd found most interesting. Our Art History assignment was due in two weeks and I didn't have a single pencil stroke to show for it. If I needed some inspiration, it was quickly clear to me that I wasn't going to find it here. Professor Gilles had a gift for relating the power art had to enlighten and enrich, a power I, as a musician, had felt drawn to as I first read his book. But now, rereading certain sections, I couldn't help but feel they'd lost some of their traction. How could a man who spoke so provocatively about the meaning and power of art be such a coward in his own life? And, more distressing, how could anyone in a position to help a vulnerable young man in pain, pain much more harmful than his physical injuries, turn his back on that responsibility?

"Good read?" Patrick was beside me. He was in his forties, a college-town lifer with long hair tucked behind his ears, armfuls of tattoos, and a pleasant face.

"Oh, hi," I said, standing to greet him. "Yes—no, I've already read it. I was just reviewing some things."

"May I?" he said, signaling with a hand at the chair opposite me. I nodded. "Jamie tells me you are a musician."

"Yes, I'm in the program here, studying under Jennifer Rivera. She encouraged me to look for some local gigs. But it was Jamie, actually, who suggested I bring you a demo."

I pulled the CD from my bag. The song I'd recorded was about confrontation and I called it "Throwin' Words at Da Moon." It had haunting undertones and a complicated melody. In Tori vernacular, more "Precious Things" than "Crucify."

"Did you have a date in mind? Sometime next week, maybe?" he said.

At first, I didn't understand. "For a show?"

"Isn't that what you wanted?"

"Don't you want to listen to the song?"

"Yes, I look forward to it. But it won't affect my decision. I trust Ms. Rivera's judgment."

Before I left, I set up a performance for the following Friday night, when I knew Ian would be out of town.

SCENE: INTERIOR. IAN'S BEDROOM. NIGHT.

IAN is lying on his bed in the dark.

Jamie Jamie Jamie Jamie Jamie's eyes hair neck shoulder Jamie
shirtless Jamie smiling Jamie Jamie sliding off his jeans boxers
socks Jamie naked kissing Jamie Me Jamie Me Jamie Me in the
shower wet Nate arms Jamie neck legs Me Jamie Me Jamie hair
naked arms chest stomach thighs Jamie Nate Jamie Jamie Jamie
Nate no not Nate JAMIE Jamie lips eyes kissing Nate Me Jamie
Jamie Nate Me Nate Jamie Me Nate Nate shirtless armpit shoulder Nate stomach stomach stomach Nate Me Nate Me Nate nip-
ple stomach pushing Nate Orton Nate Orton Nate Orton NATE
ORTON NATE ORTON NATE ORTON Nate- Nat- Na- Na- N—
    Fuck.
    I cleaned up and went to sleep.

Casey Boyd nailed that quiz on regression analysis
Casey Boyd has 6 quarters, 4 dimes, 2 nickels, and 11 pennies to work with
Casey Boyd !!! Upset alert!!!

From the souvenir shop at the airport I bought a bottle of water, a Gatorade, a *Sports Illustrated*, and a paperback copy of *Moneyball*, each in separate cash transactions that netted me $2.11 in loose change. Six quarters, four dimes, two nickels, and eleven pennies. With these I spent the flight rehearsing the playbook for the big Virginia Tech game. At least, it was a big game to us. To Vegas we were 10½-point underdogs. And to the Hokie fans, if the media had it right, we amounted to a weekend off between other opponents who posed a more realistic threat to their undefeated season.

The ritual pregame dinner was at a place called Sal's Steakhouse in Blacksburg, Nato's hometown. The meal had been organized by Nato's parents, who were the friendly neighbors of Sal himself. Mr. and Mrs. Orton sat together at the end of one table, looking at first a little stunned by the thuggish minorities swaggering into the room. Team dinners are like large family holidays, but with less drinking and considerably more profanity, though the latter was curbed in this case on account of our hosts.

The meal unfolded almost without a hitch. Almost. A few seats down from Nato sat Pile Driver, in all his unnuanced glory, an almost constant flow of idiocy streaming out of his big, bald, empty head.

"You slip it to that pretty blonde we met at Third Base?" he boomed loudly when Coach Everett had stepped away to the restroom. The main course was arriving, and Pile Driver leaned over his plate to get a wise-ass look at Nato, dipping the point of his collar in some red wine reduction in the process.

I'd have advised Nato just to say yes, whether this was the truth or not, and change the subject, the idea being that it's a rare situation where the effort required to teach Pile Driver any sort of social lesson is anywhere near worth the trouble. But Nato said nothing. And not just a fuck-off-I'm-ignoring-you nothing. This was a loaded silence, a bones-tightening-inside-his-cheeks sign of dislike that I think, to use a strong word in Nato's world, qualified as hatred. None of which, of course, Pile Driver was equipped to detect.

"Remember that girl, Smalls?" he turned to say to Todd, who was staring back at him dumbly. "She was ready to play, if you know what I'm saying." Everyone, including Mr. and Mrs. Orton, knew what Pile Driver was saying. "Hey, Nato?"

"Goodman. Forget it, man. Shit," said Darius.

Goodman didn't quite forget it, but he did shut up and eat his steak. And Kyle had the good sense to make polite conversation with the Ortons about life in Blacksburg.

Later, as we got off the bus at the hotel, Coach Everett told me to meet him in his room.

"How you doing?" he said when we were alone.

"Good."

He raised his eyebrows skeptically.

"I'm a little nervous, but I'm always like this after the team dinner. It usually takes me an hour of studying the playbook before I settle down."

"Don't read the playbook anymore tonight. You know all the plays. That isn't your problem."

Problem?

"Have a seat," he said. I sat. "How do you think the team is doing?"

"The team? All right, I guess. Everyone seems fine."

"So you're doing good but the team is doing only fine?"

"I wasn't comparing—"

"I know, that's the point. Casey, a football team needs followers, and we have them. I mean that in a good way. Our team has all the right pieces. Do you know what we need?"

We needed more rushing and passing yards per game and more disciplined blocking—a general beefing up of the W column, basically, but I didn't think that was what he meant.

"More leaders?" I said.

"No. We have our leaders. What we need is for our leaders to do some leading."

"Look, I've been trying to—"

"Let me ask you something. What do you think about on the field? I mean, what goes through your head during the final seconds before the ball is snapped?"

"I guess I try to picture what the play should look like."

"*X*s and *O*s, that kind of thing?"

"Yeah, I guess. And coins. You know, the way you show us plays using coins."

He nodded, as if he expected me to say this. "When you're on the field, do you try to see everyone's assignments, or only your own?"

"Everyone's. I try to see everyone."

"That's what I thought." He leaned back in the chair. "Do you remember when you and Ian used to run plays in the backyard?"

His voice, I thought, had faltered at Ian's name, a scratchy blip at
the back of the throat that would have been imperceptible had I
not been aware of any reason to listen for it. "You got to a point
where Ian would drop back with the ball and he'd have his eyes
closed while you ran a route. Did you know he did that? Maybe you
agreed on the route ahead of time, maybe not. I never could figure
that out. But either way, he was throwing with his eyes closed. And
you didn't turn to look for the ball until the last possible second.
More times than not the ball would be there, wouldn't it?"

"You saw us doing that?"

"I've tried to figure out a way to teach that to my quarter-
backs and receivers, but I never found it. You remember that feeling, don't you?" I nodded. "That's what I want you to think about
before every play. Don't picture your playbook. Don't think about
coins. Listen to your instincts. The ball will be there. Get it?"

I nodded. "Got it."

"I'm hard on you because I need you," he said as I got up.
"You're one of the leaders."

"I'll—"

"No, no. Don't tell me. Show me. Now, go get some sleep."

~ ~ ~

In the locker room, we got dressed and waited for the coaches to
enter with their final pregame instructions.

"So what the fuck, man?" Pile Driver said. "Did you fuck
her?"

Nato didn't even look up. "No. You go ahead, if you're so
interested."

"Hey, easy. I'm not trying to interfere. All I'm saying is you'd
have to be a homo not to jump on that."

190

In the next moment, which passed before Goodman could do anything about it, he was halfway inside his locker, eyes popping and two handfuls of his shirt bunched in Nato's white knuckles. It wasn't a fair match weight-wise, and in the next moment the advantage of surprise was neutralized and Nato was shoved backward. He came charging back with a final angry body check before the guys nearby could pry them apart. Nato seemed to find himself after a few seconds but Goodman, disguising his embarrassment behind outrage, almost lost it.

"I was fucking *joking*. Jesus, man. You're wound real tight lately."

"Settle down," said one of the guys restraining Goodman.

"Get off me!"

"Not until you shut up for a minute. Do us all a favor."

"You're clearly crazy," Nato muttered, returning to the business of his shoulder pads.

"Oh, *I'm* clearly crazy?" Goodman said, squirming under the weight of two teammates who knew better than to let go of him just yet. "You wanna be clear about something? Maybe it's time to be clear about this. There better not be any fucking homos on this team."

I watched Nato's face, but his expression didn't change.

We were interrupted then by Coach, who had just entered the room in time to catch Goodman's last remark, and the room was seized by a shameful silence. I guess some of the guys knew about Ian. No one cared enough for it to be a scandal, but something like that gets around. Last I'd heard from Ian, he'd told his parents and it wasn't yet clear what side his father was going to come down on.

"Grow up, men. Or at least act like it," was all he said. And we acted like it.

Casey Boyd posted a new photo: "me and dad"
Casey Boyd endlessly watching game film
Casey Boyd became a fan of THE Florence University

Dad surprised me a week later by flying in for our game. He wouldn't take a day off work even though he had them, but he'd hopped a late Friday red-eye into Albany and drove down to River Bend in the morning. And there he was outside the stadium, leaning against the wall near the players' entrance.

"This must be Krista," he said.

I gave Dad a hug and confirmed Krista's identity.

"Casey. You could have told me your dad was coming," Krista said, jabbing me in the shoulder. Then she said to my father, "I've heard so much about you."

Dad could not say in return that he'd heard much about her.

I was not sure how important to me Krista had come across in our father-son long-distance dialogue. I knew I hadn't been very forthcoming. Dad and I didn't talk about these sorts of feelings. But still, I felt a sting of anger when I saw Dad wasn't buying it, Krista and me. I could tell he did not see her as daughter-in-law material. He had that calm parents get when they believe their kids are going through a stage they will soon outgrow.

"I can't believe you really flew all this way for the day," I said.

"Spend a life putting airplanes together, might as well take advantage of the damn things."

"Do you have a ticket for the game? Wait here, I'll figure out how to get you one."

"It's okay. I bought one online. Good luck, son," he said as he wandered off.

Before I slipped into the locker room, I turned to get another look at him. He was alone, gazing around with an expression split between wonder and pride at the sight of campus, the ivy trimmings and green lawns, the tens of thousands funneling toward the stadium, the smells of barbeque and an autumn afternoon, the sounds of marching bands and carefree students.

Not often, but sometimes in moments like these, the sheer unfairness of it sneaked up on me. She died of breast cancer. Statistically, an ordinary tragedy.

Haile, *mezzo-soprano*

I'd performed in concert halls, opera houses, Broadway theaters, and outdoor band shells. But I'd never performed by myself for this many people, not even at the café in Hyannis. This occurred to me only moments before I stepped out onto the small platform in the corner of the coffee shop. Through a gap in the curtain I saw the microphone, poised expectantly over my keyboard, its head cocked slightly upward as if anticipating the music. My music. The room was as full as I'd seen it on a Friday—groups of students reading and chatting, a short line of customers at the bar, a few people hovering indecisively by the door, holding out to see if there was going to be anything worth seeing. Everyone turned toward me with curiosity as I sat down at the keys.

I don't remember Patrick announcing my name. I don't remember walking out on stage. What I remember was the moment, the crack in time between when I opened my mouth and the first note slipped out. It was a moment I shared with deer staring into headlights, skydivers stepping into the sky, and astronauts strapped to idling rockets. In all the moments I'd spent on stage, I'd never felt at once so primed for disaster and so near to striking glory. Then somehow, as it always does, time rolled forward and my first note rose up to meet it. That's what I remember. I can recall the attentive silence that fell over the crowd and eventually the applause that invited me back to the stage for an encore. But that first moment stayed with me, alive in my blood.

~ ~ ~

The show had been a success. I couldn't pinpoint anything that might have made it better. But somehow I felt unsatisfied.

"What's wrong with me?" I asked Jamie. We were standing on the bridge a few days after the show, watching the clouds crawl across the surface of the river.

"You're playing it safe," he said without hesitation. I gave him a sharp glance. "You are. Have you ever been in a situation where you didn't know what would happen next?"

"Yeah. On the night of the show. There were definitely moments when I wasn't sure I could go through with it."

"I don't mean on stage. I mean in real life. When your feelings and secrets and dreams and everything you love is at stake."

"I came here," I said defensively.

Jamie shook his head. "You're here because you're running from something."

"And you're one to judge. What are you doing that's so risky? You say you want to be in New York. Well, what's stopping you?" Jamie pushed his elbows off the railing and turned away from me. "Wait. I didn't mean—" I caught up to him and he whipped around to glare at me.

"You asked me what I thought you were doing wrong. Did you want me to say you're perfect, you've reached the pinnacle of your career because you played one show at a coffee shop in the middle of nowhere? I happen to think you're better than this."

"I'm sorry, Jamie."

"Forget it."

"No. Really, I mean it. Tell me. What do you think I should do? Please. I won't be defensive this time."

"It doesn't matter what I think you should do. You have to figure that out on your own. Look, can you picture yourself three years from now?"

"Sure."

"Don't. You'll only hold yourself back. When I look at who I was just a year ago I never could have expected to become who I am now. We have an amazing ability to grow and adapt much faster than we think. But you can't do that without occasionally letting yourself be vulnerable."

"Hmm. I was pretty vulnerable with Ian." I was trying to be funny but Jamie didn't laugh.

"Were you really? Ian was safe. That's what you were attracted to. Now he's even safer. Safe is nice, unless it lasts forever. It's not a way to live a life."

"What are you saying?"

"Take a risk, Haile. Do something you're afraid to do. For example, try talking to someone you don't know anything about."

"Like who?"

"Casey."

"Who?"

"You know who. Ian's roommate."

"What do you know about Casey?"

"I know he comes by the shop sometimes to ask about you."

"Really?" I said. "No. You must be thinking of someone else."

"Right. 'Cause so many football players talk to me. I get them confused sometimes."

I shook my head. "Whatever. I know all I need to know about Casey."

"You're getting defensive again. That's my advice, Haile. Surprise yourself. That's what you're missing."

I was about to refute him, but I stopped myself.

"How are *you* doing?" I asked as we strolled up the Great Lawn toward the library.

Jamie was quiet for such a long time that I began to worry about what he might say. Finally, he spoke.

"This was the first time I really wanted something and couldn't find any possible way to hold on to it. He just drifted away, completely beyond my control. I guess a part of me could see it coming all along. The way he was always just a little distracted, his mind on a tennis match or a football player or some film he'd seen for the tenth time."

"Do you have any regrets?"

"You mean, other than that it couldn't last longer? I don't know. Maybe there was one thing. We made a promise to each other. I was going to take him to a concert and he was going to take me to a tennis match. Neither ever happened. I know it sounds silly but I feel like if we had only had a chance to do more of that—to understand each other's passions—maybe we would have been less likely to take each other for granted."

"You think he took you for granted?"

"I think he got bored. Whenever he stayed over he was gone first thing in the morning. He never wanted me at his place. Maybe he just wasn't ready, so he let himself drift away."

"What concert were you going to take him to?"

"What?"

"The deal you guys made? What concert would you have taken him to?"

"Oh, that. I wanted to see the Traci Rice Trio. They're coming next month."

"I know! I can't wait," I said. "Hey, I'll make you a deal. Go with me instead?"

"All right, deal," he said. "It's a date."

~ ~ ~

I approached Jen's front door in radiant good spirits. I looked forward to a long evening of conversation, to the smells of olive oil and garlic and onions with which she always seemed to be cooking, to a fire and some music as the daylight became valley shadows and then turned the windows to black mirrors, reflecting the warm sight of the rooms back on us.

So wrapped up was I in my state that I failed to notice, when I let myself in, that I did not smell her cooking. I flipped off my shoes and hung my jacket. It was only when I was in the hallway adjacent to the living room that I heard the music. At first, the song felt familiar in the spontaneous way any song can when you're feeling good about your place in the universe. But at the archway where I stopped when I saw Jen sitting motionless in her chair, listening to the music flow through her immense speakers, I realized that the song was *actually* familiar. Not just melodically familiar, but technically familiar: a sequence of notes that made my fingers twitch with muscle memory.

I stood paralyzed with panic as the room trembled with the soaring progression of notes. The music was from the Beethoven recordings I'd made with the Atlantic Quartet. It was the piece I'd been unable to play on stage on my last night with the quartet.

Jen was in her listening chair with her eyes closed. Her black hair flowed over the back of the chair as if she was lying in a bathtub and wanted to keep it dry. One thin arm rested on the side cushion, stretched loosely to full length in the direction of the end table where three fingers brushed the stem of a wine glass. Disheveled papers were pinned beneath it.

Her voice startled me.

"What are you doing here?" I knew she wasn't asking me why I'd come into the house. She'd invited me to dinner.

"Jen—"

"Why? Why are you here?"

"I want to make music."

"You don't call *this* making music?" Her speakers, I realized, were remarkable. In the gaps between our words the music poured thick and pure as if we were hearing the strings live in a studio. "The dean requires me to enter midterm progress reports into each student's school records. I was more than a little surprised to learn that I don't in fact have a student named Haile Laine, though not as surprised as when I discovered a little more about a person named Haven Libby." Jen reached for the papers on the end table. "I didn't ask for these, so I hope you won't feel that I've gone behind your back. The dean gave me these copies of your transcripts from Juilliard." Her last word hung in the air heavier than the others.

"Are you mad at me?" It was a stupid thing to ask, but I felt desperate to know where this all was headed. Would I be kicked out of the program? Expelled from Florence?

"No. I'm confused. And a little hurt. But my feelings are beside the point."

"Jen, I didn't mean for it to be a secret. I even tried to tell you. I just—"

"Is it because of this?" Now I saw that she had other papers, not just the transcripts. As she shuffled them to the top, I only needed to see the first few words of the headline to understand that she had discovered everything. The article in her hand had been written by the critic from the *Los Angeles Times*. It had run in the paper the morning after my final appearance with the Atlantic Quartet. "Promising a Show Stopper, a Young Violinist Delivers—and Disappoints."

I didn't want to cry in front of Jen, but I was too tired to hold back any longer. I felt the hot streaks cooling on my cheeks and then finally the sensation of relief, unclenching within me like the petals of a waking rose.

"Come here," Jen said, standing. She didn't seem alarmed by my tears, which only made it easier to collapse into a full meltdown. "Here, sit down." She guided me into her listening chair and sat herself on the small stepladder I'd seen her use to reach volumes on the highest bookshelves. "Tell me what happened. Can you do that for me?"

I nodded, realizing now that I was able to admit it to myself just how much I'd wanted to tell everything to Jen—or to anyone who would understand.

"My mother—" I was going to start by saying that my mother had viewed the Atlantic Quartet as my big opportunity. The audition had been her idea. Pulling me out of Juilliard had also been her idea. And it had been her idea to take time off from her job to become my manager, which really only meant that she would be what she had always been—an ever-present mother with a law degree. But now when I tried to talk about her, I choked on the word. The thing is, I missed her. I missed having someone who supported me unconditionally, who wasn't afraid to get in people's faces and insist that I was talented and that they needed to pay attention. Her behavior may have been at times inappropriate and humiliating, but somewhere along the way I'd taken for granted that a part of me depended on having an ally like her. Since I'd come to Florence, I'd been on my own.

"I walked out on stage," I said, after I'd taken Jen through an abridged version of my life story up to my final night with the Atlantic Quartet. I'd been talking quickly, but now I slowed down. "It was just like every other night on the tour. We walked out on stage—we were in the Walt Disney Concert Hall in L.A. and it was sold out—and we took our seats. A hush fell over the room. Usually at this point, I shut out everything else and focused only on the music. But that night I couldn't. I kept hearing things from the audience, a cough here, the creak of a seat there. I thought of all the critics sitting in the front rows and I imagined that they already had in their minds the story they were going to write about me. There was nothing I could do to change their opinions. Maybe that's why I simply couldn't play. Maybe it was my body's way of warning me that I couldn't win by playing their game. My only chance was to do something totally unexpected, like standing up and walking off stage. That isn't why I walked off—I'm not that brave. The way it actually happened was that I didn't do anything at first. For several minutes, I just sat there. I was supposed to lead the group into our first piece, Beethoven's Opus 132. The others had already brought their instruments up to position and I could feel them waiting for me. But I couldn't move. Eventually my hand started trembling. That was the point I knew, physically, that I couldn't play. My bow hand felt numb and powerless and my instrument felt too heavy to lift to my chin. That's when I got scared and I just got up and ran."

"That was a year ago," Jen said. "And then I first saw you perform last spring. How did that come about?"

"I left the Atlantic Quartet and my mother sent me up to my grandparents' beach house on the Cape. She thought it would help me recover so that I could return to Juilliard in the fall. I was up there by myself. I'd never had free time like that and it got boring pretty quickly. My grandparents have an old piano and I just started writing these songs. I never expected that I'd *do* anything with them. But I kept working on them and my friend encouraged me to play some shows. I guess, looking back, I probably wanted this all along. And then you handed me your business card and suddenly going back to Juilliard to play the violin didn't seem quite so inevitable."

On the speakers, the Beethoven opus came around to its main theme, and for a minute neither of us said anything. We just sat and listened.

"Haile, you can't turn your back on *this*," she said, jabbing the air with a finger in the direction of the speakers.

"You think I should go back there?" My belly knotted with panic.

"I don't know," she said softly. She turned away to look out the window. The valley had fallen into dusk. I remembered now that Jen had first come to Florence fleeing the rejection of not being accepted at the Juilliard School of Music.

"Jen, I was honored to go to Juilliard. I really was. But it wasn't my dream. It was my mother's." There, I'd said it.

"And this is your dream?"

"Yes," I said, feeling strength in my voice. "You've seen me perform my music. You see how I love it. That's why you noticed me, isn't it? I think being here is exactly where I need to be."

"All right. But, Haile, listen to this music. Really listen to it." She closed her eyes and threw her head back for several measures. "You have a remarkable capacity to feel music. But you have to let people in. Let us see what you have. Don't run from the thing that allowed you to play music like this. Use it. It will be difficult after what happened, but if you have the courage to take that journey, people will want to come along with you."

Haile, *presto*

I watched Ian descend the aisle, thumbs hooked in his backpack straps, completely inside himself. He turned sideways to scoot into our row. I wanted to be mad at him for hurting Jamie—I *was* mad at him for that, and for other things—but he had a lonely, rattled look on his face that took the sting out of my anger. I could tell he'd spoken to his parents.

"How'd they take it?"

"'How many *T*s are there in bloodletting?'"

"What?"

He rolled his eyes and looked away as if my incompetence had become a burden. "Never mind. It's from a—"

"A movie. Right. You know, someday you're going to meet a nice, normal boy and you're going to scare him off with this, whatever it is—this code of obscure moviespeak."

"It's from *Superman*."

"Whatever, it's obscure enough. It was thirty years ago."

"You don't want to do this now," he said, only half committed to trying to change the subject. But then he couldn't help himself. "The music you listen to is five *hundred* years old. Someday you'll meet a boy who'll run off when he realizes he has to measure up to Tchaikovsky or Beethoven." This hurt a little and Ian knew it. "Look, I'm sorry. I didn't mean that."

"You did mean it. You just didn't mean to say it aloud." I let myself laugh and waited until Ian acknowledged with a smile that what we were doing was stupid. "Okay, first of all, Tchaikovsky was gay. Which brings up a second point: I'm no longer wasting time waiting around for nice boys. I'm done with boys, men, the whole filthy, lying species."

Now it was Ian's turn to look hurt. "I've told you I'm sorry. The good news is that all guys aren't assholes like me."

"That's the point, Ian. All guys *are* assholes. Except, I thought, for you."

"You want to go to dinner sometime?"

"You're free?" I said, sympathetically.

"I guess so. I've been telling Jamie I'm too busy to hang out."

"Busy, huh? And *are* you too busy?"

"Sure. It's hard work being such an asshole." He shook his head. "I suck at this. I don't even know if he gets it, that it's over. But I don't know what to say to him."

"Oh, he gets it. I think he got it before you did. Maybe you and he aren't meant to work out, but be nice to him. He was good for you."

"I know." Ian blew up his cheeks like a balloon and then deflated them in a long sigh. "Things aren't as clear as I thought they'd be."

I wanted to tell him about Professor Gilles and Danny Cole, but I was too conflicted about what I was supposed to do with Danny's paper. His words, though coherent, were clearly the words of a deeply troubled young man. And if his plan had been to stage his suicide in a way that would out Gilles, as his paper indicated, he clearly hadn't succeeded. Why had he set the church afire? Surely that would have destroyed whatever proof of their affair he intended to be discovered around him. This gave me pause. If he'd been capable of such a basic misstep, who was to say he hadn't imagined their whole relationship?

After class, as we were all filing out like livestock getting a shot at the other side of the fence, Professor Gilles came to the front of the stage and waved Ian over. I hovered quietly aside.

"Is your father the Mike Everett currently employed as our head football coach?"

"Yes," Ian said.

"I see. Fascinating. Do you find you enjoy the battle between yourself and your father?"

"Battle?"

"For attention, for success, for recognition. Maybe battle is a strong word."

"No, I don't enjoy it."

Gilles seemed disappointed. "I'm only curious. I may write my next book on the subject."

"On my father?"

"No, no. On my grandfather and myself."

Gilles had a few generic questions about how Ian felt the tennis season was shaping up—he seemed to follow most of the school's sports teams—and then we left. I decided to try to approach Ian about what he thought of Gilles in a more roundabout way.

"What the hell?" I said once we were outside. "I was standing right next to you and he never looked at me once."

"And if he had, you'd be calling him a dirty old man."

"Maybe I still am."

"Please. You're kidding. Haile, he's married."

"Right, like *that* proves anything." Ian said nothing. "Do you think there's anything weird about Gilles?"

"Weird?" Ian said, less intrigued by the notion than I was.

"Yeah, like creepy."

"I don't know. Not really."

"What about our assignment for his class?"

"What about it?"

"Don't you think it's kind of, I don't know...personal?"

"I haven't thought about it."

"Liar. It's due in less than two weeks. You already told me you started working on it."

"I threw that away. It was—" Ian hesitated.

"It was what?"

"Nothing."

"It was too personal, wasn't it? You threw it away because you were embarrassed to show it to anyone. See, that's what I mean."

"No. It was stupid, that's all. Look, it's just an assignment. No one says you have to take it personally."

"Really? I think Professor Gilles is encouraging us to do just that."

"So what?"

"I think it's creepy. Especially if he's—come on, what's your read? Do you think he's gay?"

"Now being gay is creepy?"

"Yeah, if you're hitting on students while you're married."

"Does it really matter if he's gay or not? If anything, it's just sad. Anyway, I think he's just a little crazy from being a Gilles and living in this valley for so long and he's caught up in his populist art theories that everyone congratulates him on."

"You know what, forget it," I said.

"Haile."

I didn't respond. Ian didn't know what I knew about Professor Gilles and I wasn't sure yet if I should tell him. We parted ways outside and I split off in the direction of the library.

There, the first thing I did was use the computer to search for *The Wrath of Achilles*. When the image results came up I clicked on the first one and stared at the screen. The image, created by Leon Benouville in 1847, was a startling depiction of a nude young Achilles, seated in a solid, high-backed chair and apparently on the verge of leaping to his feet at the arrival of Agamemnon's envoy. What leaped from the image, however, was the subject's self-absorbed, piercing stare and naked form. It was easy to see the figure as erotic.

"Excuse me. Where can I find this?"

I hadn't heard him coming and I felt my face flush at being startled. "Oh," I said when I saw who it was. I took the slip of paper from his hand, unable to keep from noticing the thick, wiry black hair on his forearms.

"Mathematics books are on level three," I said. My ears and face felt hot and I told myself it was because I'd just walked across campus in the sunshine.

"Thanks." Casey smiled, not moving to leave. "Did Ian ever tell you that I thought you two were together?"

"No. There's plenty Ian forgets to tell me."

"He's not a big talker."

"Is there anything else?"

Casey shoved his tongue into one cheek. "Can I ask why you don't like me?"

"Sure."

He looked flummoxed, but only for an instant. "Well?" he said, waiting for my answer.

"To be honest, I haven't given it any thought. We don't have much in common."

"How do you know? What kind of music do you like?"

I should have ignored him, but the way he'd said it, like a challenge, made me want to prove something instead. I think I wanted to prove that he didn't intimidate me, or impress me, but maybe I was only trying to prove that to myself. Self-conscious of Ian's earlier comment, I skipped over the classical greats and rattled off a quick list that included Alicia Keys, Tori Amos, and, of course, Traci Rice.

Casey cringed. "Popular stuff."

"I don't find it necessary to dismiss good music just because it's popular."

"But you do that with sports?" He grinned.

"Your math book is on the third floor. The stairs are over—"

"What if I didn't really come for the math book?"

"Right. Well, in that case I'm pretty sure we don't have what you're looking for. Maybe try up the street at one of the sororities."

"I get it. You've already made up your mind about me. That's fine. I won't ruin your fantasy. Which way did you say to the sororities? Ah, here we are."

The girl who I recognized as his girlfriend came bouncing through the door and I realized he'd been waiting for her all along. I felt a swell of humiliation. Worse was the dull stab of resentment I experienced when he kissed her on the cheek and called her Baby. (Ian by contrast, calls her The Bitch. Remembering that made me feel a little better.)

After they'd gone, I turned back to the computer, fighting the sting of jealousy. *The Wrath of Achilles* still filled the screen.

I studied the painting, remembering something Professor Gilles had said once in class: art is most powerful when it represents something to the viewer, when it symbolizes more complicated emotions, emotions that can be difficult to put into words.

And then an idea rose up in my mind so complete in its conception that I couldn't believe it hadn't occurred to me before.

I spent the rest of my shift at the library thinking of everything I had to get ready before I could call Ian. I'd have to think of something to say that would convince him to help me. But I wasn't too worried about that. Now that I possessed a clear vision for my art project, the smaller details seemed easily surmountable. I was desperate to get started. Patience, as they say, is a virtue, and artists have no business being virtuous all the time.

My only moment of hesitation came as I hurried home. I was crossing the Great Lawn when I paused in my tracks, suddenly hearing Jamie's words replayed in my head: *Have you ever been in a situation where you didn't know what would happen next?*

SCENE: INTERIOR. LOCKER ROOM. AFTERNOON.

IAN is under the stream of a hot shower. In
the background we see the blurred bodies of
a half dozen other naked STUDENT-ATHLETES.

In the shower with the other guys, I looked at three things: the
floor tiles, one-inch gray squares separated grid-like by grimy
trenches; the showerhead, where water appeared continuously
like a flashlight beam; and my shampoo bottle in the wire rack,
which told me in plain English and cursive French that the bottle
contained almond shampoo with essential oils and shampoo of
almond with oils essential, respectively.

That there is an established subgenre of gay pornography
set in locker rooms is misleading. Erotic events do not in fact
blossom spontaneously in circumstances riddled with fear and
anxiety. Maybe at a frat party (also a popular pornographic subgenre), where at least alcohol is involved. But definitely not in
the locker room. My own teammates were no longer mysterious
enough to interest me, and showering with the swimmers, as
was the case today, introduced no special tension since all swimmers naturally are accustomed to being around more skin than
clothing.

I showered at school after practice because I was already late to meet Haile. We were spending more time together again and she'd called to ask me to come over after practice. I climbed the stairs to her apartment.

"New chair?" I said.

"No. It's a very old chair. I'm borrowing it."

"How'd you get it up here?"

"Don't ask. The battle we had on the stairs almost ended expensively. I thought you were coming from practice."

"I did. I had to stay after and work with Coach on my baseline footwork, which has for some reason gone to hell."

"Where's your racquet?"

This was not a question she'd ever asked me.

"In the car."

"Get it."

"What for?"

"We need it."

I made my confusion obvious but she gave me a look that said I should just get the damn racquet. I descended to the driveway and returned with my racquet bag.

"Oh, what are these?"

"Sweatbands." I slipped one off the racquet handle and onto my forearm to demonstrate. She looked disappointed.

"Do you have one for your forehead?"

"Yeah, in the side pocket."

She retrieved the headband.

"It's perfect!"

"For what?"

"My art project for Gilles. You're going to be my model."

"I am?"

With her hand, Haile shook out my hair, which I'd let grow longer and wavy over the semester. I didn't say anything. I like when people touch my head. She slipped the headband over my hair. I resisted as a matter of dignity, but she saw I was without conviction and went on arranging things as she saw fit.

"No," she said. "Wear it higher on your head. Like this. Oh, and take off your clothes."

"What?"

"Come on. It's just us girls." She giggled and brought a hand to her mouth. When I didn't laugh along with her, she tried pouting. "For the sake of art, then?"

"Is it something you feel strongly about?" I said this in my best British butler accent, but the *Arthur* reference was lost on her. How does a person in the current century go through life without seeing any good movies, even by accident?

She removed a large sheet of paper from a sketch pad and arranged it on the desk. I looked around, feeling stupid.

"You want me in the chair?" I said.

"Yes. I know exactly what I want. You don't have to do anything. Just sit there."

In the end, it wasn't for art that I did it. I guess I felt I owed it to her. I felt there were parts of our friendship that needed evening up. Guilt, I think, is the common word for this, but at the time I was stripping down it helped also to think of myself as open-minded and daring.

One by one, in no hurry, I pulled off the shoes, socks, shirt, and jeans that I'd put on only a half hour earlier. My heart was bouncing around the room. Standing at the foot of her bed in my boxer shorts, I paused as if this final article might require some special procedure. Haile looked at me, eyebrows raised, and then turned away as if to grant a moment of privacy. I removed the boxers and set them folded in a pile with everything else.

"The watch, too," she said.

The chair was wooden but there was a flat pillow cushion and a white sheet draped over the seat. I turned, exposing myself to her, and sat.

"That wasn't so hard, was it?" she said. "No pun intended."

"You're highly unprofessional."

"Neither of us is getting paid."

She leaned the racquet against the chair to my left and set a tennis ball on the floor by the chair's front leg. Then she walked to the bookshelf and returned with three books that she stacked on the floor below me, angling them forty-five degrees off center with the spines facing out.

"Put your right foot on the books," she said.

I did as I was told. She made a slight adjustment to my knee, bending it slightly more than ninety degrees so the foot was directly below the front of the chair. She extended my left foot farther out in front of me. Satisfied with the position of my legs, she turned her attention to the white sheet bunched around my hips. She lifted one corner of the cool fabric and draped it over part of the chair back near my right shoulder. The chair had no armrests and I clasped my hands modestly in my lap. She grabbed my right arm gently, flushing my flesh with goose pimples, and placed it atop the curved back of the chair. The precise way in which she arranged my limbs made the pose seem deliberate. She bent my elbow and rested my fingers against my hair above my right ear as if to support my head. Finally, she formed my left hand into a fist and set it on the seat cushion a few inches outside of my thigh.

"Comfortable?"

"Given the circumstances."

"Good. Don't move."

I was shaking slightly. When she leaned in to adjust the headband, I shuddered.

"Are you cold?" she asked.

"A little."

She went to the thermostat and tapped the dial a few degrees until the heat clicked on. Then she sat down at the desk. There appeared to be some indecision over her first pencil stroke (I remembered that from my own project) but it lasted only a moment. From where I was sitting, I could not see the page.

I got through the first few minutes by concentrating on not shivering, which I realized was more due to nerves than the temperature. The attic room felt increasingly warm. A distasteful slickness formed against my back and on the undersides of my legs where I perspired against the wood. But I said nothing, afraid to delay what already had the potential to be a long process. I assumed Haile did not draw often and I knew she wanted it to be good. While she worked, I studied her for signs of blushing.

"Don't smile," she said seriously. "Open your eyes wider."

It didn't take long until I was comfortable to the point of boredom. By the time she set down her pencil and sat up, my mind had wandered far from the business at hand. Any urgency to get dressed had been forgotten, so when she said we were finished I sat for a moment rotating my limbs, which had gone stiff. Ah, that word! Stretching and stirring seemed to have an effect disastrously similar to waking the body in the morning. No sooner had I stood than my cock performed a shocking little bob, lifting itself slightly away from my body. I tried at first to ignore this activity, believing I'd caught it at an early and reversible stage. Quickly, though, I recognized the improbability of striking it neatly from my mind and sought frantically to force it out with distracting thoughts—thoughts of baseball statistics, bad tennis injuries, a show about ants I saw on *The Learning Channel*, and finally, desperately, dead fat people. None of these worked and only served to shock me further with my own capacity for vividness.

"What does this mean?" she asked academically. She was standing between me and my clothes, eying the determined little bastard at my midsection as if we'd been working on a crossword puzzle and suddenly might be getting somewhere.

"I don't know," I said. "Nothing."

"Do you shave this?"

I tried to get around her but she ran her hand sideways across my chest. Her touch cooled my skin and a goose bump returned to the site of each clipped hair.

"You're shaking. Are you nervous?"

"Should I be?"

Without looking at it, she grabbed my cock with her hand.

"Wait," I said.

She didn't wait and I said nothing else. The only contact we made apart from where her hand clenched me was when she touched my chest again firmly, once, to push me onto the bed. The afternoon had been a series of concessions and this was only one more. I gave up trying to stop what was happening and focused instead on expediting the swiftest possible outcome. My eyes were closed through most of it. I came on my stomach without much fuss and her hand slowed and then stopped. She went away and came back with some tissues. Then she looked at me. I didn't know if the silence needed breaking or if we were way beyond that.

"Ah, it *was* written," she said.

"Shit," I said.

While I dressed, Haile went to her drawing and I watched her for a sign that she'd captured what she wanted. But her face betrayed nothing. When I approached she slipped the page beneath the cover of the pad.

"I don't get to see it?"

"Not today."

"I feel used," I said.

And Haile smiled.

Casey Boyd taking care of business
Casey Boyd changed his relationship status to "Single"
Casey Boyd wrote on **Ian Everett**'s wall: "I'm going to need a beer when I get home."

"You're early," Krista said. It was an accusation. I was standing in her bathroom doorway and I could tell by the way she didn't look at me and by the way Jess, one of her roommates, had glared at me when she let me in, that what I'd come here to say was not entirely unexpected.

"Yeah," I said. Jess had left us alone. "I was hoping we could talk for a minute."

"A minute? I thought you were coming bowling with us."

"Well."

"Casey, do you love me?"

The right answer to this question was of course the one I couldn't truthfully provide, so I said nothing. After a healthy beat of silence she flipped on her blow dryer. I watched her dry her hair, the dryer roaring in our ears and me with no choice but to wait it out while I thought about how much of an asshole I was. This went on for four or five minutes. When at last she silenced the dryer, she turned to me.

"Have you noticed how little time we spend together?" she said.

217

"Krista, you know my first priority is the team."

"Jess thought it might be something else. Or someone else. Do you have anything to say about that?"

"Maybe Jess should mind her own business."

"Casey?"

"No. There's no one else. Is that what you want to hear?"

"That wasn't a very convincing denial."

"It wasn't a denial. There's nothing to deny."

"Well, that doesn't change the fact that people start rumors. Jess is my friend and she was kind enough to tell me to my face. Imagine what people are saying behind my back. Do you know how humiliating it is for me to have to make up excuses for why I never spend time with my boyfriend?"

"I'm sorry."

"Oh, what a relief."

"I know you're angry. I wanted—well, what I came here to say is that I think it's better if we agree that this is over."

When she started to cry I felt relieved for some reason, as if her tears brought with them the finality I'd been searching for for months.

"Get away from me," she said between sobs.

Jess appeared, glaring again, and squeezed by me to hug Krista.

"If you want to talk—"

"Just get away!" Krista screamed.

I took a step back. Of course, I was dying to get away but I didn't know if I was expected to say something else. I was so used to trying to interpret the difference between what she says and what she means and I wasn't sure yet if I'd broken free of those responsibilities. Finally Jess gave me a look like, *Yeah, dumb-ass, she means it,* and I let myself out.

Haile and *The Art of the Fugue*

The morning after Ian posed for my drawing I woke up feeling uneasy. My plans for the drawing had consumed so much of my focus over the previous twenty-four hours that my mind had blacked out everything else. Now, no longer blinded by a singular purpose, I wondered whether my ambition had outstripped my artistic ability. What if no one got it? And then another, darker fear entered my mind: What if they *did*? Then what? The potential consequences of what I'd done drifted forth in plain-as-day detail. Would Professor Gilles give me a bad grade? Would I fail his class? Forgetting about myself for a moment, I wondered what it would mean for the dean. If my drawing had its intended impact, it could have the potential to tear apart their family.

Climbing out of bed and standing over my drawing, it occurred to me for the first time since I'd gotten the idea for it that maybe I should just throw it away. There was still time to create something adequate enough to maintain my grade but that would just as easily be forgotten. Isn't that what everyone else in the class was going to do? Why was I so obsessed with the need for my drawing to stand out? What *point* was I making, anyway? Was it my business to expose Professor Gilles's hypocrisy to the world?

Probably not. But then I thought about beaten, abandoned Danny and his letter, his last art project. I thought about him burning the church. I tucked the drawing into the large sketch pad to protect it, and then slid it between my desk and dresser, feeling better about having the option not to turn it in.

What could not be undone, however, was the bizarre post-artistic flash of sexual exploration that had possessed me to touch Ian—and had driven Ian to go along with it. Strangely, I didn't feel responsible. And I didn't blame him, either. It was not something either of us seemed to have *done*. It was just something that had happened. I couldn't even decide whether I was glad it had happened.

What I did feel was an intense desperation to know what Ian thought. Had he woken up hating me? Had he brushed it off and forgotten about it? I thought of calling Jamie, but I couldn't allow myself to be that selfish. There was nothing about any of this that Jamie would benefit from knowing.

I got out my notebook and tried to work on lyrics, but concentration was impossible. My life felt on pause until I could speak with Ian. Maybe he'd call, I thought, only half-seriously. Yeah, right. Girls can become old women waiting for guys to volunteer their feelings. Ian, in particular, would be perfectly content if I never brought it up again. I was surprised, when I finally called him, that he answered.

"You're not mad at me, are you?"

"No."

"You're not just saying that because it's the shortest word you can think of?"

"Haile, I'm not mad. Maybe a little weirded out."

"Weirded out?"

"Forget it. It's not a big deal. Whatever happened happened. I don't think I'm the first college guy to wind up naked and have it end in an orgasm."

"Um, okay," I said.

"Haile. You're not thinking it meant something, right? Because if that's the case I should definitely remind you that I'm far less confused about my sexual orientation than I once was. A hand job isn't going to change my mind."

Now I was the one who didn't want to talk about it anymore. "Right. What happened happened," I said, making an honest effort to get beyond it.

"Good."

"Want to get dinner tonight?" I wanted to talk to Ian about Danny Cole and Professor Gilles, which I'd actually planned to talk to him about yesterday before we'd become sidetracked.

"Can't," he said. "My roommates are having a party. I should stick around."

"You're having a party and I wasn't invited?"

"You can come if you want. It's probably just going to be a bunch of football players."

"It's not like I have something better to do," I said, all nonchalance. The truth was there was another thing I wanted to talk to Ian about. My mind had begun constructing elaborate scenarios in which I appeared alongside Casey, and the only versions that seemed remotely feasible involved me approaching Casey through Ian. I'd been putting this off because I was mad at Ian for not confiding anything about his own love life to me, and because I'd been afraid that the possibility of Casey and me together had never occurred to Ian and he might say something mean and obvious, like pointing out that Casey had a girlfriend.

I regretted that I hadn't really been myself on the occasions when Casey had come to talk to me in the library. I think I'd actually been kind of mean. Which is why I needed Ian, around whom I *could* be myself, to help reintroduce me to Casey. Even if it meant spending an evening with football players, and even though it would annoy me as usual to have to see Casey with his girlfriend.

I decided to ignore my pride for the evening and I made my way to Ian and Casey's house after dinner.

Ian spent the early portion of the night moving quickly between rooms as if he was looking for someone, and I lost track of him soon after I arrived at the party. Standing by myself, I drank a vodka cranberry faster than I should have, and then grabbed another because holding a plastic cup made me feel slightly less self-conscious. Casey moved easily through the crowd, talking and laughing as if he was friends with everyone. I could have approached him on my own but I was hoping to catch him talking to Ian. Krista, thank God, was nowhere to be seen.

Where had Ian gone? I hadn't seen him for fifteen or twenty minutes. Taking my eyes off Casey—I'd been watching him from a distance, hopefully not in a way that seemed obvious—I pushed my way inside and looped through the kitchen and living room. Eventually I found Ian sitting alone on the front porch. He was sipping from a fizzy, caramel-colored drink in a clear plastic cup.

"Maybe you didn't notice, but there's a party happening out back." He looked up at me with humorless eyes. "What's wrong?"

"Nothing."

"No way. You're not getting away with that answer." I sat down in the chair next to his. "What is it? Is it me?"

"No." He finished off his drink, tipping back first the cup and then his entire head. He rattled the ice and I watched the liquor-thinned soda drain from the bed of shrunken cubes at his lips.

"Are you sure? Because if you want to talk about yesterday, I think it would help if I explained why I wanted to draw you like that. There's this painting—"

"It's not that. Really, I'm fine. I think I'm gonna go for a walk."

I looked over my shoulder through the window, toward the back of the house where the muted sounds of the party carried on without us. I didn't want to leave Casey, I thought, even though it was a stupid way to think about the situation. If I left, I wouldn't be leaving Casey. He hadn't invited me here. It was possible he hadn't even noticed me.

"I'll walk with you," I said. "Unless you want to be alone."

"No, it's fine. I could use some company."

"Let me grab my sweater."

I'd left my sweater on Ian's bed. I was halfway up the stairs when I heard someone on the landing above me. We were steps apart before I realized what was happening. He stopped first, preventing us from colliding, and when I looked up I saw surprise and recognition in his eyes. I stepped casually aside as if to make room for him to get by.

"Hey," he said. "I didn't know you were here."

"I am—I was. I'm leaving."

"Oh. Well, I'm glad you came." His broad hand rested on the banister and from the sight of his tanned forearm—what *was* it about his forearms?—my mind leaped to an image of our bodies sliding past each other, not quite touching. Inches apart on the narrow stairs, I could feel the physicality of his body *right there*, his particular Caseyness eclipsing my world. Whatever else happened on this staircase, I told myself, I wouldn't allow us to touch. The choreography of *not* touching would require a much more intimate level of cooperation than would carelessly brushing passed one another.

"Me too," I said. And that was it. The whole thing had happened in a matter of seconds. And though the moment left me tingling with excitement, it also left me with the familiar aftertaste of regret, the frustration of missing an opportunity to say more. *Me too?* I mean, what did that even mean?

~ ~ ~

"Let's go this way," I said to Ian when we reached the fork in the road just below campus's main gate. He made no protest when I touched his elbow to guide him onto the dirt road. Moonlight cast our shadows underfoot, short and stumpy and featureless. The moon had emerged from a phosphorescent halo in the trees along the ridge and climbed with lunar punctuality to shine crisply overhead. In the close quarters of the party, my liquor buzz had been tinged with something unpleasant that I couldn't quite put my finger on, like a string of notes imperceptibly off key. But outside, in the fresh air, the buzzing had transformed into a pitch-perfect chorus, urging me forward with an inextinguishable lightness.

When we reached the woods, Ian stepped in front of me to get around the end of a fallen tree. I watched the line of his shoulders from behind. Ever since I'd drawn him, it was difficult not to see him like this, in lines and sections of light and shade.

"What are we doing here?" Ian said.

We had arrived at the clearing by the fire-gutted church. I hadn't been back here since I'd discovered Danny Cole's paper. I guess I thought the clearing would look different to me now, more significant, like the site of a memorial. But if anything, the remains of the church seemed more overgrown and obscured than I remembered, as if nature herself wanted the past to be forgotten.

Staring at the ruins, I realized an inconsistency in what I now understood about Danny Cole's death. In his paper, he had said this spot, where they would find his body, would provide all the clues necessary to link him and Gilles in an affair. But I had never heard Professor Gilles mentioned in the same breath as Danny Cole. Somehow, though I doubt it would have surprised anyone given the rumors about Gilles, their affair remained a secret. What had gone wrong in Danny's plan? From what I'd heard around campus, it was generally accepted that Danny himself had lit the church on fire and then hanged himself inside while it burned. But the fire didn't make sense if he intended the spectacle of his suicide to be his final art project for Gilles. A fire would destroy everything, including whatever evidence of their affair he'd had with him or had displayed around the church. He wouldn't have lit that fire himself. That meant someone else must have set the church ablaze after Danny was already dead. There was only one person with a motive to burn that church—and whatever it contained.

With this knowledge, all my hesitations about the potential consequences of my drawing vanished. I felt a strange exhilaration.

"What?" Ian asked me. "Why are you smiling?"

"Huh?" I turned to face him. "Oh, I was just thinking of something. I'll tell you about it later." We stood watching the water drift silently by. "You don't mind, do you? That you'll be naked in my drawing in front of the class?"

Ian shrugged. "You think you're a good enough artist that I'll even be recognizable?"

"Please, I made you look better than you actually do. Everyone will be jealous."

I remembered the last time we were here and how I'd reacted when Ian suggested we go swimming. Maybe it was just the alcohol, or Jamie's words—*Have you ever been in a situation where you didn't know what would happen next?*—or simply my new anticipation about the art project, but my former self, the person I'd been weeks ago when I first stood on this riverbank with Ian, that girl felt small and distant and insignificant. What felt absolutely crucial was the strong tug of the present.

I sat down on a stump to take off my shoes.

"What are you doing?" Ian said.

"We're going swimming." I slid my shirt up around my torso and over my head. "Are you coming?"

"Whoa. Jesus. Sorry," he said, turning away when he caught sight of me in my bra.

"Now we're modest all of a sudden."

"Oh, my God. You're serious." Ian stared at me now, watching me with an expression that was neither ashamed nor lecherous. His face was lit only by moonlight but I noticed the recognition of something register in his eyes. "You know something?" he said. "You've really changed."

I don't know if he meant it that way, but this felt like the nicest thing Ian had ever said to me.

"Have I?" Maybe I'd changed and maybe I'd simply become more myself. If it felt this good, did it matter?

I followed Ian's gaze to the river. The moonlight was broken into silvery white chunks that formed a trail across the water. The rest of the surface was black and I wondered for the first time if it would be too cold.

Casey Boyd changed his relationship status to "It's complicated"
Casey Boyd changed his profile picture
Casey Boyd putting off registering for the MCAT

I hadn't told any of my friends about her. What was there to tell? Everyone was so used to the idea of me and Krista that raising another possibility either would have seemed absurd or made me look like an asshole. Until now. Now whenever her name came floating into my head I no longer recoiled with the familiar guilt that had so many times forced me to blink her away.

"Have you seen Haile?" I asked T-Smalls, casually, as he was coming through the kitchen. I hadn't seen her since we'd crossed paths on the stairs.

"Who?"

"Haile."

"She went out front a while ago," he said. "Had her sweater. It looked like she was leaving."

Had I missed something? I quickly replayed the interaction we'd had on the stairs. She said she was leaving. Had she wanted me to follow her?

"Where you goin'?" T-Smalls called after me. "Hey, are you hiding more ice somewhere?"

"In the freezer downstairs," I called over my shoulder.

I walked the streets of our neighborhood, moving in the direction of the bridge at the entrance to campus. It was the only logical choice—there was nothing but quiet residential streets the other way.

I got only as far as halfway across the bridge when a female scream punctured the evening silence. It was more of a yelp than a sustained call. I froze, listening, and the skin on the back of my neck tingled. I thought the noise had come from upriver, but then it was answered by the echo off the bluff deeper in the trees and I couldn't be certain. I ran back across the bridge and cut left up the dirt path that forks off the main road to campus. I wondered briefly why I'd never been this way before, but as I got farther into the woods it was obvious. There was nothing here. Just the rutted dirt road, curving into the woods and deteriorating with each step. I heard the scream again. Was it a cry for help or pleasure or surprise or pain? I thought I heard water splashing, but it was impossible to hear anything over the scratch of gravel underfoot.

I arrived in a clearing in time to see Haile's head emerging from underwater.

Light came only from the moon, but it was brighter here than in the woods. Ian was standing shirtless a few feet away, waist-deep in the river. My initial mixture of fear and surprise amounted to something very much like jealousy. But even that vanished quickly. Haile was standing now, and in the moonlight I could see that she too was shirtless.

"Jesus," I said to myself, looking down.

"It's not too bad!" Haile called. Whatever effect my appearance had on her, she disguised it masterfully. "A little brisk at first, but you get used to it." This gave me no guidance as to what I was supposed to say next. She dunked underwater and when she came back up and saw that neither Ian nor I had moved, she called up to me, "Come on, wuss! Aren't you coming in?"

"I'm not going swimming," I said, slowly realizing that I might.

"Suit yourself. But it's not a spectator sport like your football. Either you're coming in or you're heading home."

"I didn't bring anything to wear."

"Don't be ridiculous."

I saw now that two full sets of clothing were discarded on the bank. Regretting every movement, I began to remove my own clothes and then tiptoed down to the water.

"What are you doing?" Haile said.

"I'm coming in, I guess." Wasn't that obvious?

"Not in those. What are you, shy? You haven't got something we haven't seen, have you?"

I looked first at Haile, who was very beautiful, contoured with a sheen of moonlit water, and then at Ian. Was it permission I was looking for? I wanted him to say no, fuck this, we're getting out, let's all just go back to the party. But Ian only shrugged and turned to dive underwater. As he left his feet for full submersion, I was given brief confirmation of his own nudity. I picked my way back up the bank, minding the jagged rocks underfoot, and removed my boxers without further ceremony.

The water was in fact icy, a ridiculous temperature to be paddling around in, and I feared getting sick. How would I explain *that* to Coach? I wanted to know what Ian was thinking, but a more powerful impulse told me not to make eye contact with him under any circumstances. Haile went on as if this was the most natural thing for all of us to be doing. Only after several long minutes did I realize she was as nervous as I was. The same panicked confusion that drove Ian and me into static silence manifested itself in Haile in hyperanimation. She tried to organize a race between us, to the other bank and back, but Ian and I proved uncooperative. Pouting, she tried a new tack. "Throw me again," she said to Ian.

Ian disappeared underwater and when he came up Haile was balanced in a somewhat shocking position on his shoulders, her body wobbling above his head. With a great spray of water and a shout of glee that echoed off the nearby bluff, she flipped forward, traveling several feet in the space above the water, naked and dripping and more beautiful than anything I'd seen, before she was silenced by her own crashing reentry.

"Higher," she demanded upon surfacing, whipping hair from her face. Her hair was the deepest black and when she collected it into a thick cord to squeeze out the excess water, it looked as if she'd dipped the back of her head in a pot of shiny oil. "Let me stand on both of you. I'll go twice as far."

Ian looked to me for guidance, his eyes pleading for some way to end this safely.

"All right," I said, giving in. "Get your left leg here on my shoulder and put your right on Ian's." Haile liked this plan immensely. As she arranged herself between us, I tried to keep my eyes from locking on her breasts. In position, she patted us each on the head, as if to say, *Down you go.* Her foot was on my shoulder and I clasped her ankle for balance. It was the first time I'd ever touched her.

We agreed on a count of three and ducked blindly beneath her, beginning the count in our heads. For whatever reason, either Ian's impatience or my own hesitation, his side of the launch unleashed an instant before mine and Haile wound up sideways, rotating unacrobatically in midflight. But her joy was undamaged as she broke harmlessly through the water's surface. She reemerged with her face tilted back, eyes fluttering, breasts draining the runoff from her face and shoulders.

I had forgotten entirely about the temperature of the river until my body found cause to defy it. Haile was looping back around us when she brushed me lightly, a moment measured in length by the flesh from her hip to her ankle as her leg ran lightly across the small of my back. Recognizing the danger below, I brought my knees to my chest, sinking lower in the water to conceal the erection, praying that the harsh elements would neutralize the blood flow. But then Haile drew us into shallower water and, planting her feet to stand, rose until the water level lapped against her midriff, precarious and teasing, like the gown of the Venus de Milo.

SCENE: EXTERIOR. RIVERBANK. NIGHT.

IAN stands waist deep in the river, apparently unclothed. Moments later HAILE emerges
from underwater. She is laughing and obviously enjoying herself. Ian looks up in
horror when CASEY appears suddenly in the
clearing.

He had failed to mention this to me. He had always listened quietly when I spoke of Haile, never asking about her directly. He'd
been careful never to expose any clue.

Not until he decided to undress himself in front of us on a
riverbank at ten at night and walk into the water did I understand: he wanted her. He had wanted her for a long time and the
certainty with which he felt this was humbling compared to whatever he had told himself he felt for Krista.

When he tiptoed over the rocks and waded modestly into the
water, I made the decision to leave, understanding that my presence could only contribute an awkward tension. But before I could
excuse myself, Haile grabbed hold of my shoulders and pulled her
body into my back. We'd done this prior to Casey's arrival and
each time she wiggled into position there was a moment when I

felt her breasts at my shoulder blades. I ducked and braced myself as she climbed to my shoulders. I could feel Casey watching me.

On our third go at the joint launch, Casey and I ducked side by side underwater and Haile lost her balance as she was getting set. In our struggle to keep her upright, our shoulders braced together and Casey was forced to grab my thigh just above the knee in an unsuccessful attempt to keep from stumbling forward. Ultimately, the whole lopsided pile of us hurtled forward like an amateur circus disaster. When my feet were reunited with the riverbed and my head broke free of the surface, I felt at the swirling waters around my torso an improbable erection. One moment the waters induced shrinking to the point of wonder and mild concern, and in the next the thing was revived like an underdog coming off the ropes swinging. I curled into a fetal position, thankful for the dark, chest-deep water.

I think Haile was drunk, but there was something stronger at work too, something she was afraid or unprepared to face on her own. Even though I could see the potential for damage if I stayed, I knew she didn't see it. She wanted me there. So fearlessly and playfully did she move around us—touching my arms and shoulders, sometimes gripping both Casey and me at the same time so that it felt we were touching each other through her—that I could not predict her next move. I admired and hated her boldness. I was having fun and it was ruined by how terrified I was to show it. When she waded into shallow water there seemed to be two types of time passing before us: the time when her breasts were below water and the time when her breasts were above water. She seemed oblivious to the difference but I knew Casey distinguished these periods in his own mind as clearly as night and day. I had wrapped myself safely in the black waters like a blanket pulled to my neck when Haile drifted over, half-walking, half-gliding.

"Stand up," she said.

"But it's colder out of the water," I said.

She put her hand on my shoulder for balance or maybe for something else. I was aware of Casey out of the corner of my eye. He was turned away from us dipping his head underwater to wet and smooth back his hair.

"Do you know what I'm thinking?" she whispered.

"I very much doubt it," I said.

Then, without any slow lean or fluttering look, her face was suddenly on mine. The softness of her lips hit me only after I'd pulled away, unfolding my body to shuffle backward.

"What was that—"

She cupped her hand over my mouth.

Next she went to Casey. He was crouched nearby in an almost sitting position with his arms hugging his knees just above the water. As Haile approached him he watched her intently, no longer ashamed to admire her body. When she kissed him he did not react at first, as if he distrusted her every move. After a few seconds, his lips parted and he kissed her back. She lifted him gently, grasping his shoulders, so that he rose upward to stand at her level, barely thigh-deep in the water. I was only a few feet away. When his waist emerged, a third dimension of time was introduced to me. The shadow of his cock angled upward pointing at her belly. I began to scoot pathetically away, searching for water deep enough to disappear beneath. Before I could clear her reach, I felt Haile's hand at the back of my head. Rather than be pulled any nearer to them, I allowed her to guide me to my feet. She extended an open hand, pressing it lightly against my chest. Casey's eyes followed her outstretched fingers and then stopped as if seeing me for the first time. I realized suddenly, more harshly than I'd expected, that in his mind I'd not been a participant in any of this. Whatever he had been expecting or not expecting, the sight of my own erection was too much. He stepped back. His torso separated from Haile in a way that made his cock unfold like the stairway of an airplane from where it had lodged upright between them.

"I can't do this," he said.

"Do what?" Haile said lamely, looking surprised, as if he'd broken the rules of a game we were playing.

"Wait," I said. "I'll leave."

But Casey was already out of the water, pulling on his jeans and then walking toward the road as he tugged his shirt over his head. Haile waited until he had disappeared into the trees before she waded out of the water and went to gather up her own pile of clothes.

"I'm heading home if you want to walk with me," she said.

"I think I'll stay a while longer," I said.

The chill of the water was sinking deeper under my skin but it seemed tolerable compared to what I had to face with Casey when I got home.

Casey Boyd offline

When I got home the only vehicle outside our house was T-Smalls's truck. My first thought was that the cops must have come. It didn't seem late enough for the party to have broken up on its own. Fuck. This was not what I needed. I needed a hot shower. My hair was limp and ratted and a chill reminded me that I couldn't afford to get sick.

Inside I found Jerrell, Afa, and T-Smalls sitting around the living room coffee table. Their heads turned when I entered. The television was on, but there was no sound. I waited, expecting them at least to ask me where I'd been or why I looked like I'd fallen off a bridge.

"What's wrong?" I said.

"It's Nate," Todd said.

"Nato?"

"His father."

"His father what?" I said, feeling that I already knew the answer.

SCENE: INTERIOR. THE HOUSE. NIGHT.

IAN enters. JERRELL, AFA, and TODD are seated
in the living room.

An extra twenty minutes in the river had not delivered me from
my cluelessness over what I was going to say to Casey. I felt
relieved, at least for a few moments, to see that he wasn't in the
living room with the others.

"What's up?" I said.

"You know Nato?" T-Smalls asked.

I tried to answer in the affirmative, but without any breath the
syllable failed. I'd been waiting all week for the party at our house
because I was certain Nate Orton would be there. Of course he
would. I hadn't hoped for anything beyond that, but that would
have been something. And then he failed to show up. Only when
I'd realized he wasn't coming did I decide to take a walk. I don't
know why Haile had wanted to come with me, or why Casey followed us. I'd only been trying to get away.

"His father died," T-Smalls said.

"How?"

It was a dumb thing to say but I suddenly craved information.
Afa tapped his head.

"What's that called again?"

"A brain aneurysm. He was out running. He ran every day, apparently."

T-Smalls seemed to be the one with information. Afa was painfully empathetic. His eyes were wet. Jerrell had been stone silent and now he got up to go to his room.

"Did Casey come home?" I said.

"He's upstairs."

Casey's door was closed and I stood outside without knocking. Through the wood I could hear the soft notes of his guitar. I felt certain now that I had let him down. Casey talked very rarely about his own family and I knew that when he did talk it was because he needed to, to keep from breaking down. I liked to think I'd always been available on those occasions. Until tonight, of all nights, when I'd created circumstances that made it impossible for him to want to talk to me. And for what? So that we might stand naked together in a river? I felt sick with irresponsibility. And still I managed to be selfish. I wondered where Nate Orton was right now. On a plane? In a house nearby? I'd often wondered where he lived. Surely, he'd go home. I wanted the opportunity to comfort him and eventually had to remind myself that I'd never even spoken to him in my life.

"Casey," I said through the door. The guitar paused for a moment and then the notes resumed.

I went back down to the living room. Todd and Afa were talking about people they knew who had died. Neither of them seemed to know about Casey's mom, or at least they hadn't mentioned it. I sat for a minute on the couch and learned that they'd all met Mr. and Mrs. Orton on a road trip a few weeks earlier. They reported that the man had seemed healthy, adding an additional tragic layer to the late turn of events. I couldn't bring myself to ask how Nate was doing, but I gathered from their conversation that he was going home for the week. I wondered if my father was driving him to the airport.

I was far from ready to sleep but no longer wanted to stick around for their conversation. I put on a jacket and baseball cap because I hadn't showered or changed since the river and stepped outside. I sat on the front porch thinking until T-Smalls left, turning slowly out of the cul-de-sac in his Jeep.

Upstairs Casey had stopped playing the guitar. The gap under his door was dark.

And somewhere was Nate Orton. Heading home.

Casey Boyd wishes the protein bars the trainer gave him didn't taste like ass

Casey Boyd commented on **Todd Fleming**'s photo: "your mother would be proud of this moment"

Casey Boyd posted a final score: Colorado State 17, Florence 20

SCENE: INTERIOR & EXTERIOR. EVERETT HOUSE.
DAY.

The house buzzes with activity. SUSAN EVER-
ETT is in the kitchen preparing food. RELA-
TIVES sweep in and out assisting with the
preparations. IAN arrives.

The barbeque was held on a Sunday following a home game in
early November. The air hinted dryly of winter. On clear days,
bare arms and legs still registered warmth from the direct sunlight, but more and more you were inclined to bring out the
sweaters and long sleeves unworn since early spring. I went over
to the house early to help and I thought Mom seemed more comfortable around me. When I stepped into the kitchen to ask where
I should set up the plates and cutlery, she ran a hand through my
hair.

"You look good," she said.

"I'm great." I told her I would put the plates on the patio table.

Dad spent the morning on what is called a radio tour. With
the Tech win and their surprising win–loss record, Florence had
announced itself as newsworthy. Sports commentators were eager
to position the team as a BCS Cinderella story, which, mathemat-
ically speaking, was not likely but was nonetheless a prospect that

gained momentum in the press. As such, Dad was obliged by the university's sports information director to spend three hours in his office granting interviews by phone to Sunday morning radio shows around the country. From her kitchen, Mom listened to these on the satellite, editorializing wherever she saw fit.

"He sounds like he's come from a funeral," she said. "A winning streak is no excuse to be somber. It's unsportsman-like." And then, speaking at the radio: "Mike, honey, don't beat around the bush. Those refs were dreadful. Fans in the upper decks could have called that game more fairly." And, "You know why I listen to this? It's because I learn more from how he answers these radio people's questions than when I ask him something myself."

The Evans family arrived as the early NFL games were kicking off on television. Mom permitted the games to be on but didn't want anyone sitting down to watch them. It wasn't supposed to be that kind of party. Coach Evans spoke proudly of his children away at college—one who was playing college ball and two who were not but seemed loved just the same.

My sister Nikki had flown in two days earlier and attended the game with Mom. At the barbeque, Nikki talked politely to everyone, always smiling and gently touching people on their arms out of pushy kindness. She spoke of college, which is what everyone asked about, as if it was something she faced bravely, a wild parentless experience that had been hard to adapt to. She giggled condescendingly at any mention of her peers who wasted away their educations getting drunk or having sex, activities to which we all could assume she was not personally privy.

The relatives had come the day before, and by the time prep-arations for the barbeque were in full swing everyone moved through the house with comfortable independence, except for the four children, aged two, four, seven, and nine, who had been sent indefinitely to the backyard where their racing and ball tossing and hide and seek would damage less property.

Dad has five siblings and Mom six, and most of them have produced exactly two children each. It's a generational thing, this drastic cutting back in the production of offspring. While practical on many fronts, having only two children has exposed my parents to risks they never dreamed of when they were imagining pleasant backyard reunions like this. I bet now they wished they'd had a few more of us, just as a hedge against the decay of the family name, which suddenly seemed in serious jeopardy. Of Dad's two brothers, one died in a construction accident and the other had produced the two offspring, one per sex, who were now wheedling a confiscated toy from their mother. I was sitting in my lawn chair, rotating in my hands a small football that I'd picked out of the toys Aunt Linda had dumped on the lawn. When I realized my cousins weren't going to cease their tantrum until they were separated and distracted with some new activity, I stood and wandered down the lawn to play catch with Gus, aged seven. I could feel Dad watching me from his chair by the beverage cooler as I held out the mini pigskin to the little man on whose shoulders now rested the fate of the Everett family name.

A part of me wanted Dad to see me playing football again, even if it was just tossing the ball in the backyard. To all others my father stands for success, and I could sense his fear that I would, if I hadn't already, spoil this family tradition. Despite its miniature size, the football felt good in my hands. Throwing a football is more intimate than striking a tennis ball. With a football, you can feel the thing in your hand. You can sense right in your fingertips the delicate difference between a thirty-five- and forty-yard bomb.

After ten minutes of catch, Gus said he wanted to go play with his cars and I was left holding the ball in the yard by myself. When I turned to the house, Dad looked away. But I could tell he had his eye on me.

"Hey, Dad!" I called out.

I zinged the ball up the lawn in his direction. He had time only to register its approach and respond instinctively. This meant that he dropped a raw hamburger patty and caught the ball. It was something he drilled into his receivers' minds. Sacrifice your body (or in this case a burger) if that's what it takes, but for the love of God don't let that football hit the ground. I waited for a long moment while he held the ball in his hands.

"I've got to start grilling," he said finally, setting the ball aside.

Mom came out with a platter of asparagus, which she wanted grilled for a side dish.

"Shouldn't those be steamed?" Dad said. "I never heard of grilling them."

"It's a barbeque we're having, honey. Oh, and make sure there's room on there for the portabellas. We have vegetarians to feed."

They'd had this conversation before and in previous versions Dad had grumbled plenty about having to accommodate vegetables in an area he considered appropriate only for red meat. He wondered aloud why people couldn't just show up as guests at a meal without specifying what and how everything had to be prepared. But when Mom disappeared to toss the salads I watched how he took great care with the asparagus and mushrooms, tending proudly to them as if they were the house specialty. They might have come to his grill inferior, but under his supervision they'd be leaving as manly specimens of backyard culinary achievement.

I viewed myself as the cause of all this posturing. His only son was a homosexual and so it suddenly wasn't enough being a famous football coach, a former college player, and a male husband to a female wife. If there were any further way to demonstrate the model of heterosexuality he'd maintained for the two-plus decades of my life, he would spare no effort.

I had instructions from my parents not to divulge anything to my sister, presumably to protect her innocence. I suspected the real reason was that they were holding out hope that this was a stage I would quietly outgrow. They figured the fewer people who knew, the faster it would evaporate.

I, on the other hand, was growing very eager to tell Nikki. After everyone had eaten, Nikki and I were sent to the freezer in the garage to get the ice cream. Once we were alone Nikki had something she wanted to confess. She was thinking of dating a member of a Christian rock band called Saved.

"Should I tell Mom and Dad? I know, it doesn't sound like me at all, a guitarist in a band. But he's very sweet. They play at our church, and he's in a few of my classes, too."

"I'm sure Mom and Dad will be thrilled. Look—"

"He's from Idaho. And get this, he's never been to Seattle! Boise is the biggest city he's ever visited. But they're trying to get a gig there. Wouldn't that be cool? They're building a fan base all over eastern Washington and northern Idaho." The destinations rolled off her tongue grandly as if they were full continents teeming with people. "All of my friends from church love them. I can't wait to show him Seattle. His name is Cody. Oh, I wish Mom and Dad hadn't moved so far away. This place is weird."

"Jesus Christ," I said.

"Ian!"

"Sorry."

She gave me a playful shove.

"Why are you in such a bad mood? You're like Dad lately."

"Okay, you want to know why? There's something I have to tell you. Not because you need to know or because it's any of your business. But because I'm sick of worrying about who I'm supposed to tell and when."

"What is it? What's the matter?"

"Nothing's the matter," I said. I took a breath. "I'm gay."

Nikki scrunched her face. "I don't understand."

"Yes, you do."

"Wha—wha. Why?"

"Jesus, I don't know *why*."

"Don't use the Lord's name in vain."

"That's seriously what you're worried about?"

She clasped both hands over her mouth as if to suppress a scream. Tears, just like that, streamed down her face. When she removed her hands her eyes were closed, her lips moved silently in prayer. When this performance was over, she spoke.

"Oh my. What are we going to do?"

"There's nothing to do."

"Do Mom and Dad know?"

I nodded. "That's why they're acting so weird."

"Why wouldn't they tell me?" she said. "They shouldn't have moved so far away. *You* shouldn't have moved so far. Did someone at school put you up to all this? Oh, we're going to get through this. There are things you can do, you know. And I'll pray for you."

Apparently no longer a part of the conversation Nikki was having with herself, I went for the ice cream. I told her to get a hold of herself and not to make a scene when she rejoined us outside. In fact, she was quiet for the rest of her stay, brooding with puffy eyes and unwilling to admit to the adults that anything was wrong.

Haile, *forte*

After class I waited for Casey. He came out of the building with Darius and Pile Driver, and when he saw me he led them purposely in the opposite direction.

"Hey. Can I talk to you for a minute?"

They kept walking.

"Casey? Hey!"

"What?"

"Can I talk to you?"

"Go ahead."

"Will you listen? Please. Just for a minute?"

Casey stopped walking but he wouldn't look at me. Darius and Pile Driver moved on, snickering as they wandered off.

"I'm sorry. Okay? I just—I wanted to tell you that. Everything has been my fault. I guess I wasn't expecting, I don't know—*you*. It took me a while to realize it and I'm sorry."

I felt better and assumed my words would have a similar effect on Casey. But I had to crane my head to one side just to force him to look me in the eye. The instant our eyes met he turned the other way.

"Can I go to practice with my friends now?" he said.

"Are you accepting my apology?"

"No. That's not how it works."

"Can we just talk?"

"What could you possibly have to say that you think I want to hear?"

"Look, I told you. I'm sorry. I want to start over. Isn't that what you want?"

"Too late. Too fucking late." He started to walk away before he turned back to elaborate. "I've done nothing but show interest in you. First you pretend to ignore me. Then you draw me into some bullshit mindfuck with you and Ian. Well, fuck you. I'm over it. Too bad if the timing is inconvenient for you." He glared at me. "Still want to talk? Or can I go to practice now?"

His face blurred suddenly in front of me and I brought my hands to my face, humiliated by my tears.

"Oh, Jesus," he mumbled before he walked away.

I didn't stop running until I'd locked myself in one of the practice rooms in Shostakovich Hall where no one, I hoped, could hear my pathetic sobs.

Casey Boyd posted a link: "Mel Kiper: NFL mock draft"
Casey Boyd in a tricky position here
Casey Boyd starting to see the bigger picture

Mrs. Everett answered the door. Susan. She had petitioned me repeatedly in high school, when I came for dinner or stayed over with Ian, to call her Sue. But I never could. At the door she demanded a hug before I was allowed to enter.

"Hi, Mrs. Everett."

"Oh, Casey."

This wasn't my first visit to the house but it was the first time that there remained no visible signs of the move. She appeared more at ease, more a resident of the place, finally settled in with the first imperceptible coat of dust.

She offered to get me water or soda. "He's expecting you, but he's having a chat on the back porch," she said confidentially, more out of tact and politeness than a need to be discreet. The porch was off the living room and I said I didn't mind sitting to wait. She returned to the kitchen and I flipped through one of the magazines on the coffee table.

I realized I could hear their voices. The door to the porch had been left open.

"And you?" I heard Coach say.

"I'm okay. I'm more worried about my mom. But she's managing, I guess. The tougher moments come and go."

"Well, take it easy. There's no hurry. Practice with the team if you can, or tell me you're taking the day off. Don't even think about whether you'll be ready for Saturday's game. We'll do whatever seems right when we get there."

"I'll play," Nato said. He'd said it so confidently that I almost thought it was another person who spoke next, a few moments later, with a tremble in his voice that made me wonder whether he might buckle under his emotion. "Coach, I—" he sniffed, regaining control before he continued. "The last time I saw him. It was—we'd just won the Tech game. Everyone was so high, so together finally, and it felt like something had been fixed for good. You know, like that feeling would just keep on going. It never occurred to me that something could go so wrong. And I saw them, my parents, after the game. I'd decided the night before that I was going to talk to them. And there I was with them after the game in the parking lot, and I didn't do it. I didn't say anything."

"Nate, look at me. There was nothing you should have said. That's not how it works. The last time your father saw you, you were coming off the field after playing a spectacular game. He was happy. I could see it in him the night before, too. It was one of the proudest moments of his life."

"But I—I'd planned on saying something. I had something to tell them. But then the game—you know how it is when we win, how the world just seems better, like everything will be okay? Well, I was going to tell them, but when I saw them there I decided to wait. I decided I shouldn't say anything until after the season. And then my father—"

He exhaled unevenly. I could tell by the way he wasn't making much sense that these were not emotions he'd tried to put into words before. And I felt guilty for overhearing them. Nato had come to Coach, not me.

"Sorry. I don't know what to do. I thought this would go away, but suddenly, tonight, it felt like it couldn't wait. I know this has nothing to do with football but, I don't know, I guess I thought you might understand, because of your son—well, and the way you said we needed to face distractions off the field."

"Whoa, Nate. You've had a hell of a few tough weeks. This isn't the time to try to sort everything out. Don't beat yourself up." Coach had been cautious before, as if these sorts of off-the-field things weren't his arena of expertise, but now he seemed to want control, he seemed driven suddenly to arrive at a fast resolution. "Here's what we'll do. If you feel well enough to play, I think you should. We could certainly use you out there. But right now you need to concentrate on getting rested and healthy. Don't create any more distractions. How's that sound?"

Nato must have nodded silently, either satisfied or giving up on the conversation. I heard a creaking and suddenly he pushed through the screen door. He stopped short when he noticed me. I said hey, but he only looked at me blankly and left, as if maybe what I'd overheard made things worse for him but that it didn't matter because he was well past the point when his life could really deteriorate any further. I heard Mrs. Everett go to the door but Nato had already let himself out. A moment later she appeared in the living room, concern and curiosity on her face.

"Oh," she said when she saw me sitting on the edge of the couch. "You can go ahead out."

Coach greeted me without standing and I sat in the chair I presume Nato had vacated. For a minute he stared into the backyard, his right hand in a fist with his thumb working the side of his index finger as if it itched. I figured he was still thinking about Nato and I felt silly for coming here with my nonissues.

"Did Kyle talk to you about timing on your out routes?" Coach said, ending our silence.

"Yeah, we were working on that today."

"It looked slow. Keep working with him."

I'd come to get Coach's advice about entering the NFL draft but suddenly it didn't seem like the right time to talk about it. Instead, I started reviewing the various BCS scenarios that would get us into a major bowl game. The BCS has its own special kind of math, at the same time fascinating and enraging. Coach told me that my BCS math was basically a waste of time and that we'd be fine if we took care of winning our last two games. It wasn't a long conversation. He never said a word about Nato, but I could see in his distracted gaze that even though Nato had left, he hadn't really gone away.

Haile, *allegro*

The rain started to pick up and I felt a kind of excitement, a twisted hope that the weather might really deteriorate and catch us all off guard. There's something about a full-blown storm that's better than a light, irritating bout of rain. If the weather's going to spoil an afternoon, it might as well aim to impress.

I was at the window in my apartment when my cell phone rang. I let myself hope it was Casey. I assumed it was Mother. But it was Jen.

"Haile, are you home? Good. Are you sitting down? No, don't sit down! Just come over to the house."

I ran across the driveway through sheets of rain, dodging the pocked surfaces of puddles with agile hops. Daylight had gone early and the distant thunder was the only evidence of a world beyond the tight pocket of visibility. In the entryway, I could feel warm drops of water seep through my hair to my scalp. A few rolled forward down my face as if the crown of my head was shedding large tears. Jen led me into the living room.

"Okay, I'm sitting."

"I've had some conversations with Traci Rice's agent about the show next week. I didn't want to tell you before it was confirmed. But I just got off the phone with Traci."

"That's so cool. Can I meet her afterward?"

"Meet her? Haile, she wants you to open the show."

"That isn't funny."

"I'm as serious as a Brahms sonata."

"No way. Jen, they don't even know me."

"They want you to do a half-hour set before they come on. And they want you to come back during the encore."

"They want *me*? How did they even—?"

"It's been hard not to say anything to you. The short version is that they've been touring with a pedal steel guitarist who usually opens the show for them, but he's got his own gigs next week in New York and Boston, so they asked if we had any local musicians. I gave them your audition tape."

The only demo I'd made was the one I'd thrown together for Patrick, who had granted me the show at his coffee shop without even listening to it. Was she talking about *that* tape? I hadn't made it for *Traci Rice!* I managed to ask if Traci had indicated whether she liked it.

"Yes! Like I said, she called me herself. She's FedExing us a CD overnight so you can start practicing. She said to play your own stuff for the opening set and she wants you on the violin when you join them for the encore. They need a head shot for the printed program, and whatever sort of bio you want them to include."

I had stopped listening to her. A gust of wind sluiced rain across the window.

"The violin," I said.

"Haile?"

"You told them I play the violin."

"I mentioned it, yes. I thought it would help your case if I was honest with them. I said you were one of the best in the world."

I shut my eyes. "Can I think about it?"

"Not for very long. They're waiting to hear if you're available."

Available. Was I available to open a concert for Traci Rice? The answer should have been obvious. Jen grabbed both of my shoulders and looked at me with empathetic eyes.

"Do you ever miss it?"

"No," I said quickly. "I played music for people four times my age who'd heard it all before. I don't miss feeling like there was nothing I could add, no matter how well I played."

"I meant the violin. Do you miss the violin?" I didn't say anything. Jen sat down next to me and ran a finger over the tips of the fingers of my left hand. The calluses were almost gone. "Remember that day you played the violin in class, for Kim's ensemble? Why did you stop? You had something to add then, and when it started to come out you pulled it back. But it was there. I know it, not only because I heard it, but because I could see it on the faces of the others."

"That was—I think it was an accident. I'd never played the violin like that before, without music in front of me. I was just trying something."

"We should all have such accidents. Poor Kim has given up on trying to write a score that sounded the way you did that day. It's okay to have accidents. Notes aren't landmines, Haile. You can grope around until you find the ones you like. Your fingers will guide you."

She released her hold on my left hand as if handing control of it back over to me. I touched each finger to the tip of my thumb, watching the mechanics.

"Can I e-mail you the head shot, then?"

Jen smiled. "That will be fine."

Casey Boyd joined the group "Achaean Football Fan Club"
Casey Boyd became a fan of probability theory
Casey Boyd was tagged in an album

Looking ahead to Saturday's confrontation with Pitt, Coach Everett had spotted things on the game film that indicated our opponents were particularly susceptible to turnovers. And so Coach Carroll, the defensive coordinator, was training his players to swipe at the ball on every tackle, to force the quarterback out of his rhythm, to anticipate the direction of the ball before it left his hands. "The moment a receiver touches the ball, you deck him like he just came on to you in the showers," Coach Carroll instructed.

In the back of the locker room, just out of range of Coach Carroll's barking, I tried to talk to Nato. We were lacing up our shoes, taping fingers, strapping shoulder pads, preparing for an afternoon of run-throughs. I don't know why it had taken me so long to say it.

"You're welcome to hang out at our place later if you want. Or if you ever want to talk. I think I speak for the other guys on that, too."

"Thanks," he said without looking up.

"I just—well, Coach is difficult with some things. But he means well."

"Look, I don't know what you heard last night, but forget it, okay? I don't know what I was saying."

"I understand."

"I don't think so. How would you understand? When a parent who you happened to like dies, it fucks with your head, okay? I'm fine. I don't want to talk. I just want to play." Nato got up and left and it was very hard to continue thinking that any of this was my problem.

Since it was Thursday, we were practicing only with helmets and shoulder pads. The weather lacked extremes. It was overcast, a light gray canopy that seemed too high to threaten rain. The air was cool but not biting, an unmemorable November day that happened to come two days before a game that really, really mattered.

On a play called Slick Screen Right, Nato and I are supposed to line up on the right side of the field and run a screen pattern that's really more simple than slick. With all my recent work on blocking, this play had seen a lot of reps and had become one of our favorites. I cut infield to set the block and Nato took Kyle's quick pass up the sideline for as long as he could get away with. In this case, he ran for an easy twelve yards before he stepped out of bounds to dodge the rapidly approaching defenders.

The play should have ended there. But when Nato put his foot down out of bounds, the defense didn't stop. DJ Boone wrapped himself around Nato's legs like a car hitting a tree, and Pile Driver got himself horizontal in the air above Boone, his helmet aimed at Nato's side. Beneath the smack of the helmet-to-body contact came a more grisly pop and I knew immediately that an arm or knee was worse for the collision.

"Hey, what the fuck?" Kyle yelled.

Pile Driver climbed to his feet and slapped Boone on the helmet as if they'd come up with an important goal-line stand in a big game. Nato sat up slowly, not anxious to go any further. I held out my hand to help him to his feet.

"He's fine," Pile Driver said. "Get up, fag. That wasn't even full speed."

I'd been very kind—maybe even cowardly—toward Pile Driver for a very long time. This was too much. "You were late to the play, dude. We're used to making up for your dumb-ass penalties in a game, but we can't make up for Nato if he gets injured."

Pile Driver ignored me and started to walk back to the defensive huddle, until he was stopped in his tracks by Coach Everett, who'd come unglued at the sight of the late hit. While he gave Pile Driver an earful, I turned back to Nato.

"I'm fine," he insisted. "Just knocked the air out of me."

"I thought I heard something pop."

"Naw, it's fine."

I raised my hand for the trainer. "You want Roland to look at it?"

"Fuck, no. I have to play." Nato stood, and whatever he wanted to say about it, it was obvious from the angle of his left shoulder pad that he did not have full use of the arm.

"You don't have anything to prove, man. Sit out a few."

He started in with a look that I could go to hell, but then he turned away when the pain demanded some immediate attention. He bent over as if to catch his breath, but I could see it was really to hide a grimace.

Dr. Roland, the head trainer, arrived and introduced some sanity to the situation, immediately withdrawing Nato from the practice. It wasn't until the next day, on the bus to Pittsburgh, that we learned the injury would keep Nato out of Saturday's game.

SCENE: INTERIOR. COFFEE SHOP. DAY.

IAN enters wearing a backpack. He has a
baseball cap pulled low over his eyes as if
he's trying to disguise himself.

It was Saturday and I needed somewhere quiet to sit and do homework. I didn't want to go home where I might run into Casey. I
no longer knew what to say to him. So I went to the coffee shop,
thinking it was Jamie's day off.

I was sitting at a window table when Jamie walked in. He
didn't see me at first but I knew I couldn't sneak out without being
obvious, so I watched him get a cup of coffee and waited for him
to spot me. I couldn't avoid him forever. He walked over and sat
down across from me as if the meeting had been planned.

"You've been avoiding me."

"No," I lied. "I—okay, maybe a little. I'm sorry."

"You're sorry. Look, I know you're *busy*. But since I've got you
here I might as well ask. Do you remember the deal we made
once? I was going to come watch you play tennis and you were
going to come with me to a concert."

"Jamie, that was a long—"

"Well, I'm coming to watch you this week. I know, you didn't
invite me, but it's open to the public and I'm going."

"Jamie—"

"Anyway, the concert is Tuesday. I'd still like you to come with me. As friends, or whatever. Then I'll leave you alone."

"It's not that I wouldn't like to go. Really. But maybe you should take someone else."

"That's the point, Ian. There isn't anyone else I want to go with. Usually I go alone."

He set the ticket on the table in front of me.

"Jamie."

"Keep the ticket and think about it. Maybe I'll see you there."

"I didn't mean to avoid you," I said. "I was afraid you were mad at me."

"I am mad at you."

"Does that mean we can't be friends?"

"No," he said. "We can't be friends because I don't want to be friends. Don't you see that? I always wanted more than you. I wanted you more than you wanted me. I know there's nothing either of us can do about it but don't tell me just to turn this off so you can feel better about us being buddies. I'll get over it—sooner, I hope, than later—but I can't just turn it off."

I wanted to apologize again but I was afraid of insulting him further. There was no closure. Why couldn't we just agree to agree that I'd been an asshole about the whole thing?

"You're going anyway, right? For her," he said.

"Going where?" I said.

"Jesus. To the show."

"For who?"

"Haile."

"Haile's going?"

"Ian! She's playing. Oh, my God. How did you not know about any of this?"

"What?"

Jamie was shaking his head as if I'd really outdone myself this time. He must think I went around all day letting people down.

"She said you weren't at her last show because you were away for tennis. That's probably true, but I assumed you *knew*."

"She had a show? You mean with people from her music program?"

"No. By herself. It was right here."

I was about to say I should leave but the way he was looking at the empty stage in the corner stopped me.

"Is she good?" I said.

He looked at me like I was crazy.

"Yeah," he said. "She's good."

He pulled a program from his bag and set it in front of me. *Traci Rice Trio at the King Theater. Tuesday Night. Special Opening Guest: Haven Libby.*

"Who is Traci Rice and Haven Libby?" I said.

"The Traci Rice Trio is my favorite band—and Haile's. Haven Libby is Haile."

On the back of the program was a picture of Haile accompanied by a short bio that said she was from San Francisco and had trained at Juilliard and was an internationally acclaimed chamber violinist.

"I have to go," I said.

I was halfway up the Great Lawn beneath the statue when I felt the ticket Jamie had given me in my pocket and stopped. I hadn't planned to take it but I must have put it in my pocket in my rush to leave. I decided against going to the music building and confronting Haile. I had a better idea.

Haile, *vibrato*

In all of my phone conversations with my mother over the semester, I'd been very careful to protect my Florence life from her. This hadn't proved too difficult. She was uninterested in whether I was happy at Florence and denied me any opportunity to argue that, in coming here, I'd made a good decision. Her main concern, and thus the thread she expertly weaved into each of our conversations, was to usher me swiftly beyond the silly stage I was going through and get me back to New York and Juilliard. Even on the days and nights when my resentment succumbed to a mysterious daughterly impulse to miss her and I cried tears of guilt for having failed her, it never had occurred to me to invite her here. Florence had been my decision. And so far it was a success, at least in the sense that my life here belonged to me in a way it never had before.

Everything I knew told me to keep her away.

We were about fifteen minutes into what had become our weekly Saturday morning phone call when I said, "Guess what?"

"Hm?" she said. I could hear water running in the background and imagined her in the kitchen making coffee or rinsing dishes. I could picture her morning face, un-made-up.

"I'm performing next week," I said.

There was a gulping hiccup of a silence—I'd surprised her, if only momentarily—before she regained her composure.

"What does that mean?" she said, her tone icy with judgment.

"The Traci Rice Trio—you remember? That group I'm always listening to? They're coming for a show and Traci wants me to open for them." This time her silence was real. This was something she truly could not have expected. I knew I had to press on before she could utter something hurtful that would tangle us in a familiar, ugly finale of words we'd later regret. "Will you come and see me? The show is going to be sold out. And"—I hoped I wouldn't regret bringing this up—"I'm going to be playing the violin for part of the show."

"I see."

"Mom?"

"I have work. I can't get away."

"Mom, the show is in the evening. You could come out after work and be back to the city by midnight."

She chuckled. I think there's a general misunderstanding that chuckling reflects humor when really, at best, it is a mark of indifference. At worst, chuckling is the sound of demented cruelty. She chuckled, and then she said, "Everything is so wonderfully simple in your mind, isn't it?"

"Mom, what—"

"You expect me to just drop everything so you can feel like I support whatever it is you think you're doing? Do you even know how much I've done for you? And now this—you run off on some childish whim like I never existed."

"That's not true. This is what I want to do, Mom. It really is. I think you'd see that if—"

"What you want to *do*? What *you* want to do? You're twenty years old. You have no idea what you want to do. If you know so much, how come you don't understand what you're throwing away?"

"I'm not…throwing it way," I said. But explaining myself now, even if I thought I could, was futile. The conversation was essentially over. Now we were just taking out frustrations. "You know what? Never mind. I shouldn't have thought to invite you in the first place. Why would you want to see a performance you had nothing to do with?"

"What is that supposed to mean?"

"You know exactly what it means," I said, aware that our argument was building toward an unprecedented level of hostility. "You want me to feel guilty about what you've done for me. But you weren't really doing those things for me, were you? Everything was what *you* wanted. I'm done feeling guilty. Do you get that? I. Don't. Want. You. To. Do. Things. For. Me. Do something for yourself, something real, something that makes you happy instead of making both of us miserable. If you think Juilliard is so fucking crucial to existence, you should apply yourself. Leave me out of it, okay? Mom?"

I don't know how much she'd listened to before she hung up. As soon as I realized the call was already disconnected, the tears sprung loose and I was left with a sinking guilt as dark and bottomless as I'd ever felt.

Casey Boyd playing Guitar Hero
Casey Boyd posted a final score: Florence 17, Pittsburgh 22
Casey Boyd turned in his lame art project

Ian was sitting on the steps of the math building where he'd told me to meet him. I'd come straight from an ugly practice that had made me more anxious about the team's condition than I'd been after Saturday's well-deserved loss. Once again, another Saturday rapidly approached and the shattered pieces of our team weren't exactly falling into place. I said hi to Ian but remained standing. We hadn't talked much since the river, and that was just fine with me. Across the lawn, the King Theater was lit up, the stairs dotted with people climbing to the pillared entrance.

"Must be something going on tonight."

"Yeah," Ian said. "Here."

"What's this?"

"Your ticket."

"For what?"

"The show."

"Come on, man. Is this why we're here? I don't even know what this is." I looked at the ticket without really reading what it said. "Look, maybe we need to let things cool off for a while. I mean, the other night—shit, I don't know how to talk to you about any of this. I just don't want there to be any misunderstandings."

"There's been plenty of misunderstandings," Ian said. "But not this time. Go in there, Case. Trust me."

"You're not coming?"

"No. It's sold out."

"Dude, I'm not taking your ticket."

"It's yours. Thank me later."

This was how I ended up descending the aisle on the floor of the King Theater, looking for Row G, Seat 1. I was fortunate to have an aisle seat. The seat next to mine was occupied by a guy I recognized because he worked at the coffee shop.

"Ah, he sent the roommate. I was beginning to wonder if anyone would show up," he said. I nodded politely and tried to look busy getting comfortable in the seat. There wasn't a great deal of leg room. "I'm Jamie."

"I'm Casey."

"Yeah, I know. Ian hasn't been very good at making introductions, has he?"

"You know Ian?"

"Never mind. It's just that I was stupid enough to think that he might actually come himself."

"Look, I don't even know what I'm doing here. I don't usually come to these things."

I was thankful when the lights began to dim. I wished I'd grabbed a program so I could monitor how long I had until intermission, which seemed like a safe time to leave.

Haile, live in concert

Traci Rice. Traci Rice sits on a couch in the green room, sipping herbal tea from a foam cup. Her face glows like a magazine ad, brown and unblemished. Her mouth is rimmed with thick, glossy lips that seem always in motion, though she listens more than she speaks. Mostly she smiles. Between her mouth and her green eyes, she can produce a thousand smiles, each one natural and meaningful, like a good actress nailing every take.

We're finished with sound check and Traci is still hanging out in her street clothes, an orange tank, tight jeans, and knee-high maroon boots. Her bandmates are in the dressing room or out back for a smoke and I feel, more by the attention she pays me than the absence of others, that I have her to myself. I'm going on first—soon, the house has already been opened—and I'm dressed to take the stage in a strapless knee-length red dress. I've slid a few bracelets onto my arms and reddened my lips. We're talking about recording when we're interrupted by the assistant stage manager, Andrew, a waif of a college male in a ribbed turtleneck and fashionably torn jeans, all black.

"Sorry, hon," he says to me, "there's someone here to see you."

I excuse myself and Traci says, "Rock 'n' roll," in case she doesn't see me before I go on. In the corridor, Jen spots us and relays word that we might start a few minutes late if people are still filing in. Something stops her in midsentence.

"What?" I say, turning to look. We're almost to the wing off stage right.

"Nothing. I just thought I saw the dean."

"Yeah, that's her," Andrew says. He is above rolling his eyes, but he achieves the equivalent with a subtle adjustment to his posture, cocking his head and hips almost imperceptibly in opposite directions as he exhales. "She's asked me three times if there's enough bottled water in the dressing rooms. Is she looking to drown someone?"

"She's looking to be in charge," Jen says under her breath. Then, to us, "Just ignore her. Politely, if you can. She likes to feel involved, though I have no idea why she suddenly wants to be involved in *this*."

My stomach clenches at the mention of the dean. Two days ago I turned in my drawing for Professor Gilles's class. I'm not seeking justice of any sort other than poetic, which is what I understand to be the assignment's purpose, but there is still a part of me that wonders, whenever I think of the dean, if what I'm doing is reckless, or outright cruel.

"Hm-mm, we're coming," Andrew says to someone on his headset, and then, to me, "Babe, we gotta go."

Someone is here to see me. Without any conscious effort my mind runs through the wild logic that could make it Casey. To stop this line of thinking before it works itself into a legitimate hope, I ask Andrew who we are going to see.

"I have no idea, hon. I just work here," he says moodily, holding open the door to the backstage area, a black forest of curtains, pulleys, guitar stands, and speakers. The lights are still up and she spots me before I see her standing by the cargo elevator.

"There you are!" my mother says, performing a dangerous running shuffle in heels over the sound cables taped across the floor. She wraps her arms around me before I've decided on an appropriate reaction. She is weeping in soft choking sniffles and I am reminded of the reserved way she bites her lip when she gets emotional in public. I hug her back and worry that I'll lose my composure minutes before I have to step out on stage.

"You came," I say.

"My God, look at this place." She gazes around us.

"Mother."

"But it's dreadful."

"Is everything all right?" Jen says, coming up behind me.

"Jen, meet my mother. Mom, Jennifer Rivera."

Jen's eyes widen before she can manage her surprise. "Oh, my. Haile didn't say you were coming tonight."

"Jen is my music teacher."

"I see." My mother's face drops as if she's identified the enemy. I realize now that she hasn't come only to see me perform. She's come with the belief that this is a place I need to be rescued from and that she has the power to rescue me. "Rivera, is it? I've never heard of you."

Jen is no match for my mother and I hope she realizes it straight off before she's tempted to take anything personally. "We're very proud of your daughter," she says. "I'm thrilled you were able to come tonight to share in what she's accomplished."

"Accomplished! You can't possibly imagine what my daughter has accomplished."

"Mom, don't."

From nowhere, Andrew pokes his head into our little circle to say I'm going on in three.

"Haile," Jen says, "don't let us keep you from your preparations."

"What is this 'Haile' business?" Mother says.

"It's just a stage name," I say quickly, though I know that doesn't make complete sense to her, since I'm about to go on stage as Haven Libby. "I have to go. And you should find your seat. There's only a few minutes." Jen offers to show my mother to her seat and I'm finally left alone, just in time to take a few deep breaths before the lights go down.

I hear my name being announced and then a great applause rises from the audience like a crashing wave and I'm sucked out onto the stage as if by an undertow.

~ ~ ~

Obvious distractions aside, the music portion of the evening was indeed a breakthrough. The crowd came to see Traci but the theater was already mostly full at the start of my set. I was given thirty minutes, enough time for five songs, since I tend to talk to the audience between them. I'd performed before, but this music was different. It was my own music, music that would determine my future.

There's a certain humility to performing. Even if the audience knows and loves you ahead of time and is prepared to go wild the instant it catches sight of you, there is still a point during the show when you have to entertain in a way that is unexpected. You have to put yourself out there and do something risky or self-deprecating or embarrassing. Fans want to be treated to something special, to the real you. You can't win them over until they've seen you slightly exposed. That's the key to performing live, and by the second half of my set I felt comfortable enough to creep out onto that ledge.

My set list went as follows: "Throwin' Words At Da Moon," a soulful reggae song about confrontation; "Major D in D Minor," a jazzy tune that Ms. Rivera liked; "Freak On," a funky piece about being different; "Sump'n Sweet," also funky, about not wanting to be anywhere but where you are; and finally, a cover of "The Times They Are A Changing," which I'd been tempted to jokingly dedicate to my mother but instead just said was one of my favorite songs when I was growing up. The applause was humbling, but that might have been because I'd never performed for so many people. Actually, I'd performed in front of much larger crowds, but the average age at a chamber music concert is north of sixty and any room with a thousand college students is going to make more noise than that no matter who's pushed out on stage.

Every minute of the show was better than any other minute of my life before it, but the ultimate highlight was the last song in Traci's encore. I'd planned to come out and play the violin for two of the trio's songs, but after hearing my rehearsal Traci asked me to sing a section of "No Woman, No Cry" with her, which they'd started using as the final song in each of their shows.

By the time I sing my last note I've forgotten about my mother. It's another thirty minutes, enough time to talk to an arts reporter from the campus newspaper and change into jeans, before I find Jen just outside the stage door on the side of the building.

"Is my mother with you?" I say, though it's pretty obvious she's not.

"No. She had to catch her train back to the city," Jen says, and then adds, as if she can read my mind, "But she stayed for the entire show."

"Really?"

Jen nods. "I'm sure she was proud of you." And then I remember that she hadn't exactly been polite to Jen.

"Well, now you've met. You see what I mean? I guess I shouldn't have expected to find her out here waiting for me."

"No," Jen says. "Maybe not. But I think he's waiting for you." She nods in the direction of the sidewalk between buildings.

When I see him, I realize I'd never stopped hoping for it. He's alone, and at first I think this is probably better for my chances at being forgiven, though I'm not sure yet if that's why he's here. He is standing against a railing, away from a group of girls who are waiting to get Traci's autograph. I give Jen a hug and tell her thanks before I go to Casey.

Casey Boyd speechless

More than the shock of seeing her walk on stage is what comes out of her. This is a girl who I've heard whisper to me over the library counter, a girl I've heard murmuring through Ian's wall and squealing in the river. I think I know her, and while I know she is capable of surprising me, I had no reason to believe there would be any more surprises.

And here she is, stunning.

At first I'm scared for her. I can't breathe when she sits at the piano. She will sing and I worry that with this many eyes on her something will not be perfect. The notes will be revealed and someone will have expected more. Right off it doesn't seem fair. But when the notes come out of her there is no indication she is afraid to attempt them. She is confident and polished. Each sound is sweeter and more powerful than anyone could hope for. I am mesmerized. I live a full, rich life in every note. I think of how I knew her before this—and I thought her very beautiful then—and I'm glad to never have to go back to that.

Late in the performance I have not at all gotten used to the sound. The half hour is a single moment. When it ends I want more. It is not enough to have been in the room, to have witnessed perfection. Though there is no sign of it, I imagine that behind this perfection lay years of hard work, the mining of deep passions, battles with doubt, and a triumph over vulnerability. Though seemingly inevitable to the audience, every word and note was to her at one time a complicated decision. I know this in the way I know how eleven men work for months to get the ball in the hands of one open receiver. It is these parts of her that I'm now interested in. I would sacrifice the perfection of the performance to see everything else, to glimpse the real thing, to be a part of the whole beautiful, frustrating, painful process that occurs in her head.

Haile, *pianissimo*

The glow of my bedside lamp is a flattering yellow. The show has left me charged and feeling like the day has no right to end. I'm on my stomach on the bed, chin resting against my intertwined fingers, feet performing a slow flutter kick against the comforter. How can there be standout days like this when each day contains the same volume of time? Why not make them all so perfect?

"What are you thinking?" Casey says. We are fully clothed. He is reclined on the bed next to me. He started in a sitting position but has slid down against the pillows, lengthening his body.

"Have you finished your art project?" I say.

"I guess."

"I want to see it."

"I handed it in. You'll see it in class this week."

"What is it? No, don't tell me. It'll be a surprise."

"It's not worthy of any big surprise."

"What do you think Ian did for his? He wouldn't tell me. I hope it's not boring. Yours isn't boring, is it?"

Casey winced. "You'll probably think it is. I do."

I look up at him. "Casey. Now that you're listening, I want to say it again. I'm sorry about the river the other night. The whole thing was a disaster and it was entirely my fault." The truth was that I'd thought I was being bold and spontaneous when in fact I'd been careless. It was not my place to test Casey and Ian's legs of the triangle. I'd been craving a little risk, but that particular risk was not mine to take.

"Forget it. It's okay."

"What I mean is that you shouldn't hold it against Ian. It was my mistake to involve him. I thought I needed his help to get you to notice me."

"You didn't see that I'd already noticed you?"

"I guess I did. I just didn't believe it. Will you forgive me?"

"Of course."

We lie without speaking until the subject quietly expires.

"What do you like about me?" I ask.

"Is that an insecure question or an egotistical question?"

"Sorry. You're right. It was stupid. What I meant is that we don't make obvious sense together."

"Maybe giving it a try makes more sense than avoiding it any longer."

I lift myself onto my elbows and without further deliberation we kiss. His head lifts away from the pillows and his hand touches my cheek. When we part it isn't to separate. We remain as we are, the full length of our bodies touching through our clothes. I feel unprepared to make a decision about whether we should sleep together.

"What's this?" I say when my finger finds a lump below his elbow.

"It's bone. I broke my arm when I was in middle school."

"Playing football?"

"Playing football badly. I was guarding this guy, backpedaling, and I tripped when I tried to spin around. It was a quick, clean fracture, but I guess it didn't heal as cleanly as it broke. Or I didn't let it. I was too impatient to get back on the field. Have you ever broken a bone?"

"No."

"Good. I would hate that." He ran his hand down the length of my arm to where it rested on his leg. "How 'bout a speeding ticket? Ever get one of those?"

"No. Why?"

"You want to know what I like about you? You're smart. You stay out of the most basic kinds of trouble."

"That just means I have common sense." Then I thought about the three of us in the river and added, "Sometimes."

"No. You're smart. But there's one thing I can't figure out. How did you end up here?"

"It's *my* bed."

"I don't mean here. Why did you leave New York?"

"Long story." I know I'll eventually tell Casey the whole story, but I don't want to risk spoiling the evening. "Basically it's because I'd never broken a bone or gotten a speeding ticket. I had to *do* something. Smart girls don't get where they want to go just for being smart. What about you? Most football players pick the easiest course load they can get away with. Why premed?"

"It's an honorable field," he says.

"That isn't a reason."

He shrugs. "It's safer than banking on a career the NFL."

"Safer? That's worse than not having a reason. I don't believe you."

"What do you want me to say, that I'm doing it to find the cure for cancer?"

"Are you?"

He pauses before he says, "I don't know."

"I'm sorry."

"For what?"

"You're uncomfortable. I feel like I'm being mean to you."

He kisses me on the forehead. "It isn't mean to ask questions. But I'm not used to someone unloading all the uncomfortable ones at once."

"You don't seem very much like a football player."

"Are you trying to compliment me? Be careful."

"I thought I needed to understand football before I knew whether I liked you. But really, I only needed to see how much you love it. If you want to play professional football, I think you should go for it."

"Thanks for the permission. Have you got a team in mind? Maybe you could write a letter of recommendation."

"I'm being serious. Don't you see how we're told all our lives to dream big, but in reality most incentives encourage us never to be too risky? Why's it such a risk to go after something you want? I think in the end it's more risky not to."

"I don't know. Maybe it's because failing is such a pain in the ass. Or maybe people just can't decide for sure what they really want. I mean, are you ever really sure?"

I put my head on his chest and feel it throbbing healthily.

When I've almost fallen asleep he runs his fingers through my hair and says, "I should go." I don't agree, but I don't stop him either. I follow him across the room to see him out, and in the doorway we kiss. Yes, I think, this makes much more sense than avoiding it any longer. In fact, it makes much more sense than that.

Casey Boyd all guitar heroed out
Casey Boyd is now friends with **Nate Orton**
Casey Boyd changed his profile picture

We are in a group in the lounge of the student center bullshitting our way through the last fifteen minutes of study hour. It is no different from how we spent the first forty-five minutes.

"Where's this girl you're chatting with?" I ask T-Smalls.

"El Paso."

"Texas?"

"Are there other El Pasos?"

"There are other girls. The fuck are you gonna do with a girl in El Paso?"

"Layin' groundwork. If we win this weekend and two other teams lose, then we go to the Sun Bowl. And when we get to El Paso I don't want to have to bang one of these Florence school spirit girls who follow us around the country. Alla them have already screwed half of you and I don't want to think about your monkey asses when I'm enjoying some pussy."

When I catch sight of Nato coming out of the computer lab and heading for the front door I tell the guys I'll see them later.

"Wait," Afa says. "Aren't you giving us a ride?"

"I can't. Catch one with T-Smalls, okay? I gotta go." I grab my bag and jacket before anyone can ask where I'm going.

In the parking lot, Nato is nowhere to be seen, but I'm right in assuming he's probably headed back to the athletics facility. It's a short walk and most guys leave their vehicles by the practice field where we have guaranteed parking spots. When I catch up to him I ask about the shoulder.

"It's better," he says. "I wish I could have taken some more reps in practice today."

At practice, Nato tossed the ball around with Kyle but the trainers wouldn't let him on the field, even after he'd pleaded his case for giving the shoulder a try. The coaches know as well as I do that we need Nato healthy to win Saturday's game, but I'm worried about more than just the shoulder.

"How 'bout everything else?"

Nato looks at the ground ahead of us. "Sorry about what I said the other day. One of the guys told me about your mom. It was shitty of me, even if I didn't know."

"Don't worry about it. It's been a rough few weeks. You were close to your dad?"

"Yeah. Or I thought so, but—you know, something like this happens and you wonder."

I nod. "You know, talking to Coach last week was the right thing to do."

Nato shrugs as if he's had his doubts. I continue.

"I've known Coach for a long time. My dad and I get along fine, but I used to wish I was a part of Coach Everett's family. Ian and I were buddies and I used to stay at their house just to feel like I was a part of it, you know? Anyway, I don't think he's dealt with things lately as easily as he's accustomed to. But you were right to go to him."

"You're friends with Coach's son?"

"Yeah. We've been best friends since high school."

Nato falls quiet. We've come up along the fence that sur-
rounds the stadium and when we're even with the side gate, I stop.

"Want to try that shoulder out?"

Nato looks at me, gauging whether I'm serious. "Okay. You
want to go to the practice field?"

"No, let's go in here." I pull from my pocket and hold up
the key to the stadium that Sheriff Paddock gave me before
Homecoming.

SCENE: EXTERIOR. FOOTBALL STADIUM. NIGHT.

The parking lot surrounding the stadium is
deserted. IAN approaches in the shadows.

The main entrance is locked. Pocketing my hands, I lean against the gate and roll my head back and forth over one of the iron bars while I wait. I'm not early. It's a few minutes after nine. There are security lights along some of the sidewalks, throwing long shadows. Otherwise it is dark. Some laughter carries across the parking lot and a car speeds away, taillights jerking into line as the tires grip the pavement. In the distance a few student-athletes trickle back from study hours or night classes to fetch their cars from the parking lot.

It occurs to me that for a building accustomed to filling and emptying itself of seventy thousand people there are likely a half dozen other entrances. I check the locker rooms and find them locked. Same with the doors to the elevators that rise to the press boxes. Then I remember the tunnel. At the side of the stadium is a wide entrance that is used for marching bands, ambulances, horse-drawn mascots, lawn mowers, and trucks carrying conces-sion supplies. I assume the tunnel goes directly to the field but it pitches down at an angle that doesn't permit a view straight through. At the gate there is a security hut that resembles an outhouse with windows, but it's unmanned at this hour. The lock on the gate is disengaged. I glance up and down the sidewalk before I let myself in.

The field is magnificent when it comes into view at the end of the tunnel. The grass is perfect, the walls of empty seats climb right up to the stars. Only three of the megawatt lights are lit, spaced high above each end zone and over the fifty-yard line, like three moons too bright to look at. Because it was Case who told me to meet him here, I spot him right away. He's throwing the ball to someone else at midfield and at this distance I don't recognize the other person until he makes a sharp cut and runs underneath Case's pass. I know immediately who it is from the way he moves. Case calls out my name and I have no choice but to walk toward them.

"This is Nate," Case says.

Yeah, I know.

"Hey," I say. "I'm Ian."

"Hey."

"Remember that play we did at State? Senior year?" Case says to me. "The pump fake-out route and then you hit me on the fly? Let's see if you've still got it."

I have to think back to what Case has just said when he tosses me the ball and jogs away along an imaginary line of scrimmage. I don't look at Nate and he isn't looking at me and yet it feels as if each of our attention is fully on the other. Case is tilting forward on his front foot, awaiting my signal. My fingers grip the laces instinctively but the ball starts to feel heavy. Suddenly I can't imagine hitting a moving target downfield. My arm feels asleep. But I won't be able to live with myself if I fuck this up, so I give the ball a slap and Case bounds forward. We haven't done this in four years but he doesn't take so much as a step that I don't anticipate. I cock the ball and almost lose it in the pump fake. My fingertips are slick with moisture. I wipe my hand on my shirt and re-grip the ball. Case is twenty yards up the sideline, then twenty-five. When I let the ball loose it wobbles ever so slightly in its trajectory. But it's catchable, and without anything too athletic on Case's part the ball drops neatly into his hands.

He jogs back and flicks me the ball like a well-trained dog.

"Well," he says. "I gotta go."

Nate's eyes cloud with panic. "Yeah, I should get going too," he says.

"No, no. You guys stay as long as you want," Case says. "Get that shoulder back in shape. It's not every day you get to play in here without seventy thousand critics on hand."

We both look at Case, like *What the fuck are you doing,* but he just slings his bag over his shoulder and wanders toward the tunnel. I'm thankful for the football in my hands, to keep them from shaking. Nate Orton and I stand motionless. The farther away Case gets the more urgent is the need to say something.

"You injured your shoulder?" I say, even though I already know this.

"Naw," he says. "It's a little sore, but I'm fine once I get it loosened up."

I'm talking to Nate Orton. My chest feels like it's overinflated and imploding all at once. I hold the ball up as an invitation and he shrugs as if to say what the hell, though he's still looking back across the field at Case. We toss the ball for a few minutes, maybe an hour—it's impossible to tell. One minute would have been enough and this was longer than that. Nate wants to try a few routes, the ones he's missed while sitting out practice. After a few hard throws I stop him to ask about the shoulder. "Good as new," he says. Of course, I should know it's pointless to ask a football player if he's too hurt to play. I throw to him some more and then tell him he doesn't need any more practice.

"My dad will kill me if I have anything to do with that shoulder not being ready on Saturday," I say.

We sit down on one of the sideline benches and listen while his breathing slows. Finally he speaks.

"I almost told Coach the other night."

"Told him?"

Nate looks at me.

"Oh," I say. It barely comes out as a sound.

"But I couldn't say the words," he says. "It's weird. I thought all along that it didn't matter, that I could just keep it to myself forever. And then suddenly it was killing me. I was ready to tell him. But I got there and Coach and I were talking and I couldn't do it."

"Yeah, it's a really fun conversation," I say. "Have you told anyone else?"

"No."

"What about Case?"

He shakes his head no and shrugs. "I guess he kinda figured it out."

"What about the other guys on the team?"

"I can't tell them now. It's a crucial part of the season and—"

"There's never a good time."

"It's not that simple," he says defensively. "I want to play in the pros and having something like this out there isn't going to help my chances."

Nate has a point. Unless you rank among the very top picks in the NFL draft, something as minor as chronic ankle soreness can drop you to the bottom of the draft boards. Nate is a good receiver but he's not going to be a first-round pick. I can imagine the team brass deliberating his pros and cons on draft day: The Orton kid's got good hands. Good vision. Good speed. He's tough. Came from a good program. So that puts him even with about fifty other guys. Oh yeah, right here's a little note says he's a homo. We don't want to deal with that, right? Next.

"But what do I know?" he says. "I've wasted so much energy keeping it a secret I'm not even acting like myself anymore."

"You have good instincts," I tell him. "You should probably use them."

"That's the problem. The instincts I've grown used to trusting tell me that I should have left an hour ago with Casey. But I'm still here."

Nate looks at me and then our eye contact is too much and he looks away. We are silent for several heartbeats. The vast bowl of empty seats around us reminds me of something.

"Win the crowd," I whisper, more to myself.

"What?"

"Have you seen *Gladiator*?"

"Yeah. Why?"

"In one scene Russell Crowe's character, Maximus, is being sent into the coliseum to fight. Proximo, the old gladiator who won his freedom, advises Maximus to win the crowd. He tells him it's not about how many fights you have to win or how many obstacles they'll put in your way. 'Win the crowd. Win the crowd and you will win your freedom.' "

I'm prepared for Nate to laugh at me but he only tilts his head slightly to gaze around the stadium.

The sensation of pressure on my arm is at first only confusing. I've been aware of his body since the moment I first recognized him on the field. The thought that there would be contact between us beyond a handshake seemed as remote as my fiftieth birthday. So when his hand clasps my arm above the elbow I feel almost nothing. I've prepared no emotions I can trust. When I turn toward him I'm not expecting his face to be so close. His breath touches me, first grazing my cheek like a feather, only warmer and alive. I feel goose pimples rise on the back of my neck and along my arms. Finally, I'm aware of what's happening and I'm able to participate in the kiss. When we're through he looks surprised and a little frightened.

"I—I don't know what I'm doing," he says.

"Exciting, isn't it?"

Nate smiles. To see him relax in front of me is as good as anything. Nate Orton is a guy who has not let his guard down in a long time. We walk together through the tunnel to the parking lot.

"Do you need a ride?" he asks me.

"No. I think I want to walk."

I watch him climb into his silver pickup and pull out of the lot. And that's it. The best hour of my life is over.

In our living room, my housemates are playing Madden on the PlayStation but Case gets up to follow me into the kitchen where I fill a glass with water from the tap.

"How'd it go?" he says.

I can tell by his discreetness that the others don't know what Case knows about Nate. I take a drink of the water and shrug.

"His shoulder's fine," I say.

Case's expression is blank at first but then he smiles. "Thanks for doing that," he says.

I don't know what Case thinks I've done but I'm pretty sure I'm the one who should be thanking him. Right now, though, I still don't trust myself to talk about it. And anyway, I have no intention of trying to explain this feeling to anyone. It's mine.

Casey Boyd teamwork on three: one…two…three
Casey Boyd averaging 6.4 receptions and 73.8 yards per game
Casey Boyd dazed and confused

SCENE: INTERIOR. WEIGHT ROOM. DAY.

IAN is lifting free weights with his tennis teammates. Across the weight room, NATE is spotting another football player doing a set of squats. Ian and Nate make eye contact and Ian smiles. Nate is more cautious, containing his smile so that no one can see.

At the end of the workout they pass each other. Ian says hi. Nate, conscious of his nearby teammates, is too afraid to acknowledge Ian's presence. He looks away.

SCENE: INTERIOR. NATE'S TRUCK. DAY.

The truck pulls into the cul-de-sac in front
of Ian's house. NATE puts the vehicle in
park. IAN sits in the passenger seat, not
yet reaching for the door.

"So."
      "So."
      "Do you want to come in?"
      "No. I can't."
      "You can't or you don't want to?"
      "I can't. You live with my teammates. What if they see us?"
      "No one's home."
      "I can't, okay? I can't take that risk right now."
      "All right. I understand."
      "So."
      "We could go somewhere in your truck?"
      "Ian!"
      "I'm joking. Relax."
      There is a brief pause.
      "Ian?"
      "Yeah?"
      "What did your dad say when you told him?"

"'Well, that explains a lot.'"

"What?"

"That's what he said."

"Really?"

"Yep."

"Shit. Do you think he meant it?"

"No. I guess not."

"Has he said anything to you since?"

"No. Not really."

Long pause.

"So. I guess I should go inside."

"Yeah, I guess so."

"Thanks again for the ride."

"I'll see you soon?"

"Sure."

"Maybe we can have dinner sometime."

"Sometime?"

"Yeah. Like tomorrow."

"Tomorrow's good."

"Okay, then."

"I'm going inside now."

"Wait. Can I—"

I kiss him before he can finish asking.

Casey Boyd confused
Casey Boyd wrote on **Darius Parker's** wall: "no idea what just happened in class…wtf?"
Casey Boyd attending "Final pep rally: Florence vs. Iowa"

"We're ready to begin. I'd like to remind you all to respect the efforts we've gone through to keep this anonymous. My TA has assigned each of your pieces a number so we can keep track of the grades without having to use your names. Please resist the temptation to identify your classmates if you happen to have discovered independently which artwork is theirs."

The stage is set up different. Professor Gilles's podium, usually front and center, is off to the side. In the middle, black curtains have been hung like screens to conceal the art projects until they are revealed. It all has the look of a production unworthy of itself and I feel certain it will only exaggerate the mediocrity of the art, if we're really calling it that.

Haile leans over and I can smell her hair. "Why are you always playing with those coins?" I can't look at her without thinking of how she looked at the concert, her voice, her posture at the piano, her eyes when she saw me waiting for her afterward.

"They help me think." To kill time before class I'd been using the coins to rehearse the playbook.

"I don't think you need them," she says, shuffling the coins out of order. Just what Coach Everett would've done, it occurs to me. She turns her attention back to the stage when Gilles starts in again.

"Now, you've all been given a sheet on which to evaluate the artwork. Rank each on a one-to-five scale, with five being the highest rank. Remember, it is not the artistic talent that matters but the impact it has on you. The two students with the highest marks—as awarded by you—will be displayed for a month in the library. Shall we begin?"

One of the TAs emerges from between the curtains to dangle before us what might generously be called a mobile. It is exhibit number one: dozens of fractured pieces of a wine bottle suspended by fishing line to make it appear as if the bottle is exploding. Perhaps a commentary on alcoholism, perhaps not even that profound. Not, in all honesty, very moving either way. I give it a two on the scale, since I can at least appreciate the effort taken to measure and string up all the fucking fishing line.

We wait for the next exhibit. And then the next. They come out one at a time for an hour and twenty minutes, and Gilles reacts vaguely to each. "Ah, I see the direction this was headed." "An original use of repetition here, I think." "I've never seen something quite like this." "Hmm, that's big." The class's reactions are more predictable. We see hilarity in the most extreme artistic disasters: the unintentionally deformed sculptures, the failed resemblances of self-portraits (of which there are many; we are a self-centered bunch), and the lousy scribbles of students who are without a talent even for trying hard. Anything relating to sex or nudity receives thunderous approval.

293

When my own offering is brought forward by the TA my face flushes and I struggle not to react in a way that will give me away. I don't want Haile to know. For the assignment, I'd drawn Krista, a portrait from the neck up, and pasted pieces of magazine ads over her head as if they were spilling out. I chose the images to represent what I thought she thought of me. This was all before the break-up, of course. The images in our heads have changed now. The drawing, though, turned out far better than I'd hoped, even if the facial features are somewhat more abstract than I intended. Other than a few murmurs, the class has no special reaction to my drawing. They are saving that for what comes next.

As the next picture is unveiled, a great laugh explodes around me. Fingers point, necks strain, heads nod in appreciation. The image is a pencil drawing depicting the Garden of Eden. It is meant to resemble an etching we were shown on the first day of class. *The Fall of Man*. The difference here is that instead of Adam and Eve there are two naked dudes standing beside the tree that bears the forbidden fruit.

"Very clever," Professor Gilles says.

It doesn't occur to me until I pick up on the way Haile is laughing and nudging Ian that it is *his* drawing. For his part, Ian is as red as a tomato, blushing at the audience's approval. I am suddenly jealous at how he's entertained the whole auditorium, and how he can command Haile's attention seemingly without even trying.

When Ian's drawing is put away and others are presented, class begins to drag on and I wonder if I've missed picking out Haile's. On stage we are shown an outline of Texas inlaid with a crucifix and a football and I feel embarrassed for Pile Driver because I know it's his.

As students begin to pack up their notebooks and planners in anticipation of the end of class, a large sheet of paper is carried out from behind the screens. When it is turned toward the class, the room falls still. Everyone's rush to leave is forgotten. Murmurs build to giggles. Once again, nudity is involved, this time in the form of a guy sitting naked in a large chair. There is something calculated about the drawing. The figure in the chair resembles Ian unmistakably. I glance over at him. His eyebrows are raised but I can't say whether this out of surprise or amusement. Haile is sitting very still beside me and when I glance at her she isn't looking at the artwork. She's watching Professor Gilles. Gilles stares at the drawing with his mouth hanging half open, his hands abandoned at his sides, his eyes slightly squinting. In the drawing, the naked figure is resting his right foot on a stack of three books. Looking closer, I see that the books are identical. The title, barely legible from this distance, stares back at me in triplicate: *The Search for Meaning.*

"Who did this?" Professor Gilles says suddenly, turning to the class.

If people had been thinking of splitting early, they'd now changed their minds. This kind of tension isn't walked out on.

"Who did this?" he repeats. His voice is frighteningly calm on the surface, like the waters of a deep, dangerous river. Getting nothing from the class, he turns to his assistant. "Tell me who turned this in. I want to know who is responsible for this."

"Professor, I don't have the master with me. You asked me to keep it in a safe place—"

"Who did this?" he says again to the class. His voice has a desperate edge, enough not to care what we think of his outburst. He takes a final, helpless look at the drawing before he turns sharply and disappears through the side stage door.

I realize that there is only one person in the room who understands what's just happened, and it's not the frightened TA. It isn't Ian either, because he's pulled his eyes away from the stunning drawing on stage, in which he appears, and looks questioningly at Haile.

Haile is staring at the door where Professor Gilles made his abrupt exit. She exhales suddenly through her beautiful lips as if she'd been holding her breath.

Casey Boyd holding the team together. Barely.
Casey Boyd watching more game film.
Casey Boyd posted an article: "Florence Achaeans earn a shot at the Sun Bowl"

We're outside running through the game plan in a light rain. It's two days before the Iowa game and there is reason for optimism. Nato's back on the field with a functional shoulder, Kyle's arm is accurate, and I've yet to drop one pass all week. But something is off. A strange tension lurks beneath the emotionless execution of plays we're capable of running in our sleep.

I come off the field for a few snaps and go for a drink of water. The cooler is at the end of the bench and as I fill a paper cup, swallow its contents, and refill it, I strain to hear what is being said by Pile Driver and DJ Boone, who are huddled together nearby. They are laughing at something, blissfully ignorant of how their conduct appears to their teammates. I remind myself that on a team with one hundred guys, you're not expected to like everyone. They're here to do their jobs and I'm here to do mine.

After the play finishes on field, Pile Driver and Boone are sent back into the action. Kyle's made his call in the huddle and Coach Everett is feet from me on the sideline, watching intently with his hands on his knees as if something he's looking for might come down to a matter of centimeters. The ball is snapped. Kyle drops back and then steps into a pass. The play unfolds on the far side of the field, and from my perspective I can see how it will end before the ball is even in Nato's hands. Stalking him from the snap, Pile Driver and Boone are now racing to the play, their bodies angled forward in a way you don't often see in practice when you're gunning for your own teammates.

Nato leaps to grab the ball and he isn't able to make it back to the ground before his feet are cut out from beneath him. By the time the sound of the collision reaches us, their three bodies are strewn across the turf.

I leave the sideline automatically, prepared to start a fight or break one up, whatever's needed by the time I get over there. But this time it's Nato who is first to his feet.

"I'm fine," he says, not accepting any help up. "But fuck this. I can't take this bullshit anymore." He'd taken off his helmet and now he throws it at the ground as he turns to walk away.

"That's fucking twice," Kyle yells. "Did you not hurt him bad enough last week? What's this about? Because it's not helping me run my offense."

When I look to Coach Everett for direction, his head jerks slightly as if he's coming out of a daze. "Goodman. Boone. Get off the field," he barks.

"What for? Everyone's okay," Pile Driver says. His grin, as devoid of shame as it's ever been, compels me to get involved.

"You heard Coach. Get off the field," I say, taking a warning step in his direction.

"Look, pretty boy. You know what this is about. Stay out of it. Or I'll start assuming things about you, too."

"We're a team here. Why don't you fucking act like it?"

"Fuck you." Pile Driver takes a step in the direction of the field but I'm blocking his way. Instead of going around, he tries walking right through me, forcing me to stumble backward. When I have my balance, I take a swing, fully intending to give him a last meal of knuckles and teeth and blood. The punch lands on the edge of his mouth and before he registers any pain, he's lunging back at me, by far the fastest I've ever seen him move. This time he leads with his fist instead of his shoulder and catches me in the face as I duck instinctively away. Had it been a direct hit to my nose I probably would have broken something, but most of his knuckles connect high on my cheek, near my ear, or at least the ringing makes it feel that way.

I'm prepared to fight back but three guys have grabbed Pile Driver and someone is pulling me back by the shoulders. When I turn I see that it's Nate Orton. I thought he'd left for the locker room but he must have come back when he saw me taking swings on his behalf.

And maybe Nato's right. This isn't the time to fight. We risk enough injuries just playing the game by the rules. For a few moments no one moves; everyone looks to Coach Everett. Coach Evans and Jerrell are still restraining Pile Driver. When I turn to catch Coach's eye I'm surprised to find him looking directly at me. He starts to bring his whistle to his lips. *This is my moment*, I think. Before he can blow the whistle, I hear my voice bark into the silence.

"Everybody get in here. Now!" I say, ignoring the blood that I can feel and taste like someone is rolling pennies into my throat one at a time.

No one moves. But Coach has paused, holding the whistle in front of his face. At first I'm afraid he's going to ignore me and tell everyone to get back on the field. But instead he says, "Huddle up," and gives me a slight nod.

Obediently, everyone gathers around and suddenly I have no idea what to do. I try to say a few things about there being the biggest game of the season in two days and suggest that now would be a good time to get our shit together. Then Nato stops me. He steps to the center of the huddle and sweeps his head around. I can feel him looking each of his teammates in the eye. I look nervously at Coach, who is standing back, watching.

"I'm here to play," Nato says. "Saturday is our last regular season game together. For some of us it could be the last game of our college careers. I'm here because I want to win this game. If anyone doubts that and has something they want to say to me, say it now. Say it to my face." He turns to lock eyes with Pile Driver, who looks down at the turf. "Tell me to my face why you think I shouldn't be here. Otherwise, I'm not going anywhere. We've got work to do. Kyle?" Nato flicks the ball to Kyle, who catches it and turns red, horrified to have any attention cast on him in this moment. A flash of fear crosses Nato's eyes as it occurs to him that maybe he's on his own. "Kyle? You ready to play, or what?"

Kyle is speechless. A few of the guys shift their weight nervously from one foot to the other. Coach hovers in the background, a permanent squint on his face. The rain patters against our shoulder pads.

Finally, it is Jerrell who steps forward.

"I'll play with you," he says. He slaps Nato on the shoulder pad and jogs to his position on the field.

Afa is next. He lumbers forward, grinning as always. "Man, I'll kick your ass myself if you try to leave."

"Yeah, I'm cool, too," Kyle says finally, though it's clear he's mostly confused about what's just happened.

Coach turns to walk back to the sideline, but then he stops as if he's remembered something that needs to be addressed before we can continue with practice.

"Goodman. Boone. You two get off our field. Your season's over."

The rest of the guys jog to their positions. The field is spotted now with puddles and I can feel my cleats gripping the soft earth. I feel numb. Ten minutes earlier we seemed on the verge of self-destruction. And now, although we've lost two defensive starters, if someone would've asked me if I thought we were going to win on Saturday I would've told him I was willing to bet everything I had.

"Boyd!" Coach barks my name in a way that's always made my heart jump. I hate being singled out on the football field. The only reason you're ever singled out on the football field is because you've just fucked something up. What Coach says next he says in a much quieter voice so that only I can hear him through the rain. "*That* was leadership."

Haile, *diminuendo*

"What are you thinking?" Casey says. This question has become our first inside joke as a couple. It started because Casey has a habit of saying, "What are you thinking?" every time a silence opens up in our conversation. To tease him, I ask him the same thing whenever I catch him daydreaming. The joke is that when he asks me, I always tell him exactly what I'm thinking, no matter how random or blunt. And when I ask him, he usually hesitates before making up something benign and appropriate.

This time, though, I can tell by the way he's asking that I must have had a troubled expression on my face.

"Professor Gilles." I keep seeing the look on Professor Gilles's face when he first saw my drawing unveiled.

"You mean his reaction in class? Do you want to tell me now what that was all about?"

"Did you read Professor Gilles's book?"

"Hell, no. Isn't it enough that I show up for class every day?" he says, and then adds, "Well, almost every day."

"In his book he writes beautifully about why art matters. I was drawn in completely. I found it inspiring. It was like he put into

words what I'm always trying to do with my music. And then..."
I trail off, not sure where to go from here.

"What? What is it?"

And then Casey becomes the first person I tell about Danny
Cole's paper. I explain how I came across it in the library, not
quite by accident, but not with any malicious agenda. I explain
how burning the church, in which Danny had collected all the
evidence of their affair, had effectively buried the secret with him.
I explain how Danny's paper said that Gilles's favorite painting
was called *The Wrath of Achilles*. And I explain how I'd felt that
my drawing could finish what Danny had tried to do.

"I guess I was disillusioned about Professor Gilles after reading Danny's paper. How could these ideas he so wonderfully
articulated have any meaning if he was such a fraud in his own
life? I needed to prove that that...that *power* of art...existed without Gilles, that it existed in me, that I had command over it. I
guess I do. But do you think my drawing for class was a mistake?"

"No way. I think it was amazing. I mean, the rest of us just
turned in these lame pictures that no one else cares about. Yours
actually got everyone's attention." We are lying on his bed. He
draws me closer to him, cupping my shoulders in the bow of one
arm.

"What if I've upset something that should have been left
alone?"

"What do you mean?"

"The dean."

"Dean Gilles?" he says.

I nod. "They've built this life together, even though a big part
of his life is a lie."

"Well, having a fucked up relationship isn't a crime," Casey
says. I wonder what makes him use that word. Aside from arson,

which seems laughably beside the point in all this, I don't know of any crime that Professor Gilles has committed. But is that the only thing that matters—that we not commit crimes? Aren't there unforgivable things that fall within the boundaries of the law?

We are quiet for several minutes. I like these pauses in conversation with Casey. They give me a chance to feel his arm around my shoulders, the warmth of his body beside me, and they remind me not to take for granted that this is happening. At one point earlier in the day I caught myself thinking of him as if I was *used* to us being together. It was a feeling I wanted to undo immediately. I never want to be used to him.

Casey Boyd staying in tonight with the lady friend
Krista Marshall wrote on **Casey Boyd**'s wall: "well that's nice. Thanks for sharing that with everyone"
Casey Boyd is attending "Florence Tennis hosts N.E. Conference Championship Tournament"

At home, I lay in bed with Haile. We are silent, putting some distance between us and the day that's ended. She has been telling me about how she got the idea for her art project. Something has been bothering me ever since the art projects were revealed in class.

"Did he really pose naked for you?"

Haile laughs. "Are you jealous?"

"No," I say in a way that I hope sounds sincere. I know there is nothing to be jealous *of* but a feeling lingers that feels an awful lot like jealousy. Maybe it's because I can't begin to understand what did happen between her and Ian. "You really liked him."

"I still do," Haile says. "And so do you. You know, you two are more alike than you are different."

I'm still not used to being with her. For many months before this she'd remained something unreal, a crazy idea I should keep to myself. Now when I feel like kissing her I can turn my head and there's nothing to stop our mouths from touching. Within minutes our hands grow exploratory and she unbuttons my shirt, top to bottom. We kiss some more and I realize this path can lead only to sex.

"Oh, shit."

"What is it?"

"I have a game tomorrow. I can't—I mean, the night before a game."

"*What?* What does this have to do with the game?"

"Sorry. I know it's crazy."

"When is the last time you had sex the night before a game?"

"I haven't."

"Never?"

"Never. Well, once I, you know, stimulated myself. And the next day I had the worst game of my life."

"You're blaming one bad game on masturbation. And this is your argument for not sleeping with me?"

"I just—"

"I'm going home."

"Wait. Fuck it. You're right."

Haile smiles. I forget all about football when our bare stomachs touch and I shiver like I did in the river.

SCENE: INTERIOR. IAN'S BEDROOM. NIGHT.

It is after midnight. IAN is wide awake,
staring at the ceiling. Asleep beside him
is NATE, bare chest rising and falling with
each breath.

Here is a football player, that symbol of American romance and
brutality, asleep in my bed. But I don't see him that way. Lying
alone in the dark with Nate I feel as if I've only traded in one form
of loneliness for another. An empty kind for one that enriches.
Nate Orton isn't who I thought he was. But none of us is. We can
never be how others imagine us.

Earlier in the day, I had gone to the coffee shop to see Jamie,
rehearsing in my head what I might say to him. Patrick came out
from the back office.

"Jamie's gone," he said. "He took the train to New York yesterday. I don't think he's coming back."

I realized suddenly that the words I'd come to say were more
for my own sake than for his.

"Good," I say, and mean it. "Good for him."

In the dark I can see the stack of magazines on my desk,
underneath which lies the thick envelope from UCLA. When
Nate went to the bathroom to get ready for bed I'd held the enve-

lope, studying it, wondering if I should wait until tomorrow to tear it open. I already knew what it said. I knew it in the way you can feel toward the end of a long grind of a tennis match that you're going to win. It's not yet confirmed but you can already see how the chips will fall.

What I couldn't predict is where things would fall with Nate. Our status changed daily. For a week after we'd first kissed in the stadium, our secret alliance had raged on with an almost desperate intensity. We'd needed each other—or rather, we'd needed the experience of having had each other. I noticed it in Nate first, and it was painful to see how quickly the rest of his life came back to him, regaining the space that I'd briefly monopolized. I'm not sure Nate ever projected our relationship into the future the way I had, and that hurt me—probably in much the same way I'd hurt Jamie.

As recently as a week ago, the thought of being away from Nate was inconceivable. And then earlier today the mail from UCLA arrived. I'd nearly forgotten about it. But the moment I laid my eyes on the heavy white envelope and the blue block letters, I realized that I, too, had stopped projecting us into the future. Maybe what had happened between Nate and me was just as it was supposed to be—two people lucky enough to spend a few moments together, living fully in the present.

I didn't want it to end, but I no longer feared that it might. It *was* ending, and I was already beginning to find a way to move on.

Down the hall, I hear Casey's door and wonder which one of them is unable to sleep. I want it to be Haile, waiting for me to sneak downstairs for a late-night talk. But when I get to the open bathroom door Casey is standing at the sink, finishing off a glass of water.

"Can't sleep?" he says.

I shrug. "Don't need to."

As he tips his head back with the glass he catches me smiling as I stare at him. He has shaved his chest. The flesh is whiter in the glare of the bathroom light and the short ends of newly trimmed hairs are only barely visible.

"Fuck you," he says.

"What? I didn't say anything."

"I didn't do it for you," he says.

And with that he goes back to Haile, both of us smiling. I slide under the sheets and shut my eyes, nowhere near sleep. The bed is smaller and warmer than it's ever been. Nate rustles. His arm comes around me and goes limp across my chest as he drifts back to sleep. A few minutes later he shifts again and the arm slides back to his side of the bed.

The UCLA decision brings me no nearer to knowing where I'm going, but I don't care. Not tonight. I feel as if I've already arrived at something.

Casey Boyd became a fan of "Haile Laine, musician"
Casey Boyd calculating the standard deviation
Casey Boyd wrote on **Kyle Brown**'s wall: "hit me deep, I'm open!"

SCENE: INTERIOR. TENNIS FACILITY. DAY.

The stands are at best half full. But the arena still buzzes with the electricity of an important tournament. IAN is serving for the match. In the stands we see CASEY, HAILE, and NATE. SUSAN EVERETT is sitting with them. We see the final point play out from a wide-angle perspective high above the court; it is clearly the view from one of the press boxes. Far below, Ian and his opponent battle for the point. Ian wins. The crowd goes wild.

The camera pulls back slightly and we see that it is IAN'S DAD watching from the press box. The roar of the crowd seems to move him. Something changes in his face. He is proud of his son. Coach Everett ducks out before anyone can recognize him.

Haile, *accelerando*

The dean's office is elegant and weighty like the deans' offices in those movies set at exclusive private schools. Most Florence professors work out of cramped, fluorescent-lit closets, few of which have windows. By contrast, the dean's chambers feel designed for intimidation. A vast immovable desk is anchored in the center of the room, behind which sits a heavy chair cradling the dean like a throne. Around us are book-laden shelves built into the walls, regal portraits, classical paintings, a great deal of wooden paneling, desktop lamps with dark green shades, and photos of the dean with famous alumni.

Conspicuously out of place in this setting are three drawings displayed on the couch, leaning anthropomorphically against the cushions. Two of them are immediately familiar to me: my drawing of Ian for Professor Gilles's Art History class, and Ian's twist on *The Fall of Man*. Seeing them again, it strikes me how, well, *good* they are. I wonder if Ian was as surprised as I am by our ability to mold our separate visions on paper. I know nothing about the third drawing, a charcoal sketch contrasting patriotic and antiwar themes, except that I remember it was among the many of my classmates' projects to be revealed in class.

"Haile, isn't it?" the dean says. "I'm hoping you can help me with something." She rises from her chair and moves around the desk and couch to stand behind my drawing. "This is your work?" I nod and resist an urge to shift in my seat. She is watching me closely. "There seems to be some controversy over which art projects in Professor Gilles's class received the most votes. Unfortunately, my husband—" she catches herself, "—Professor Gilles has taken a sudden leave and is not available to clarify things. So it has fallen to me to sort everything out."

There's a false note in her tone that confirms my suspicion that she's really summoned me here for her own purposes, to probe the motives behind my drawing—and her husband's reaction to it. I nod again. My official attitude is one of cooperation, but a growing part of me prepares for a confrontation. I think of Danny Cole's paper in my book bag. I'd tucked it in there at the last moment before leaving home, a little embarrassed for myself for thinking of it as protection. It doesn't feel much like protection now. It feels like nothing less than the nuclear option, a last-ditch tactic of mutually assured destruction. For that reason, I have no intention of letting the dean see it.

She moves from behind my drawing and rests a hand on each of the others, Ian's and the unidentified classmate's pictures. "As I understand it, Professor Gilles pronounced these two the winners before he left. He instructed his TA to have them hung in the library as planned. However, when the TA informed the winners of their achievement, one of them"—she taps the charcoal drawing—"withdrew her project in protest, insisting it was *this* drawing"—she returns her attention to my work—"that must have received the most votes. Apparently there was some kind of commotion when this was revealed in class."

She pauses briefly, studying me for a reaction. I give her nothing.

"After speaking with both the TA and the young lady who created the other drawing, I am convinced that you were, in fact, voted the winner by your peers. Which brings us to you and your drawing." She comes out from behind the couch and leans against the front of her desk. "Can you tell me why you think Professor Gilles might've objected to having this displayed in the library?" The way she scrutinizes me suggests she's already decided I'm less than innocent. Her stare is cold, her arms folded across her abdomen.

"I really can't speak for Professor Gilles…" I begin, and then trail off. *The reason Professor Gilles would object is right here in my bag.* The thought of Danny's paper seems to bolster my determination to at least approach the truth, even if my instinct is to protect her from having to face it full on. "What do you want from me?"

"Let me be straight with you," she says. "Are you having an affair with my husband?"

I inhale sharply. It takes me a moment to recover from my shock. *Does she really have no idea?* At the very least, she isn't thinking clearly; why, if I *were* having an affair with Professor Gilles, would I present him with an erotic drawing of a nude male?

It is important to look directly at her. My eyes are desperate to look away, but I buck that instinct and hold my ground. "No," I say quietly.

"No?" She studies me, as she's been doing all along, but now she appears even less sure of herself. "I see. Affair or not, I expected you to deny it. But I think you're telling me the truth. Your expression, however, makes me think you know something more. I don't intend to accuse you of anything you haven't done, Haile. But…an affair. It's not an unreasonable question, is it?"

She is asking me now not about my behavior, but her husband's. I am aware that this is not an appropriate question for a dean to be asking a student, but I feel at least partially responsible for setting all of this in motion and my guilt obligates me to give her a response. "Mrs. Gilles, I came across a document in the Gilles Archives in the library. I work there. Honestly, I was just curious about the school's history. I wasn't looking for anything… like what I found."

"What document?"

"It's not important," I say, my first outright lie. "The point is, I used it, I guess, to inspire my drawing. I was only looking to make an impact. Professor Gilles encouraged that and I—I guess I underestimated the impact it would have on him." I stop. The dean's face contorts in such pained confusion that it derails my train of thought. "I don't know what to say, other than that I apologize to you, if not Professor Gilles, for…misusing what I found in his files."

Her face hardens again with suspicion. "My husband left town suddenly and without explanation. I'm not interested in your minor lapse of judgment in snooping around in my family's archives. I need to know exactly what happened."

I picture Danny Cole's paper, each typed line so neat and orderly on the page in the face of all that violence and desperation. *Does she really want to know the truth?*

When I speak, it comes out as a whisper. "I don't think you want to know it."

"What?"

"I don't think you want to know the truth, Mrs. Gilles."

"You no longer have the luxury of speculating about what I want. You've created this, with your snooping, with your drawing, with this whole stunt. I'm demanding the truth, and now it will come out."

If it were me, would I want to know? Behind her anger, the pleading in her eyes indicates that she *needs* to know, whether or not it's something she's ready to hear. One thing I do know is that I cannot sit here and explain it to her. I will not be able to find the words, or the voice to deliver them. Besides, it's not my story to tell.

Slowly, I reach for my book bag. I'd made a copy of Danny Cole's paper and given it to Ian so that he'd understand my drawing. It's the original I've brought with me today. The dean won't know about the copy I gave to Ian, and I doubt he has any reason to give it to anyone else. I pull the paper out of my bag. It is folded in half, the way I'd found it in the box in the Gilles Archives. I stand. Something prevents me from handing the paper to her directly. Instead, I set it on the surface of the desk next to her. Then I shoulder my book bag and take a few steps back. She doesn't tell me to sit back down.

"You can read it if you want to," I say. "But I won't blame you if you decide to throw it out unread, and I won't mention it again once I leave here." Then I add, meaning it, "I'm sorry, Mrs. Gilles."

"I think you should leave now, Haile."

I leave her there with Danny's paper and my drawing, our two nods to *The Wrath of Achilles*, our two attempts to satisfy our professor's search for meaning, thinking I will never see either again.

It's not until I've shut the door to the dean's office and I'm walking down the hall that I understand, with bittersweet clarity, that I truly am sorry—for her, and for her only; not for what I've done.

Casey Boyd game on mutherfuckers!

"Take a knee." Coach looks us over as if sizing us up like a beaten ship he's not sure should be taken out to sea.

Everyone stops what they're doing: getting ankles and wrists taped, shouting and singing, suiting up for a final chance to prolong our last season. Through the walls of the locker room, we can hear the crowd stomping and yelling, restlessly awaiting our entrance onto the field.

"This year hasn't gone the way any of us could have planned," Coach begins. "But we're sitting in a position to bid for a good bowl game. We are here not by some miracle, but because together we've become a better football team. Some of you may read the sports section and you know that the media are writing us off. We've had a good run, they say, but we don't have the pieces to hold it together when it counts. They say we don't have chemistry, that you men are not suited for my system because I wasn't the coach to recruit you." Suddenly Coach looks directly at me. "They say we don't have leadership." Then looking at Nato, he says, "They question our courage.

"The papers and TV commentators are in agreement on these things. They think we're too small, they think we aren't fast enough, not aggressive enough, not disciplined. These are the experts, folks. They've followed Florence football for longer than you or I have. Let me ask you this: do they know you better than you know yourselves?"

Coach pauses here to let the silence become uncomfortable.

"The answer to that question will affect you for the rest of your life. And I want you to answer it for yourself right now, before you step onto that field. Gentlemen, it seems to me that there are two teams in this locker room: there's a team described in the media by the so-called experts, and there's a team that only each of you can imagine in yourselves. Before you take the field you better decide which team you're on. That's the team that will win or lose today. Let's go."

SCENE: INTERIOR. LIBRARY LOBBY. DAY.

IAN stands alone, looking up at his and Haile's Art History class drawings hanging on the hallway wall.

I discovered Danny Cole's paper one afternoon resting neatly on my bed. I knew it came from Haile because in the top corner on the front page, in her curly girly handwriting, were the words: "*The Wrath of Achilles*. Look it up."

I read the paper a couple times, understanding everything except what it had to do with Haile and me. Perhaps she just wanted me know Danny Cole's untold side of the story. It was not until I did an Internet search for *The Wrath of Achilles* that I comprehended the significance of the paper to Haile's drawing—and to Professor Gilles's reaction. When the image appeared on my laptop screen, my breath caught. The painting is of a nude young man in a chair. The young man is sitting in exactly the same position—down to the bend in his elbow and the placement of his feet—*exactly* the same position Haile put me in to pose for her drawing. I remembered then how deliberate she'd been with her instructions. At the time, it hadn't occurred to me that she was modeling her drawing on something specific.

The winning drawings, mine and hers, now hang in a display case in the hallway between the museum and the library, where they will remain for the balance of the semester. There had been a week's delay before the announcement in class about the winning drawings. Mine had been a surprise, to me at least, but Haile's was a given. Professor Gilles had disappeared by then. He was running the way he'd run his whole life. He simply didn't know how to stop.

~ ~ ~

On a December day during finals week, I think to stop by and see our drawings one last time. Haile strolls over from the library's information desk.

"I still can't believe the dean allowed these to be hung here," I say. "You think she's doing this to punish him?"

"I think she did it because it's the right thing to do. For herself. Maybe she'll be able to move on."

We are silent for a long moment. Finally, Haile speaks.

"You're really leaving."

"Seems more productive than changing majors again, don't you think? 'Get busy livin' or get busy dyin', " I add in my best Morgan Freeman voice.

Haile smiles. "I think you're very brave."

I shrug. "There's a fine line between being brave and being a fool."

When I told my parents that I was moving to L.A. they were not pleased. This is what kids don't understand. In their short childhoods, they've seen the direction of life change on a dime many times over. We make decisions like pinballs aiming for the bells and whistles and hoping for a big score or a bonus round.

And our poor parents' hearts want nothing to do with all the racket. It is their duty to guide us toward the stability that they've understood for decades. My parents had a thousand little questions about my move to L.A. What about tennis? Would I finish school? Would I have a job? Where would I live?

I didn't have any of the answers but I told them I would be okay. And this is what parents don't understand. That sometimes we're okay even if everything isn't all laid out for us just yet. There were some tears but, honestly, I expected worse. I expected to be forbidden or lectured or warned into submission. But beneath their dutiful concern I detected a part of them that believed me. Believed *in* me. A part of them saw that I'd become someone who would be okay.

Standing beside Haile, looking at our drawings, I think of the burned down church and something reminds me of the path behind our house where the mud is reddish orange and where, when I pass it on the way to and from campus, I've often wondered whether the hate would come crashing down on my skull one night. I no longer fear that. I think instead of the alert chill of the river water. I think of winning the crowd. I think of sunny L.A. And I smile because through all these things I've learned what I want to do next with my life.

And that has made all of the difference.

Casey Boyd posted a final score: Iowa 12, Florence 41
Casey Boyd is at the end of the beginning of the rest of his life
Casey Boyd is attending "Haile, Live @ the Main Street Coffee Shop"

I wish I could say the game had ended with me making a diving catch in the end zone, or with Stewy booting a fifty-eight-yard field goal that bounced over the crossbar as the clock went to zero. But the fact is, we flat outplayed Iowa for sixty minutes. Coach had asked us in the locker room which team would take the field. His pregame speech was followed by silence. We didn't discuss anything or vote on it or talk ourselves up. Somehow we stepped onto the field with each one of us holding the same answer in his mind.

The Sun Bowl will be my last game in an Achaean uniform. I don't know what will happen after that but maybe it's moving-on time. Odds are, I have a better chance of doing math for the NFL than catching passes in it, and with that in mind, I met with my academic advisor to change my major from premed to statistics. But who knows—what are odds but the things every guy sets out to beat? You beat the odds when you go after something you want. They don't teach you that in stats class. You have to learn that on your own. I've had NFL dreams since before I could grip a regulation-sized ball, but there are other people who want it more, who have better reasons. Nato will keep playing. Just as Haile will keep singing. They know what they're playing for. They're the type who beat odds. Maybe I'm the type to study them. And maybe I'm all right with that.

For the remainder of the semester we sit in Art History with dumb expressions while on stage a TA soldiers on drone-like through a prepared lecture. I rarely see Pile Driver. Since he was booted from the team, he skips more classes than he attends. Football, his reason for staying above water in school—and, I suspect, in life—ended with his final, late hit on Nato in practice. More often than not, I find myself feeling bad for the guy, but then I remember how many chances we gave him and how many times he chose instead to let us down. The word is he's decided to retreat to his hometown in Texas and won't be returning to Florence next year.

As for Professor Gilles, the school's official position is that he is taking a leave of absence for a book tour, which is plainly bullshit to those who saw his behavior the last time he appeared before us. The most recent rumor gaining traction is that he simply can't leave the house. The word "breakdown" is whispered between rows in the auditorium but I don't think it's anything as legitimate as that. I think he's a coward. In any case, what keeps us showing up day after day is the fear of missing the action if he finally does return.

After practice one afternoon, I call Haile to tell her I'm on my way to pick her up. I don't want to make her late for sound check, but I get an idea and decide to take a quick detour through Main Street. I park in front of the florist and hurry inside. I tell the woman at the counter I want a rose.

"Red or yellow?" she says as if neither choice impresses her.

"Red." The roses are in a pail and she separates one from the others. I watch her slide the stem into a cone of stiff tissue paper.

"It comes to $2.11, with tax."

I reach for my wallet, but then I stop. A smile comes over me. I shove my hand into my front pocket and come out with all its contents. Emptying the fistful onto the counter, I thank her for her trouble and turn to leave. I've left a lot of coins on the counter and she's not happy about it.

"Hold on, please, sir. I'll have to count this."

"It's all there," I say, the door falling shut behind me.

And it is all there. Six quarters, four dimes, two nickels, and eleven pennies. I don't need 'em anymore.

Haile's coda

I call Mother on a crisp December afternoon before the start of holiday break, not knowing exactly what I'll say. I want to assure her that I'm okay. But she either knows it or she doesn't. I tell her instead about the songs I'm doing for the end-of-semester concert tonight and then I mention that she should come see one of my regular shows at the coffee shop.

"Oh, what would I wear?"

"Jeans, Mother. Jeans would be fine."

We're about to hang up when she stops me.

"Baby," she says.

"Mom, I'm okay. Really."

"I know. Let me finish." There is a terrible pause on the other end of the line. But finally she says, "I had dreams for you. What I forgot to account for is that you might have the courage to have dreams of your own. I…" I hear the hitch in her voice and wish impulsively that she was near enough that I could give her a hug. "I'm proud. I love you."

I tell her through tears that I love her, too.

Casey's already a few minutes late, but I don't worry because he called to say he was on his way. While I'm waiting, I pull a thick volume from the bottom row of my bookshelf. *The Iliad*. I'd bought it over a month ago intending to start it immediately, but by the time I'd gotten home and crawled into bed the mood had passed. Now, while I have a few minutes, I decide to give it another shot. I get through only a dozen lines of the Homer poem before I hear Casey's car. He knocks, which he finds necessary though I've told him otherwise. When I look up, he's standing in my room with a red rose.

"What's the occasion?"

"I had to get rid of some loose change," he says.

"Oh, how sweet."

"Jesus, you're reading *that*. How do you even start something so long?"

"Like anything else, one sentence at a time. Would you like to hear the first line?"

"We should go. You have sound check. Sorry I'm a little late. I had to stop." He holds up the rose and I see he wants to be congratulated for his thoughtfulness. I take the flower and give him a kiss.

"Just a line. I think you'll appreciate it."

"All right. If you'd like. But read it out loud. You'd do it better than me."

I read him the line and then I lay the stem of the rose in the first page like a bookmark:

Sing, Muse, the wrath of Achilles the son of Peleus,
*   the destructive wrath, that brought a thousand griefs upon the* Achaeans.

Acknowledgments

I can say without hesitation or embellishment that my parents are the most supportive pair of human beings anyone could wish for. This book simply would have been impossible without their unwavering love and support. Mom and Dad, thank you. It could not have been easy.

Major thanks to my sister, Kelly. In addition to being an enthusiastic believer, she got through a long, early draft of this book and thought no less of me for its flaws (or at least she didn't show it). Love you, sis!

Chris, I don't know where you came from, but your support, love, and laughter keep me going. Thank you for everything you are, and for giving me so much to look forward to.

Teresa and Gail provided a place to stay for a significant period of time while I was working on this book. And, really, does it get any more basic than that? Thank you both. I owe you for that and so much more.

I'm incredibly grateful to the team at Amazon, who discovered, improved, and fought to raise the profile of this book. Terry, Katy, Jessica, and the many others who touched this book behind the scenes, and especially my outstanding editor,

David Downing—thank you all for your guidance, wisdom, and professionalism.

A lot of smart, generous people read drafts of this book and contributed valuable feedback. *The Fall* still would've been written without them, but it wouldn't be half as good. I am especially grateful to Laurence, this book's first reader and earliest supporter, Nat Brown, Molly Barton, Kevin Callahan, Lucy Carson, Dan Lazar, Vanessa Hansen, Elizabeth Parker, Aubrey Smith, Elizabeth Duffy, Eric Brassard, Brian Olsen, Jamie McCarty, Ben Baur, Dan Cordova, Sean Marier, Travis Bone, Jacob Kiani, Jake Mason, Jon Bergman, Victor Davidson, and Josh Berkowitz.

And finally, a shout-out is in order for Vagabond Blues in Palmer, Alaska, which, it seems obvious to me, is the best coffee shop in the world. For the bargain price of a coffee and a cinnamon roll, I was allowed to sit for many hours, day after day, while writing portions of this book. If you ever find yourself in Palmer, don't leave before you drop by.

About the Author

Ryan Quinn attended the University of Utah, where he was an NCAA champion and an All-American athlete. After graduation, he worked for five years in New York's book-publishing industry. A native of Alaska, he now lives in Los Angeles. *The Fall* is his first novel.